* * * * * * * * *

F L E S H and *Gold*

* * * * * * * * * *

FLESH and *Gold*

Phyllis Gotlieb

A TOM DOHERTY ASSOCIATES BOOK
NEW YORK

FLESH AND GOLD

Copyright © 1998 by Phyllis Gotlieb

This book is printed on acid-free paper.

Edited by David G. Hartwell
Designed by Nancy Resnick

A Tor Book
Published by Tom Doherty Associates, Inc.
175 Fifth Avenue
New York, NY 10010

Tor Books on the World Wide Web:
http://www.tor.com

Tor® is a registered trademark of Tom Doherty Associates, Inc.

Library of Congress Cataloging-in-Publication Data

Gotlieb, Phyllis.
    Flesh and gold / Phyllis Gotlieb.—1st ed.
        p.   cm.
    "A Tom Doherty Associates book."
    ISBN 0-312-86523-6 (acid-free paper)
    I. Title.
PR9199.3.G64F57 1998
813' .54—dc21   97-29852
                                                               CIP

First Edition: February 1998

Printed in the United States of America

0 9 8 7 6 5 4 3 2 1

For the First Readers:
Calvin Gotlieb, Donald Maass, David Hartwell,
Virginia Kidd, John Robert Colombo,
Terence Green, Elisabeth Vonarburg,
Ursula Le Guin

PROLOGUE *

Khagodis: *Nohl and Ferrier*

"My knife is missing," Nohl said.

"What does that matter?" Ferrier turned his eyes from the smoking volcanic peak on the horizon to the east and watched the waters of the bay dancing in glints of light from the lowering sun. On Khagodis the air is so thin that the stars are sometimes visible in daylight; now in the flaring blue Ferrier could see three of the system's other worlds. He had hooked the oxygen tube into the corner of his mouth and it bubbled slightly.

Amber lights glinted on Nohl's scales. With a pearl talon he flicked away an insect buzzing near his eye and looked down at the thin figure whose head came to his elbow. Ferrier was wearing white against the equatorial heat; his short jacket was closely fitted, and had double-breasted black buttons. Nohl was thinking that Ferrier's eyes were like the buttons, fixed and sharp on white skin. A thin skin over arrogance and greed.

"I lost it down there." Nohl nodded at the folding waves

and at the same time clawed at his shoulder harness as if he expected to find the knife there; his stunner had not been taken. "I went because one of them had a foot caught in the sprigweed—when I came up it was gone."

"Think they'd know how to use one?"

"They would know. They already use pieces of shell for cutting, and sharpen them, too. Sometimes they catch fish with them, by slashing, but those are not dangerous to us. A real knife . . ."

Ferrier said, "If one of them's got it you ought to know who."

But Nohl did not like to admit that he was no longer quite so powerful a telepath as he had been. Even some of the best Khagodi ESPs grow weaker with age in the sixth sense as well as others. He hunched his bulk down at the edge of the steep bank and steadied it with his tail. "Kobai knows where everything is." :*Come here, Kobai!*: He sent the message silent and deep, deep enough so that the Khagodi standing guard farther down along the bank moved forward. Nohl shrugged him away.

A whorl appeared on the surface before him, and two hands parted the waters: a head rose between them. The head was hairless and dark red; under the brow ridges the eyes were dark and sharply alive through the transparent sealed lids. The face was fine-boned, a woman's. Kobai snorted to clear the brine from her nose, spat and swallowed air. She grinned up at him.

"Yes, Lord Upthere?"

I know all the time Big Om stole that knife, he don't hide it from us his own Down-people, think him some big man that Big Man Om, flub his lip and go cross-eye, poke-poking the women, See Me Big Om. Don't know we take a look and see he is not so big, and kind of dumb.

About knife, yes. Way we-people get a knife is, if the Up-people drop it down. Then they put to mind: where is my knife? and call around everywhere, don't care what you are doing, weaving the net or eat or make the in-out. They ones talk with the mind and the mouth sound, not with the hands like us under the water. Sometime I think they are not so bright either. They sure are deaf. Yes I can make with mouth by swallow air, go burp-burp, the kind of way they do. But I don't like to put my head through the skin of my world and make dumb noise. Because then I got to think so hard what the word are I don't talk good. Like now, gentle ones.

Yes, yes, I go on. Where I was? Big-lord say, *Pay attention you Folk, my knife is lost.*

You think I tell, or Siko or Pers, about Big Om and this knife? No, honorables. We do not give away even the kind we have no use for. He never do us harm except for pushing his this-here at us.

So we say, *No, no, great ones, it is not here.* Let them guard their own knives.

That one big upside-Lord who likes me—he is not a bad fellow—he puts his mind in my head and says, :*Come on, Kobai, you know everything, so you must know who has the knife.*:

And I give back, *Nononono Lord Big One Upthere, I would never touch a knife.*

:*Kobai,*: says he, :*you are funning me. I think you are all hiding Om.*:

I don't give him a funny answer because he is all right. But that Om, he has to be so big. I think that time he got bit by the sharptooth make him one wild man. He only want to make a pretend fight in the water with silly Usk and all the crazylegs around the place, but he got the demon in him from that bite and he dive deep and pick up a chunk of the gold that get washed smooth and shiny down there, jump up

most out of the water with one great whack of his tail and shout in this loud thoughtvoice like we hear in the mind from them up there, *:You like your fine gold all so much you take this and keep it and let me keep one own small knife!:*
And he throw that chunk let me tell you, so hard!
But he don't shout nor he don't throw no more, never.

An instant of tableau: a jet of blood leaping out of the throat of the dark red figure half-emerged from the placid waters of the bay; the thin dark Solthree with gun lifted in one hand, the other to his bruised temple; the scaled Khagodi staring down at him, hands raised and open. On the horizon one volcano spits a jet of red fire.

The spurted blood fell slapping the water while the astonished face, hairless and gaping, slipped down and away, the huge eyes lingered at the surface for a moment and were gone.

"Stupidskin!" The Khagodi flicked the gun out of Ferrier's hand. The watchman had aimed his stunner but did not fire. "What have you done?"

The thin dark man caught up his gun quickly and arced it up toward Nohl's heavy jaws, heard the sudden movement of the guard behind him, and replaced it in its sling. "Taught them a lesson, that's what." He rubbed the bruise on his temple again and kicked at the lump of gold near his foot. "They try anything they'll get it again . . . Nohl, you are a frightened little man." He picked up his broad-brimmed hat and put it on his head; it had an esp shield set into it.

Nohl had never wanted to know what was in Ferrier's mind, but now he stood watching him a moment, scratching an irritated spot near his gill-slit and thinking how if that shield had been removed a few moments earlier Ferrier might have been lying dead, brainburned by two furious Khagodi, and perhaps Om would be alive. "I believed you had some modest store of intelligence. These people would not have hurt you."

The waters of the bay began to pucker and glitter with points of sunlight. Hands rose from it, twisted, snapped fingers, and made lewd gestures. The domed heads pushed out glistening, the huge eyes bulged, lips on the water's surface made cracking blurt sounds. The body of dead Om rose from the water on the arms of his people in a gesture of defiance as the lifted hands of the others slapped the surface. Ferrier's fingers sought his gun once more. The sweat stood out on his upper lip and ran into his beard shadow.

Nohl said, :*Get down, all you Folk! Go about your business!*:

The eyes turned on him sullenly. He was not a bad one, no. But his friends were demons.

The sea people fell away to the depths, and the bay rippled in its calm evening way; the sun dropped below the rim of the world. Ferrier took out a handkerchief and wiped his face and neck. "Anybody going to report this?" The question was more threat than appeal.

"Not I." Not with that gun a touch away from Ferrier's nervous hand. "One of the Folk might. You cannot stop that without some great violence, and no Khagodi does that kind of thing. You will be brought to book, Ferrier." There was real threat in Nohl's voice, but what he really felt was shame at his own complicity in dealing with this sniggering little man.

Ferrier took a suck of oxygen from his tank. "It's really amazing, all the people who've wanted to get rid of me . . . maybe still want, you think? You do some thinking about getting rid of that woman, that Kobai. She's the one who'd screw things up for you—yeh, I could work out a couple of ideas for her." He kicked at the water-burnished lump of gold and grinned up at the big-jawed head. "Include that in your shipment. Or my kickback. I've been arrested before. If I get pulled in again I figure you'll get me a judge who won't convict, like usual, or we'll all find out what Central thinks about the people who do your slaving for you under the water, and their keepers. You like that, friend Nohl, you tight-ass Khagodi?"

He tilted his hat and walked away. In a few moments his solitary figure dimmed in its background of flat scrubgrass terrain. Two chalkwhite moons rose above his head. Nohl watched him disappear; he admired Ferrier's courage almost as much as he detested him.

Often there were rains toward morning, but now a cool wind swept a sky intense with stars. Nohl looked out at the seas among the islands, then down at the waters of the bay: lights were moving below that rumpled surface, the biolu-minescent lanterns of the Folk. *They are like the stars. No. They are like the lights of a village where the people are going about settling things in the evening. They have much to settle.*

He thought of Kobai, a woman of no small intelligence. *Damn you, stupid Om!* he told the horizon. And wondered what would become of her and the others.

I need a new knife.

ONE *

Fthel V: *Skerow*

Starry Nova was a name stuck on the port city of Fthel V by Solthree jokers. The Russian words *stary novy,* old new, where there were no visible stars and nothing was new, gave a good sense of the grubby middle-aged facility.

Skerow was endlessly fascinated with Starry Nova. The Khagodi are brisk about playing down an exaggerated reputation for morality—along with the well-deserved one for telepathic power—but their presence has always commanded too-extreme respect and unwanted reverence. Skerow liked to visit dark and grimy cities like this one set in the cold dank center of a continent of mines and ore refineries; a city of lowered skies, lodgings rather than homes, few pleasures and fewer legal. The inhabitants paid no attention to Khagodi.

"You are a romantic!" Tony Labonta had cried, dancing in his buckled pointed shoes and balancing a goblet of the local gargle with a star-fed tidbit.

He had said this several years ago during Skerow's last

visit on the assizes circuit at a function honoring the appointment of a new commissioner of mines and resources. Skerow, a grave and sober judge, looked down from a height of over two meters on the curly head of Tony, a tiny and pugnacious prosecuting attorney known for his youth and daring. "Romantic! You are meaning to tease me, Tony!"

But he was grinning up at her with no concern about keeping his mind shut, and it was true that he saw something shy and wild in her: *farouche,* was his word for it. He had other words to describe her: *streamlined baby allosaurus,* for instance, but she was not sure what they meant, or that she wanted to know.

She put those thoughts away now, while she lingered by the window of chambers late on a slate-colored afternoon, slow about dressing herself in a judge's dignity. The robe, a long surcoat of thin crinkly leather, was an old one she had inherited from a retired associate, a Khagodi from the equatorial regions of her world, when she was not sure how long she would remain a judge. Later, secure, she had not bothered to replace it, though it smelt of salt seas and musty scales. Before she was done Thordh came in; he stood hesitating in his rippled draperies. She waited; she had never made small talk with him. At length he said, "Will you take the bench today? I would like to go back to quarters."

Khagodi judges traveled in pairs and alternated on the long wearisome circuits. Thordh had been the protégé of Skerow's old associate, and came from the same country. She herself lived among the stony hills of the Northern Spine Confederacy, and had first expected him to be a warm and effusive Southerner, but he had little to say to her, and held his esp shield down tight.

"Certainly I'll sit for you. Are you ill?"

"A little." He spoke *lingua* with a precise and refined diction. "I find the old ague rises in my bones from the chill air of this place. Here,"—offering his case of spools and tablets—"there may be some notes you do not have." With the other hand he picked up a magnificent impervious helmet of silver and bronze, and put it into its traveling case. The helm was too heavy for Skerow; she preferred her silver net, which had its own disadvantage: it rubbed her scales wrong way.

That Thordh of yours is a very sober sides, Tony had said. *He's none of mine, Tony.* The image of Tony, hair ruffled, jigging with some private joke or other, folded itself away, and she arranged her face in the sober mien of the Law.

Skerow did not need any kind of seat before the lectern; she rested on the base of her heavy tail. Sometimes she rather enjoyed her power; sometimes she found it wearisome, as today, when the robe seemed shabby and she felt like a bumpkin wearing it, and the court was heavy with the stink of atmospheric tanks for fifteen kinds of humanity; even Thordh's absence, the empty cubicle below and to one side of her, seemed looming and intrusive. Tony Labonta stood waiting, neat and tight like a duelist; she did not think of him, but called the court to order.

Defendant was a Solthree named Henri Boudreau, a smuggler caught in port, a pirate rather, dragging a long record over five worlds.

The sheriff led him into court, a man of fierce brows and mustache; he glanced up at Skerow and his eyes bulged: he snorted into the supplementary oxygen tank. Defense, an old warrior woman, drew her mouth tight. Tony's eyes narrowed. Skerow had tried many cases in this court; now, for a moment, she became disoriented.

The Warrior, a powerful black woman with elaborately coiffed hair, drew close to the railing. "I understood that Justice Thordh was trying this case."

"He is indisposed and has asked me to stand in for him." Because Defense did not seem to be ready to withdraw, she asked, "Do you wish to make some formal objection, Madame?"

"Um, no." Defense stood for one more instant of paralysis, turned to a statue of basalt; Skerow, caught in the moment by her own unease at Thordh's having so casually rid himself of the case, waited with her. Defense shook her head slightly and withdrew beside her client.

Tony brought in twenty-three witnesses, and with the hammer of his argument nailed down the case with them one by one, hardly pausing to sniff oxygen. Skerow, mindful of Tony's brash enthusiasms, allowed half of Defense's objections, but Boudreau's activities had been so blatant that the Warrior's dramatics were mechanical and tired.

When the arguments had wound up Skerow called the lawyers into chambers to discuss sentencing.

"His record stretches across the Fthel system and beyond," Tony said.

"He's never had a major conviction, or served as much as a year, with time off," said Ms. Sama, for the Defense. Again she was looking oddly at Skerow, as if she wished to say something, but not with her mouth. Of course Skerow could not remove the helm to esp: all Galactic Federation judges were obliged to use them, and particularly the powerful Khagodi.

"A question of sentence," said Skerow. "If we send him to mine the iridium and beryllium he smuggles out he will have easy access among the miners to—and probably die of— the drugs he has smuggled in. Does that seem fair?"

Tony lifted his hand to forestall an angry outburst from Sama, and smiled at Skerow, who nodded and said, "Perhaps a few years supervising the robots at an ore-processing plant where there are no drugs available and he has no soul to corrupt but his own. What do you think?"

Out in court Boudreau stood gaping and red-eyed while this sentence was read. "Five years," he whispered. Then said something silently that by lip movements might have been: *Where is Thordh?* But Skerow was not sure of reading a Solthree's lips correctly.

"Your attorney will appeal," she said. Boudreau knew this well enough—sentences of more than one year were always appealed—and also that appeals made to assize courts took years, and he might well have finished his sentence before even the clerical work was done. He turned to Sama, opened his mouth and shut it again, and returned to staring at Skerow. His face was flaming, nearly purple.

She looked at him for an anxious second before she faced the court and asked the formal question of its observers:

"Is Justice seen to have been done?"

"No! No!" Boudreau leaped from his cubicle and beat his fists against the rail.

"What—?"

He flung his tank at the lectern and shoved his foot through the railings to kick at it, screaming, "Thordh, you filthy bastard! Where are you?"

"Be still, man! Bailiff!" The bailiff aimed her lightning-rod at Boudreau. Skerow said sharply, "Don't be violent with him! Just return him to the holding area."

"You sonofabitch, he swore you'd let me off easy!" Boudreau howled. "I'll die before I get out of those hell-pits!"

The bailiff summoned two guards to remove him, and the courtroom began to stir like dry leaves before a storm. A burly Tignit with swarming tentacles sniggered through his vocoder, "Give him five more years for bribing the judge!" Attending court was one of the few legal pleasures of Starry Nova.

An elderly Solthree woman in a mineworker's uniform

said in a quiet but penetrating voice, "Give him death. His drugs killed my son."

"Quiet!" Skerow's small hoarse voice was passing its limit, and the bailiff tapped the railing with her rod: a spark jumped from it, hissing.

"Get that prisoner some more oxygen before he suffocates." She slammed her heavy tail on the floor. "Court is adjourned! This is the last session of Galactic Federation Assizes in the city of Starry Nova until next quarter." Tony was looking at her slantwise, but said nothing. The audience gathered itself up and away, grumbling; there were plenty of local courtroom scenes to be enjoyed, but no more exciting interworld ones for another quarter-year.

Skerow turned now to Sama, who was lingering to get her files together. Her voice had been reduced to a hiss and a squeak; she went down the ramp to the floor below the cubicle so that her head would be level with Sama's. "You wanted to tell me," she whispered.

Sama pulled her lips tight and shook her head.

"I will not bring down more trouble on your client's brow," Skerow said. "Five years of prison in Starry Nova is a very heavy sentence. Thordh is a different matter."

Sama looked at her and shrugged, then muttered, "Boudreau said Thordh would let him off with a short sentence, that he'd done it before. Twice." After a moment she added, "I knew that would have to come out some time, but I had an obligation to him, and he might have been boasting. Of course I haven't checked on what he said."

"Quite right. But Thordh said this to him directly? Boudreau could not have been allowed to see him in person."

"I think there was an intermediary, someone who actually spoke to Thordh."

"Yes." *He said I'd get off . . .* "Whatever it is, there's nothing to be done about it this moment," *except, of course, that I must speak to Thordh,* "officially. Good night."

In the empty courtroom she and Tony looked at each other. "I had the impression that you thought I would let that go by. Did you really believe I would be so derelict, Tony?"

"Not at all. It might be easier on you if I spoke to him. That's all I was thinking."

"I must speak to him first. He cannot be let off easier than Boudreau." Tony kept on looking at her. "But I cannot go on sleeping in the same room with the man while this lies so cold between us."

Tony snickered faintly. "I never knew you slept with him, sweetheart."

"Not in the same basin," she hissed.

"Tsk." Tony whisked himself away.

She found herself suddenly very hungry and thirsty. In the lavatory she moistened her gill-stoppers and dropped a pellet of Khagodi sea salt into her water bowl; she was just flicking her tongue at the water when the reaction hit her. Thordh. Fussy, careful Thordh. She felt slightly nauseated but drank anyway.

. . . Some notes you do not have . . .

A very sober sides, that Thordh of yours.

But this was foolish. At the least premature: an enraged felon, an attorney resentful of Khagodi authority . . .

Yet . . . with the cage off her head, and her mind free-ranging, she recalled the wisps of thought, the suspicions, the remarks aside that she had just barely caught when she and Thordh were preparing this case, the efforts she had made not to know or hear. Half-consciously to hide her dislike of the man she had known and often worked with for twenty-five years.

Khagodi: a name made by the Ancestral Saints from compounding words: *Double heart, single mind.* Or expanding them from a chance-found name, perhaps: her people carried these words everywhere throughout the Galaxy. She felt her two hearts beating their heavy uncoordinated rhythms.

Why should I feel betrayed? This one was no Saint and I never liked him. I think I am suffering from deflated vanity. Obviously my judgment of others is not as good as I thought it was.

"Oh Judge Skerow!" Before she had shut the door behind her in the corridor there was a journalist, a thin dark Solthree with a microphone, plucking at her robe. "Where is Thordh, Judge? Where?"

Skerow stared down at the insolent face beneath the broad-brimmed rain hat. She could tell that beneath it he was wearing a commercial shield to hide his journalistic secrets. "He is indisposed," she said, and flicked away the restraining hand with one pearled claw.

Kobai

She called off the limousine and walked the streets in the dirty rain. There was still a smear of dull light toward the west, but the eastern sky roared with takeoffs and landings, and their muffled thunders rolled across the city from beyond its limits. No stars to be seen. Twenty-five years of riding circuit with Thordh and others had brought her here four or five times, and each time renewed her fascination with the thick and lurid sky, the shimmering pavements, the coldlight displays advertising shoddy and expensive gewgaws. In no other city that she knew did hunched figures slink in and out of crumbling archways in such a sinister way, in no other streets could she expect to be confronted out of the darkness with such huge bubble windows that blazed with light to offer satisfaction of the darkest urges in a half-score of species.

Khagodi who live among northern hills and dry plains are usually of a smaller, tighter build than those of the south, and can walk halfway gracefully; the others have a heavy wagging gait that is tiring even to watch. In spite of this advantage in size, the shocking trial had wearied Skerow, enough to make her look for a short cut, though the residence was not far away. She searched for a street where she could go slower and out of the rain, which she liked well enough when it was clean. Now it was coming up over the soles of her sandal-boots, and the chill dampness was getting to her the way it bothered Thordh. She paused in a dimly lit stone passageway leading to an open square. It seemed clear except for the odd drifting flock of bockers and footpads, and the one nuzzer who slithered up to her, whining, "Mama, you want a pogue?"

She spat in his face while she swept her tail to knock down the huggard creeping up on her from behind. Then she moved forward quickly into the light of the stone square.

—and I'll kill you for this!

The thoughtvoice came from nowhere, sharp as a steel dart, and she stood still for a moment among the flashing, bloody-colored lights; the passersby stared, and their thoughts eddied around her.

:Who is that? Who!: No answer: the cry had come from emptiness, as if it had been waiting at the gate of her thought for a stimulus. She turned about, still searching, and behind her left shoulder found the kind of display she had been thinking about, the kind that made Starry Nova so interesting. She stood staring.

A huge bubble of light—no, an illuminated water tank formed the advertisement and window of one shop. She was dimly aware that the line of symbols on its base spelled the name of a chain of brothels famous in a hundred cities on three worlds.

There were two creatures in the tank. One lay on a bed of fake jewels: it nearly covered them, so pearly pale, all tentacles and violet-rimmed mouths: Skerow did not want to know if it was sentient.

The other was . . . a Solthree woman. No matter that it—that she—was hairless, with dark red skin and a blade-shaped tail that propelled her in angry circles, that her forehead and chin receded steeply from the firm mouth, and her huge eyes had sealed transparent lids. Those eyes were empty of thought only because she was sleeping, and twitched with angry dreams that made her open her mouth and clench her teeth. She was a human Solthree woman, not merely sentient but intelligent—powerfully built, with square hands and spatulate fingers, a navel in her belly, and milk glands. Breasts. The sight of them with their stub nipples, of her, exposed and perhaps used, in this window, gave Skerow a powerful pang of vulnerability. Was she the source of that furious threat?

The woman's head rose, her eyes came alive and sharp.

:You out-there do-nothing!: Furious enough, but not the voice that wanted to kill. *:Scaly lady-woman, you tell Lord Big One Upthere, that Nohl, when I catch a good hold of him there is not much left that the dung-fish chew on, you tell him Kobai say so!:* Her dark red palms and knees pressed flat against the glastex, she pushed her bright red mouth and tongue against it in a threat-face. *:You tell him!:*

For the first time in her life, Skerow had absolutely no idea what to do.

She knows me! No . . . she knows Khagodi, Nohl is a Khagodi name. Worse. She is from Khagodis! A captive . . .

The wild and foolish thought came: *rescue!* She calmed herself: the young woman, really a girl, seemed healthy, unmarked, maintained in the kind of water she needed. Even treated like a possession she was being cared for in a legal establishment, and any fuss Skerow might make would harm her. *:Kobai, I understand. I will help you. Tell me—:*
She felt other eyes on her. The madam, a blue-skinned Varvani woman, was standing in the doorway: she balanced her elephantine legs on gold clogs, and the enormous bosom above her chain-mail skirt was tattooed with red kissystars. The bouncer, a Solthree weightlifter, appeared behind her. She said in a deep plush voice, "Don't block the window, dear heart. You want a sample, come on in."

:You tell that Nohl!:

Skerow bared forty-six teeth at the woman, and snuffed air through her nostrils, but she very much wanted to avoid bringing further attention to herself and the captive woman. The Varvani knew nothing: she had only accepted delivery of a sullen package. Skerow told Kobai, *:I don't know him. But I will find him.:*

And without waiting for answers hurried away into the darkness.

Thordh

Because Fthel V is part of the Twelveworlds system, the Administrative Headquarters of Galactic Federation, and run by GalFed, its Outworld Residences are older and shabbier than those of worlds in other systems. They are built and furnished in Early Civil Service, and maintained threadbare and grimy. But this policy does not apply to the more exotic outworlders who need special mixtures of water or atmosphere, and particularly to Khagodi, whose basins and mudtubs need constant sealing and renewing, as well as new floors to bear their weight: Skerow's quarters in what was called The Luxury Suite were no more than half a century old.

When she came round the corner to the entrance she was astonished to find the walkway full of street people, looking up at a window; it was her own, bright with much more light than her room's dim lamps could give. Her first thought was that either the basin had broken, or the mudtub had fallen through the floor, and perhaps Thordh had been hurt. She dipped lightly into the minds of the people around her, but they knew nothing, and when they saw her, scattered.

Just inside the gate a Solthree woman in a uniform was waiting for her: local police. Behind the helmet visor her eyes told of something more serious than a broken tank, or a sunken tub. "You are Madame Skerow?"

"Yes. Where is my colleague? Judge Thordh?"

"Come."

The bright light came from floods on stands. The basin was whole: Thordh was floating in it. Red ribbons of blood swirled round him; it had come from his eyes; squirting was typical of many Khagodi from his part of the world, along with high blood pressure. As he turned in the water the light refracted from his scales, pink, green, metallic blue and sudden red. A bubble had caught in his gill where his breathing siphon had retracted until only its stub was visible; his hands were open, as if he were beseeching.

There were five people waiting for her, two Khagodi, two Solthrees, and a Lyhhrt in a workshell.

"What happened? Is he dead?"

"Yes," said one of the Solthrees. "I'm Lieutenant Strang

and this is Sergeant Ramaswamy. You know Commissioner Erha, and here," indicating the Lyhhrt, "is Medical Examiner Um." This was not the M.E.'s name. Lyhhrt were difficult to introduce because they did not have names. Strang offered a recording microphone. "Can you identify this person?"

"Yes. He's my colleague, Judge Thordh, of Khagodis. Did he die of a stroke?"

"We're not sure how. Or when." He added grudgingly, "Someone called in without leaving a name."

One of the Khagodi, an iridescent young woman, said, "The unknown person also called Lawyer Anthony Labonta, and he sent me when he could not reach you." Her name was Hathe, and she was a friend of Tony's who worked in the Public Defender's Office and lived in the complex.

Skerow turned to the other Khagodi, the Commissioner whose party she had attended years earlier; he and Skerow, along with Hathe, now made up the complete Khagodi population of the city. "Erha Twelfth," she said, for he had Lineage, "can you tell me something about this?"

Erha said awkwardly, "I don't know that I can, Skerow. I was called in . . ." He turned away from the lamps and the sight of the body. "I knew this man for most of my life . . . must we stand here looking at him?"

Without esping him, as she dared not for the sake of privacy, she knew:

You were called in, Twelfth Generation Erha, Father of Many, because someone told you that Thordh, another Father of Many, was in all of that trouble.

Boudreau: *. . . he swore you'd let me off easy!*

Give him death. His drugs killed my son.

All the images of the trial boiled in her mind, and the vision of the woman Kobai imprisoned in a bowl. She had deliberately left off the helmet to avoid an appearance of defensiveness, and now she wished she had worn it. She was shielding perhaps to an unusual degree: Sergeant Ramaswamy put aside the daybook into which he had been both dictating and tapping out notes. "When did you see him last, Madame?"

"During adjournment before the last trial, end of noon-chime three. He asked me to replace him and gave me his notes."

"Do you have them here?"

"Yes." She opened her carryall and offered the spools and tablets. "For some you will need an esp-reader. I scanned through them but there was no new material in them."

"He left after he spoke to you, then?"

"As far as I knew. I found the trial very disturbing, and decided to walk home. I never saw him again."

Strang said, "Did you know he was under investigation, Madame Skerow?"

"No! It seems I am the only one who did not!" She glanced at the body. It was drifting in the darkening water, spirit long gone, discussed with as little concern as if it were a stone of the desert. "I only learned today that there was some kind of trouble. He told me nothing." The water-refresher caught her eye. "Look!"

"What?" The Lyhhrt, previously only a statue of some vaguely hominid and sexually neutral being, stepped forward. She pointed to the rim of the basin and the inset container that normally purified the water. A thread of dark green stuff was seeping through its perforations. He said, "What is that?"

"It is not water purifier."

The Lyhhrt scooped up some of the green-stained water into a specimen jar without touching his metal hands to it.

"He might have poisoned himself," Strang murmured.

"Would he have done it so elegantly?" Ramaswamy asked. Strang gave him a look.

The Lyhhrt was kneeling at the edge of the basin delicately turning the body with a flexible wand. "Was this a moody person, Madame?"

"Self-contained and self-respecting," said Skerow. *Smug* she did not say. *That glossy stud from the Lesser Archipelagoes,* Tony had called him. He would have poisoned himself most elegantly.

"Yes," Strang said. "We will probably call on you again, Judge Skerow. I know you intend to ship out, now that the session is over, but I hope you will be staying for a while."

"Ten days, until the *Zarandu* leaves orbit."

"Good. You may remove the body, Medical Examiner."

"The van is waiting."

She dared a flash of esp at them as they left. The room was not bugged. :*What really happened, Hathe?*:

:*What makes you ask?*:

:*I have not esped you, but those persons are a little uneasy with you.*:

Hathe was embarrassed. :*I hid one small thing. Come to my chamber, where I am sure there are no spies.*:

Hathe's room had two basins, like Skerow's, but it was not offered to important people: two Khagodi would have been cramped in it. :*I never mentioned the tethumekh.*:

:*So much excitement, I had forgotten him.*: The *tethumekh,* Skerow's pet, or more truly companion, was a small primate reptile: a rare and ancient miniature given to her by her brother. It was perched on a basin faucet, flicking dead scales from its shoulder with a tiny forked tongue. "Eskat!" she hissed, and it leaped to her shoulder so that its glittering tail curled beneath her jaw. :*How did he come here, Hathe?*:

:*I found him running in the corridor. Someone . . .*: Some

murderer . . . :left the door open . . . I know I should have told the police, but I was afraid they would take away your pitiful Eskat and torment him for evidence. I will tell this to them though, if you want it.: And aloud, "Would you like to spend the night here, and use the extra basin? I have enough water allowance, and plenty of food."

"I'm grateful, Hathe, but too tired."

"Then share the evening meal with me tomorrow."

"Yes I will." Then she was taken with a feeling of mild but definite unease, because the whole atmosphere of Thordh's deceptions—and deceptiveness in general—seemed stiflingly close. "Thank you for preserving my Eskat, but if any question about him comes up, tell the truth. Thordh's death has already made Khagodi double-minded in the eyes of others."

Tethumekh

When she returned to her room she found the comm buzzing and flashing. "Hullo, sweetheart!" Tony wanted to hear about and tell her everything: "Like a kind of man's voice, like a Solthree's, could have been anybody disguised— *'Tell the police, tell the other Big Squat her Thordh's dead!'* "

Will I never get rid of "my Thordh"?

She listened to the light baritone voice, and thought of a desert windflute, and the scrap of her poetry that went with the thought:

> *in*
> *the sea of*
> *the desert it sings*

Thinking of the sea reminded her of the swimming woman. *Shall I tell him about Kobai?*

She heard in memory the words: —*and I'll kill you for this!*

Is there something about that mindvoice, some familiar echo, that links it with Boudreau? With Thordh, and Kobai too?

And Skerow . . . the final judge of Thordh. Yes, why should she not also be a target of this violence? . . . or Tony, who had a pretty little wife and two frilly daughters.

"Scramble, Tony. I want to speak to you."

"That's what you're doing, love!"

Not over the comm. "Face to face, Tony. Head to head."

"Er . . ."

"Not to esp you!" The idea amused her: Tony was only too generous with his thoughts. "I want to give you what is in *my* mind. Will you come and meet me in the Hub Common Room?"

Where there are plenty of people night and day, and particularly guards.

"All right, but let me get the girls to bed first. They and Jenny have got all excited over having the police here."

"Not in your sector, Tony!"

"Yes, yes! The Terrarium's buzzing. Give me a stad and three ticks."

"Good. I'll put my thoughts in order."

"Dear lord no, Skerow! I can't bear another headache like the one you gave me last time you did that!" He switched off, laughing.

Silence now. No, the rustle of the tethumekh's tail along her neck, its tip like a crystal of topaz that matched its eyes.

Skerow took pity on Tony, and on her own weariness, and let her thoughts drift. Perhaps her indulgence in his presence took precious time away from his family; she hoped this was not so: this friendship was one of the very few pleasures she enjoyed on this world. There had been none at all in Thordh's company; so many nights shared in a room of basins, and so few thoughts or feelings. His presence turned her shy and inhibited; that of all her peers, male Khagodi, did, and he had been a big man, just her own size. He had floated there asleep with the colors playing on his scales, perhaps three *siguu* away, tail curled around his Lineage, his ten sons and seven daughters . . .

She could not drag her mind away now: the little picture-cube had been on the shelf—how had it got into her hand? Finger touching the switch-stud like a magnet.

The holo image floated on the water of her basin. She could not bring herself to move the cube and disturb it, so very slender, so frail a girl holding the little transmitter in her pearl talons: *:It is Tapetto, Bathi! I hope you are well, and Tada. Everyone here says I am looking so much healthier, I will be home by the time Tada comes for Holidays, and I will race with you!:*

One breath of wind for those ashes. And he had divorced her for infertility.

She thought of composing a poem, but there would be too many desert winds blowing through it, and she still had a half stad in which it would be wise to make her way most slowly and thoughtfully to the Hub Common Room, all senses extended.

The tethumekh had dropped to her shoulder and was trying to groom the scales of her neck. A member of this species almost always wore around its neck a fine chain hung with a pendant that had begun as the small seed of a *kesshi* fruit. The tethumekh sucked at its rough surface to rid itself of a substance in saliva produced by overbreeding, and after years of accumulation produced a precious jewel, very much like an opal: now Eskat was building the eleventh of such jewels. He tapped it with a claw, and the iridescent bead swung in the light. This time she would not leave him loose. She scratched him gently under the jaw and slipped into his mind: it was like looking into a crystal which showed things magnified but blurred . . . his daylong memory bank:

Day always dark, no Sun to sleep in, he is bored and sucks furiously on the bead; once long ago there was a Big-one who kept him locked up and cruelly teased to make it grow. Not this Big-one. This One puts out food and water. Stale meat, strange-tasting water, some kind of small dried things, says this is good-good! He spits. When she goes and Other-one comes with that thump-step, yellow-eye looks him down, he squeaks: eeyik! Other wants to wring his neck, he is glad to jump-into-cage-pull-the-door-shut!

But now Other-one sleeps and he is bored again. No, Here Comes Somebody!

Wants to play!

No! Skerow's teeth clashed involuntarily. The *tethumekh* squeaked and skittered to the floor.

But yes, no choice but to know everything now. The murderer had not reckoned with her patience, her particular link with this animal. She picked him up very gently, he trembled in her hand and drew the faceted gem of his tail down the side of her head. She soothed his scales down carefully the right way—nice, good Eskat!—and lived along with him the rest of his afternoon.

When she was done there was almost no time to keep her appointment properly. She left without hurry just the same, caging Eskat and setting all her personal alarms. Tony would be anxious, but she would watch what was going on about her.

The hall was bright with white diffuse light, its neighboring doorways framed with black-enameled Cruxan *thaq*-wood that lasted for centuries. She kept her mind tightly closed though there was no one about and the apartment doors connected white-noise circuits that shielded both the people behind them and whoever might be in the halls. She loathed the impervious helmet; Khagodi sight and hearing were slightly duller than those of most non-ESPs, and while she very rarely esped intrusively, the low-level scan she usually maintained sharpened her senses, especially on these worlds where the skies were so thick and dark. The helm made her feel blind and deaf.

The walls of the first cross corridor were lined with grey slotted machines dispensing oxygen tanks, water-purifying cartridges, air-fresheners, meal and transportation tokens, franking-stamps, signet rings and sealing wax. The hard un-resonant floor was covered with colorless carpet tiles that looked the same whether they were threadbare or new.

At the next hallway the traffic began to thicken with people of other species who breathed similar oxygen mixtures: two prowling Ungrukh who liked a night run, shaking imaginary fleas out of their crimson fur, looking calmly at her with eyes of the same color that flashed green as they turned them to the light: they wanted fresh meat and their thoughts clearly expressed what they felt about what they got instead; a long and twisting Sziis ambassador roiling because she had been obliged to smoke too much *ge'iin* at a party celebrating the acquisition of a hovercraft factory for a colony world; a Solthree, lugging an oxygen tank, who had been trapped by a flight delay and found no room in the Terrarium. None of these intended Skerow any harm. All of them, no matter of what species, sensed her in some way as prehistoric with her massive head balanced by the long heavy tail, her powerful tread and glistening scales.

Two doorways watched by guards formed a loose airlock that led into higher oxygen country and eventually the Terrarium. Skerow put filters in her gills to thin the air and stepped on the moving walkway nervously: she did not trust ground that slid under her feet. After a while the decorative foliage shifted in emphasis from succulents to broadleaf plants; these too looked as if they had lasted centuries: although the air was much moister here they seemed to be writhing for lack of water.

The moving corridors put out branches that grew from and fed into more lanes swinging up and down to other levels. The one Skerow was traveling seemed to go on forever. Along all its length of *siguu* no other person was riding it. The traffic had melted, and the walk lay deserted from one vast stretch to another. She quickened her pace, but the exit ramp seemed to recede, or perhaps her eyesight had dulled because there were no sharper eyes to see along with.

She was conscious of movement to one side, and glanced to her right; all she saw was a mirror where another Skerow paced along the reflection of her walkway.

She blinked. There was no mirror here, and never had been, but there was another Khagodi keeping abreast of her on a walkway running parallel to her own that was about to swing down to a lower level.

Startled, she realized that it was her awareness rather than her eyesight which had gone dim. In this moment she lost the power of her shield. Her mind was naked to a thought-attack of a kind she had never in her life experienced.

Of all the criminals in her dock, Khagodi or extraterrestrial, no matter how furious and cursing they had been—some far worse than Boudreau—none had tried to attack her in this way, not even when she was bareheaded.

She was helpless: her mind was so bent back on itself that all she could see was her own reflection, as if she were surrounded by mirrors; did not know who was attacking her or why, tried to run, to thrash about, and could not even see her body or anything but her own image, could not move. Light was fading from her eyes, the whine of her blood in its vessels rose with the drumming of her hearts; she began to sink under the pressure of the mirrors.

She gasped, her jaws opened in terror and panic, but her nostrils and voice-bladder had collapsed; she was voiceless; when her teeth clamped again involuntarily they came down hard on her tongue; this time she found a shrill voice, and saw hideous stars of pain. When she could get her eyes open after that there was a dim tunnel of sight opening away from her, and at the end of it the tiny figure of Tony with his mouth open in a round shape and his hands turned out like finger-clams. The mirrors hovered at the edge of her vision ready to close in, but from the corner of her eye she saw the prehistoric figure looming, always running to stay where it was on the walkway.

When she realized this—*It must run to stay where it is*—she saw clearly through the pain that her enemy's intention was divided, and also aimed at Tony, the unknowing witness.

:*NOW YOU ARE GOING TO STOP THAT,: she said firmly.*

The other Khagodi stared at her with pale yellow eyes.

She seized her consciousness to herself with all her being, and said, :*YOU WILL STOP THAT OR I WILL BE-COME REALLY ANGRY!:* She felt rather foolish saying this, like a teacher addressing an unruly pupil, and at the same time rather savage, because of the threat to Tony—and the pain in her tongue. Her eyes locked with the Other's. She tasted blood.

The stars and mirrors crashed down on her.

She rose from the rubble of smashed mirrors to just below the surface of consciousness, and her mind began a tentative exploration, as if she were probing the extent of a sore place. The sore resolved itself into the bite on her tongue, which had swollen so much it was a painful lump that filled her mouth.

She was floating in her basin. Her head was under water but her autonomic system had extended her breathing siphon and inflated the fold of membrane at its lip into the big bubble that anchored its opening to the surface of the water; it was trembling with each of her short breaths. Someone had brought a Solthree chair for Tony, and he sat with Eskat digging claws into his shoulder, watching her. The *tethumekh* had become a decorative jewel like the swag of gold on a diplomat's uniform, making him look odd and out of place.

Strang and Ramaswamy had come and gone, and so had Commissioner Erha, but the Lyrhht Medical Examiner was bending over her. He had stayed because he was the only one who had even a notion of how to treat a Khagodi in shock. He had warmed her bath and given her a nutrient IV drip. Since she had had no time to eat the previous day's meal she was saved from nausea. Now he said, "I have put my signal into the comm here, and you may access it with the emergency code," and left.

Alone with Tony, she watched through his eyes as he watched this big drowsing woman, so shy for all of her authority. At a just-below-conscious level she understood that now she was safe and in privacy, and she began to stir: her mind boiled anew with images of lightning flashes and shattered mirrors. The *tethumekh* sucked fretfully on its bead and squeaked: *ik! eeyik!* She saw through Tony's eyes that a thread of blood had drifted from the earslit at the top of her gill; she turned to look at it and her siphon dipped and bubbled.

"Watch it, sweetheart," he whispered.

She could not force her mind back to the walkway. :*What happened, Tony?*: Her eyes opened.

"You don't know your own strength, my love. I'd hate to be around when you became really angry."

:*Did I kill her?*: She shifted and began to lever herself up on a hip and one elbow. Her siphon-bubble deflated, and the tube folded concertina-wise into its gill-slit. The water streamed from her shoulders and neck.

"Watch out for the IV! The doctors may be able to put her head together again."

"Who brought me here?"

"Five medics and four trolley-servers lashed together."

"My folly in being so headstrong . . . this flask is nearly empty, and I suppose I no longer feel hungry." She pulled the needle from her neck, filled a spitbowl with fresh water to rinse her mouth. "It . . . was Hathe then?" She spoke a bit raggedly: because of the sore. Through Tony she could see that her dark red tongue had a flaming lump on one edge.

"Didn't you know?"

"I tried to keep from knowing." Her head seemed dull, and she felt as if her body had shrunk. "I had left Eskat out of his cage, I didn't expect Thordh would come back first. Thordh loathed him, but he took care not to let him escape. Hathe didn't even think of Eskat while she was poisoning Thordh, and he thought she'd come to play . . . he followed her afterward . . ."

"Do you think she poisoned him only because he refused to let Boudreau off?"

"Not only . . . I believe someone must have bought her for that reason. To spy on Thordh. According to Sama, Thordh had let Boudreau off twice earlier, and there must have been other cases she didn't know about. Thordh was a double-tongued man; it seems that he was in the hire of smugglers. Perhaps they had doubts about him already, and when he betrayed them—by having me take the case this time—they had him killed. I wonder about him . . . whether that one last time was one too many, and he was trying to redeem himself. Or just that he felt footsteps on his tail."

"Then why would Hathe sell herself—really?"

"Must I know that? To gain some kind of power, meaning an apartment with more space and bigger basins? To get away from this ugly world? Tell me, did I truly harm her so badly?"

"Not on purpose."

"She was very powerful. It's a pity, she could have been . . . I will apologize to the Saints. I've lost a person I thought was a friend."

"So have I, and I thought I knew her even better than you did."

"When she showed herself to me on the walkway . . . after Thordh disgracing us . . . I thought—perhaps hoped—some other intelligence was putting on a Khagodi image. I was deceived—I deceived myself. Not altogether. There was a possibility that the attacker was Nohl."

"Nohl? Who's that, Skerow?"

She told him about Kobai. "When Hathe attacked me I was on my way to tell you . . ." And gave him the picture.

"My God. From Khagodis? I've never heard of that kind of person. Who could she be?"

"There is no other indigenous sentient life on our world, and nothing at all that looks in the least like a Solthree, not under the waters or in the trees or in the air."

"Poor woman! Why didn't you tell the police?"

"I'm not sure I know . . . first I was too astonished at Thordh's death even to think of her, and then I only wanted to get away from them, get them away from me, and yes, I do know—because some of my own people were behind this on a world where there are so few of them, and the citizens here don't much care for Khagodi authority figures. And, you know, the police don't either."

"There may not be anything they can do about this woman but the police ought to know just the same."

"Perhaps they know already. Brothels bring in a great deal of money."

"I never expected to meet that degree of cynicism in you, love—and so suddenly."

"Because my manner is rather awkward you believe I'm ignorant and naive. You have many preconceptions about me, Tony."

"I did. But I don't think I'll have too many more!"

The Slave

Ramaswamy looked at her with soulful eyes. "It is not a human being, Madame."

"What!"

"It is registered as an experimental animal, legally imported under the terms of the Recreations & Amusements Act, Brothels & Zoos Division. I was shown the bills-of-sale and receipts."

She looked hard at him. "Experimental animal? I spoke with her! And that is a trash law, Ramaswamy, designed to let Zamos's establishments operate. They are not running a zoo."

He shrugged. "Whatever they run, Madame, is under the authority of the local police. Traditionally they are jealous of that authority."

"If I might see her—"

"Zamos's admits her presence, but we are not zoo inspectors, Judge Skerow. As long as this being has no status as a person, is legally accounted for, with documentation, and is seen to be in good health, those people are within their rights, no matter how ghastly a pleasure is taken from her."

Skerow hissed, "There is nothing at all to be done then?"

"Judge Skerow, you may be correct in your belief that

there is a suffering person illicitly held by Zamos's establishment, but you know," he looked hard at her, "that you cannot go near it, and I cannot do anything except by catching them bloodhanded." He took out his daybook and switched it on. "If you can tell me whatever you know, or even think you know, I will consult with Lieutenant Strang and we will try to keep an eye on that place."

"I am sure she came from Khagodis. The Nohl she told me about was certainly a Khagodi—she thought I knew him. No. She was sure I must be associated with him. Experimental animal! We import most of our technology. How could we produce those kinds of experiments—animals that look like Solthrees!" Almost absently she held her hand out: Eskat landed on it in one leap from Tony's shoulder, and ran up her arm to his usual perch on her head. "Even creatures like Eskat are rarely bred nowadays because it is considered cruel, and I would never own a tethumekh if my brother had not given him to me more than fifty years ago . . ."

Ramaswamy waited. Skerow was feeling quite dim, but tried to focus her thoughts. "She called me an 'out-there-do-nothing,' had no idea where she was or who I could be—except a Khagodi—said I was to tell Nohl, Lord Big One Upthere, that if, no, *when* she caught him, there would be nothing left of him, nothing for the dung-fish to chew on. I've never seen one of those, but I know they exist, under a slightly different name . . . There were others like herself in her mind, I think, perhaps one Solthree . . . and, the fish we call scrapfish. I think they come from the Volcanic Isthmuses, an equatorial country. Some people there actually eat them, but Isthmus-men like to eat all kinds of poison. Since she called me a do-nothing, she must be some kind of worker, or even slave . . . she is hand-oriented, and would have been working in the waters of that country . . . what I think is that she's a gold-picker. Yes . . . a gold-picker. I wouldn't swear to it in a court of law, but that's what she is."

"I don't understand, Judge Skerow."

"You know gold, Sergeant. In the Isthmuses, where you'd find the scrapfish, the veins of gold that swell up from earthquakes break off in lumps of almost pure gold and roll into the seas, where the currents wash them down smooth as pebbles. People pick them, as they do on any world where gold is, and we get quite a bit of it that way—just picked up. Ourselves, we are not big gold users; we manufacture a few instruments and some bits of jewelry and export the rest. But in the same way that non-ESPs believe they can become telepathic if they take mind-altering drugs, there are Khagodi and some other peoples who believe gold enhances their esp if they eat it in compounds. That is only because it makes them toxic—just as with the others."

"Then there is likely an illegal trade in gold compounds, same as any other head drug," said Ramaswamy.

"Maybe so, Ramaswamy, and I am also sure that Kobai is a victim of illegal trade—in people. And if so, then I am forced against my will to believe that a respected man like Thordh must have been involved in all kinds of that trade, along with any other Khagodi smugglers to or from this world. And by all my Saints and Ancestors I want it stopped."

"We will do what we can," said Ramaswamy.

An Aborigine

It was noon. Skerow felt that she had not eaten and not slept: rightly, because she had taken IV fluids and lain for hours in the drowse of shock. She thought vaguely that she ought to bestir herself, if only to show Tony that he need not worry about her. Although the Assizes were over, he had plenty of other work: he dealt with international cases as well as Galactic ones, though in this cold laboring world the nations were huge mining and industrial companies.

There were no aboriginal peoples on Fthel V: Khagodi called it *tikka,* meaning Five, and all of the names given it by other worlds were analogous. The world Khagodis had a name, but in one basic way it was similar to Five. It too was a colony world, and it had no paleoanthropology.

The Khagodi did not know their home world or people; they knew only that thousands of years of exploration and digging had yielded no buried family lines of descent, not even for tethumekhs and other wild reptiles. The ancient skeletons of thumbless animals had unrelated structures and inimical chemistries. There were branches of Khagodi religions that considered these conclusions heretical: the Diggers and some of the Inheritors contended that no one had yet dug in the right place; but the Watchers and Hatchlings, who believed that their ancestors had been delivered by burning gods in enormous eggs, were probably a half step nearer the truth. Whatever their religion, Khagodi did not believe in lost gardens of innocence, or any other kind of ignorance.

Skerow's home had few gardens and many mountains that rose fiercely out of the desert. She missed its thin cool air and vast blue skies by day and the white salt light of its two moons by night. No matter how powerful a yearning for warmth and tropic greens might sweep her at times, her visits to equatorial lands left her suffocated by the heat and moisture that winds and storms would not blow away. Dismal worlds like Fthel-tikka gave her part of her livelihood, and beyond that only piqued her curiosity with their degraded cities.

Dutifully she set her mind toward work. Eskat scratched her head. There were documents to be collated with those prepared by Tony and Sama, and reports to write . . . now Hathe would no longer help with ledgers and trial records.

Would you like to spend the night here and use the extra basin?

Would I still be alive if I had? You must suppose so, Skerow, since she would not likely have wanted your dead body in one of her tubs! Hathe! How could you have given yourself in that way? And Thordh—what price did you sell yourself for? Dear Saints and Ancestors, let me not become a complete cynic in less than one day!

—But Kobai! How could she have come there? Can there be people on Khagodis breeding and importing slaves?

Work was out of the question. She opened her personal copybook and called up what she had last set down:

> *o*
> *this desert*
> *I drown in moonlight*

This is as near as can be described in general terms the form of the *seh* written by Khagodi in the Northern Spine Confederacy: three lines of one, three and five syllables in any order. It is not the only form of poetry produced in the Spines, but certainly the one considered by critics in equatorial lands to be the most dry and frigid.

What Skerow was thinking was: *alone in moonlight.* She erased and rewrote the last line with these words.

Now I can never show this to anyone. she said to herself. Far too revealing. Nevertheless she considered it in a steadfast way, and added:

> *at noon*
> *I*
> *see the burning star*

When the sky is very clear more than one can be seen. She thought for a moment, went back to the first *seh* and wrote:

o
this desert
I burn in moonlight

She was content with this but now, having used up the idea of burning, did not know what to do with the second *seh*. The comm buzzed, scrambler-tone. There were very few now who knew her scramble code.

"Skerow!" said the voice.

"Yes. Who is speaking?"

"A friend." This was a male Solthree's sharp but seductive voice.

"Do you have a name, friend?"

"Not yet."

Her fingertip hovered over the recording button, but once activated it would trip a signal on the caller's panel. Unless he was calling from a cheap public comm. She pressed the button very gently.

No reaction. "What do you want, then, aside from be-friending me?"

"Skerow dear, would you like to become a senior magis-trate?"

"I believe I already am one."

"Are you earning as much as Thordh?"

"No. But he is dead, and not earning it either." He would have gotten the code from Thordh, who used the same one.

"Thordh dead, Judge?" the sharp voice sniggered. She was being mocked.

Where is Thordh, Judge? Where? In the courthouse hall after the trial: a thin dark Solthree with a microphone and an

insolent face, plucking at her robe and pushing a microphone at her. Mocking her.

He is indisposed, she had said. Now she refused the temp-
tation of a flippant answer. The man was dead, murdered,
perhaps at the order of this person or someone like him. "I
don't care to pay Thordh's price for advancement."

"For showing a little mercy?"

This was not one with whom she would discuss justice. "I
was thinking more of the dying."

"Really? You believe he was killed?"

—I'll kill you for this!

She was already hanging up when she realized that the
particular pronunciation of *killed* was very near what had
rung in her mind, from one raveled tag-end of thought, out
on a busy street. But there was nothing to be gained now by
speaking longer.

Neither Strang nor Ramaswamy could be reached; she
transmitted the recording of her conversation to their
comms. When she finished this her mind of a sudden became wonderfully clear.

*Hathe—that woman tried to kill me. Really tried. Did
her best. And I burned her brain to smoke and sea-wrack.
This man is some kind of demon. I am sure he ordered the
death of Thordh, whom I knew for twenty-five years, and
who died horribly in my own sleeping room. He tried to
tempt me to do terrible evil. No, I was not tempted, but I let
him speak to me. I listened.*

She began to shake, her teeth rattled, the sore on her
tongue flamed. She seized at herself as she had done when
she was under attack out on the walkway, forced herself to
let her mind slip out of gear, to relax long enough to find a
flask of the mildly sedative herbal tea that most of the time
calmed the strung-out nerves of powerful Khagodi ESPs.

The latch hummed on the outer door, and it slid open. She crouched staring.

The person who faced her was the servant who replaced the towels, drinking bowls and water purifiers, and left fresh flagons of bath oils, salts and softeners for her skin. A small grey-skinned hominid in a blue robe, whose sex, species, world of origin she did not know. Thin-boned and hairless; soft pinkish eyes rested on her in a moist-rimmed gaze.

Drugged on something strong—by choice or force? . . . *perhaps Kobai has been drugged, taken away to some even more terrible place or killed—just because I found her?*

She pushed away these panic-thoughts sparked by her state of delayed shock. The servant, who looked more like a Solthree than a Khagodi, and more like a female than not, was staring at her with something of fright in her face. She whispered in *lingua,* in an accent unknown to Skerow, "I came to freshen your basin for you, Madame."

"I think I would like to sleep a little now," Skerow said weakly.

"It takes only a moment, and the water would be sweet." She was wearing a cheap mesh white-noise helmet, not for her own privacy but to show she could not receive the thoughts of others. After a pause, she added, "These flasks are safe-sealed."

Skerow looked at her closely, but she was only waiting with a drudge's patience, explaining local standards to the outworlder. Skerow pulled herself up sharply: her brains were surely still out of order. "Thank you, go ahead."

She watched the stale water being gulped by the drain, and then the fresh flowing into the clean basin, mixing the oils and crystals into swirls. On impulse she asked, "What world do you come from, dems'l?"

The servant stopped in mid-motion and stood without

moving, as if she were a robot that had been turned off. For a moment Skerow wondered if she might not actually be a robot; then she said quietly, "Why not take off that uncomfortable helmet for a moment?" The small grey creature took off the mesh cap with a submissive gesture, and Skerow forced herself to ask the question again.

And with obvious effort, the servant made herself answer: "This world, Madame."

"You were born here?"

"Yes."

"And your parents?"

"Here. We have always lived on this world." As far as Skerow could tell, her consciousness and memories of parents and world were genuine, though not sharply detailed.

Skerow whispered as if she were a conspirator: "Do people ask you this question often, dems'l?"

"No one has ever asked it of me before."

"Thank you for speaking with me. Don't forget your cap."

The servant pulled up a cloth that had been looped into her cord girdle and wiped her head with it before replacing the helm. "Yes. It was a relief to be free of its weight for a moment." She gave Skerow a little dipping curtsy as she replaced the cloth, and her eyes cooled and seemed to flatten. "May all good go with you, Madame."

And Skerow was left alone with her thoughts—or against them.

In a day of twenty-eight stads the man she had worked with for a quarter century had been revealed as a criminal and murdered; the woman who had seemed to be one of her two or three friends on this world was shown to be a murderer; she herself had barely escaped with her life and done terrible violence on her attacker; she had discovered that there was a species of intelligent life which she had never heard of living on her home world, a member of which was held captive; the working world she had believed to be without indigenous life, and which was part of Galactic Federation Headquarters, had turned out to have something very much like it; and both of these kinds of life were very much like slaves.

"The first version was better," she said to the empty air. She sank into her basin, extended her siphon and let the water flow over her eyes and mouth.

I drown in moonlight
I drown.

Zamos's Brothel: Skerow and Ned Gattes

Having slept exhausted until the evening, Skerow prepared herself a listless rehydrated meal.

It was a grisly irony that, because the Khagodi population had halved in one day, the availability of its food supplies had doubled. But the foods were still the same freeze-dried strips of myth-ox and sea-*smik*, the same preserved *kappyx* bulbs. This irony induced a mild sadness in Skerow, but it did not dull her appetite for better stuff than was usually available to interworld travelers. She had tasted a few foods grown on other worlds and liked them, but so far had found no one who liked myth-ox, sea-smik, or kappyx, so there was no question of trading.

There had been no messages on her comm when she woke, and she shrank from calling Strang or Ramaswamy to press for news. Thoughts of Kobai haunted her, of the help she had been unable to give, the near impossibility of giving it now. She was afraid that her whole trail of connections was no more than a story she had told herself, with no evidentiary basis at all.

She laid it out once more:

The first sign had been that Thordh excused himself from sitting on Boudreau's trial because of "indisposition"; then Boudreau's defense counsel, Sama, had behaved oddly when she heard about Thordh; Boudreau's reaction to a change of judges was extreme because of his stated expectations of being let off by Thordh and his claim to Sama that this had been done twice before.

The strange Solthree "journalist" with the microphone had pestered Skerow in the corridor; the flicker of thought— *and I'll kill you*—had caught her in the street—or only the tag-end of a half-heard conversation? Kobai had flashed on her like a dream, with her certainty of recognizing a Khagodi.

The day and its events had been growing darker all the time, with the murder of Thordh, the news that he had already been under investigation by GalFed for misconduct, and her reading of the tethumekh to discover his murderer (Eskat darted his little tongue at her sea-smik, and she absently shooed him away, but on taking thought offered him some). And the battle with Hathe that seemed to close the incident, all in the space of one day. . . .

Kobai, who was no vision or dream, was called an animal. An experimental animal whom she believed to be a victim of illegal trade.

The bribing voice on the comm that stirred echoes of the rude journalist and the threat thought; last, the servant who claimed to be an aboriginal on a world Skerow had always believed to have none.

There were three stories there: Thordh, Kobai, and the servant. Thordh's had a clear line line that could be substantiated by police work, more clearly if Hathe could be examined. That story was separate from the others. There was evidence enough that Kobai existed, but Skerow did not know how to prove she was a person. She had noticed the servant—for the first time in all of her visits—only because Kobai was on her mind, and made her think of indentures and slavery; she was afraid her attention had endangered both of them.

She washed out her bowl and shelved it, she mopped a spill of water from the rim of her basin, she paced and wrung her hands. Eskat jittered on her head, squeaking. She called up her report in its ledger, hissed at it and shut it down again. She looked at her face in the mirror and rolled her eyes at it. There was nothing to do but get out of this place.

She stalked the streets. Away from its blistered port area Starry Nova looked from above like what it was: a city that had been built by computer simulation. Skerow watched it through the eyes of buzzer and hovercar pilots: its concrene warehouses and glastex offices stretched beyond and beyond, their square clusters occasionally varied only by the cancerous spread of a factory with landing pads and transport terminals on its roof. Beyond the factories and warehouses were more and more that stretched out like amoebas with ever-narrowing arms gesturing at the mines with their engines and satellite towns. The cloud lowered ever closer and darker toward the winter season.

Down in the city center, the rivers of life flowed along the wet pavements, past the shops flickering with coldlight displays, shouldering the little squat runabouts that carried the mandarins of industry and policy on errands of civil or personal service; these did not pause at the narrow fronts of the stopover hotels or the grimy restaurant faces, each advertised by one yellow lamp. Establishments like Zamos's had private back roads for them, covered with arcades of imitation shrubs, and richly draped and carpeted entrances. The poorer people, bold and shy, who slipped past the gross Varvani or the comatose bouncer in the street doorway beside the window were most of them on their way home to slots in the wall of a workmen's hostel.

Skerow's thoughts brooded over the city. Citizens of five thousand worlds, GalFed and neutral, labored here in perhaps fifty thousand establishments; her mind hovered above the one where Kobai was or had been. She was a little calmer now, and did not much fear that Kobai was in great physical danger, even though she was hidden away behind the crackling white-noise barrier: the life of the swimming woman had come to the attention of too many people outside its milieu.

Three buildings away from the complex that housed the two-faced bordello, Skerow peered without seeing over the railing of a bridge into a stream that was not a river but a drainage channel; her mind's eye was watching Zamos's traffic from the eyes of passersby. Outside the bubble where the dead-eyed creatures floated there was a scuffle going on.

A Solthree mack was beating a whore, also a Solthree, though she looked anything but, more like a Pinxid with her blued skin and lips green as a fruit peel, the way she writhed and howled pitifully, and clawed with green nails; perhaps she specialized in Pinxin. Skerow knew that there was a specialist for everything. The woman was dressed in some blue smoky wrap that seemed to have caught the raindrops in it, and a fold of it had been draping her dark blond hair, but was beginning to drift away as she shrieked and twisted. Her voice rose sharply among the mutterings and gestures of a thousand languages. She was screaming incoherent words: *bass'd! muffker! cocksker!* Her face was in shadow.

The pimp was gripping her wrist with one hand and buffeting her face and head with the other. "It's me or nobody!"

his voice was tight with fury, "me or nobody!" He pulled a horn-handled knife and flicked its blade open. His hair was slick, and he wore a velvet jersey that raged with red and blue coldlight designs, and tight blue skinlo pants, but his face looked grubby because of his uneven beard stubble. Each seemed to be wearing a big fake diamond earring, but these were oxygen capsules implanted in their necks.

Skerow watched through twenty minds and pairs of eyes as their owners came within view of this couple and moved out of it: large topaz ones rather like her own, which saw them like her own, weak and blurry; mammalian and reptilian eyes, brown, green and pink, whose owners hurried to get out of the way for fear of the pimp's knife; steely ones sensitive to infrared (red thermograms throbbed with the furious heartbeats of the combatants); robotic eyes in cyborgs that saw them abstractly as flickering points on a grid; flat sound-reflecting pupils that intuited them as concepts. Two Solthree eyes flat with stupidity, their pupils shrunk by opium.

Skerow from her distance felt equally stupefied, but was sharply pulled back to self-awareness when the Varvani madam clapped her hands and the dim eyes of the bouncer livened with resolve: he moved neatly and quickly toward the pimp as the knife flashed upward at the woman's throat. At the same time the brothel's bubble window flashed even brighter as some new orange-and-yellow creature swam into Skerow's ken, and she saw then not the dueling pair but in her mind's eye Kobai raging in captivity, in the situation she could do nothing about. She sent her thought more quickly than the pimp's knife hand to disarm its controlling mind.

Out, out, lady! Out! This was not a formed thought but an almost physical repulse coming from the pimp as the thickly painted whore twisted her head away and brought her hand's edge chopping on his arm. Skerow did not exactly see into the steel trap of the man's mind but caught a mental configuration that said: *Agent, Madame, your side.*

This was the truth, and she did not want to break his barriers then, but watched the fleeting moment in which the musclehead from Zamos's knocked the knife from the rogue's hand with a mallet fist and the prostitute picked it from the air and cast it away.

The bouncer did not grab at her but unhooked his lightning-rod and advanced on the pimp, who scrambled away like a craven cur, howling, "Take the damned fireship!"

The bouncer sniggered and tossed him a gold coin, which the pimp did not hurl back at him but tucked into his waistband before he scurried off, snatching up his knife as he ran. The Varvani opened her arms to the beaten woman, and she like an orphan rested her decorated head on the huge blue bosom.

Skerow let herself drift from their orbit and waited on the bridge, eyes downward. She did not hear the steps as the pimp climbed the arch and put his elbows on the opposite railing, but her ears caught his still-harsh breaths. He was looking out toward the garish window of Zamos's as if he was waiting for the woman to come back to him.

"Ned Gattes at your service, Madame Skerow." He did not esp, but kept his shield down tight and his voice to a hoarse whisper.

She took a closer look down at him in the glancing lamplight and saw that the stubble covered a rash. He was nearly as short as Tony, but heavily muscled. "You know me. Of course. The only Khagodi woman in the world now. Don't expose yourself to more danger, Ned Gattes."

"A pimp who is allowed to run from Zamos's back door is safe."

"You did all of that very nicely."

"I was well trained."

"Is your lady safe?"

"She has no more virtue to lose than I do, and takes good care of herself."

"Do you work for the police?"

"With them. Right now I am working with yours."

She did not want to mention, or even think of, Kobai in this place, but she could not help asking: "Are you looking for . . . ?"

"A woman, yes."

The sky over Starry Nova had darkened, and, except for intermittent alarms, the city had fallen silent, even around Zamos's, like any other that had no urban culture. She heard his hand rasping over his jaw. "You have some trouble with your skin."

"Ingrown beard. I think I will kill whoever picked this skin for me."

She had to think a moment before she said, "A graft."

"Yes."

"You must have lost your own in curious circumstances."

"I did." She sensed rather than saw his grin. "The face suits pimping for cheap whores."

"Are you really a pimp?"

"Only for tonight. Usually I'm a pugilist, gladiator, whatever it's called on this world."

That was quite right; slender Tony was the fencer, this one the pug. "Then you would not have missed with the knife, if you had meant to use it."

"I would not. But I'm not an ESP, either. None of the pugs are. I'm just a sensitive with good blocking ability."

"What was the gold coin you picked up, Ned Gattes?"

"A token for fourteen percent off the price of Ophiuchi flameheads, tonight's specialty. It will have useful fingerprints and sweat traces. Goodnight, Sta'atha Amfa Skerow."

* * *

Skerow left Ned Gattes to do his work and went back to her lodgings: ate again and slept again. Then she wrote up her legal reports and one more for Strang and Ramaswamy, describing her encounter with her room-servant, and all she had seen or heard, or thought she had seen or heard, or simply thought; she was content at least that she had done everything possible to place and preserve the endangered in safety. After that she boarded the shuttle and then the *Zarandu,* bound for home. Once on board, she went, along with Eskat, into starvation mode, stasis, and deepsleep early so she (and he) would not have to eat any more dried mythox and sea-smik, or preserved kappyx bulbs.

TWO *

Fthel V: *Ned Gattes and Manador*

Ned wanted to hang about and see whether Jacaranda, his fighting partner and fellow pro-tem agent, might be kicked into the street: if she had been, he would know that she was unsuccessful but safe. That she had not been did not show either. But he dared not wait. His ability to keep moving among crowds was his best defense. It was not safety, but better than the naked dark. In a moment he was among the jostling crowds, not lost, nor wanting to be, but chatting up the whores and other pugs who pimped on the side, offering better deals to their customers, grinning his hard grin, dodging the fist and the knife.

Although Ned was very self-aware and extremely sensitive to his surroundings, he was not an ESP and had no innate talent for sensing whether he was being followed. As a GalFed agent he did not seek out heroics, but preferred to work as an observer who hung about in the scurf of the crowd's edge to report the odd or unusual. He fought for money, not for free, and his fear, besides defeat in the arena, which might be fatal, lay in being pestered by some street challenger who had seen him fight and thought he could be beaten. Now in these circumstances he did not know whether he ought to expect a shadow.

But whether as pimp, pug, or spy, he was not quite astonished when a pair of arms came at him from a doorway and a voice shrieked, "He swears me clean safe clappies, the devil-dog, and he brings me none but old combers who like to blacken me blue in the stem from pinch!"

"Hey what, Poll Tenchard!—ow!" for she had bitten his ear. He pulled her off him by the scruff and laughed, though he had nearly broken her arms in his startle. Ned associated quite happily with Poll whenever he worked in Starry Nova. Now she was the literal fleshing out of his string of employees (two), his protective coloring. She wrenched to free herself; she was no frail thing but a good strong woman of TerBorchland on New Southsea World, from where she had forfeited a bond through bad behavior and been exiled. She was light brown in the skin, had long black braids, and wore a red-and-purple skintight, all whorls and zippers.

"Poll, sweet Poll, what're you boiling for, darling-o?" He grabbed both her hands in one, kissed them, and tickled her chin, enraging her further. "You were well and goodly paid for last time, hey? Spend-all drinking kava, bet you."

"Keep your scab thumbs off me, fartbreath! That was none but a taste to work up the spit in my mouth!" Her native people spoke a Malay-rooted language, and for talking with Solthrees she had learned a bastard pidgin from watching old trivvy programs. It was not uncommon. Even the Russians spoke this, with rather less color than Poll.

"Hush, dear heart, you'll spoil my business."

"It's good for my heart if I do! Y' owe me for all the scumsuckers nozzered me this night when yer leaving me by."

"Well, Poll, you're better off for it than I am, for you've

had the gold if only in the drinking of it, and I've had none from you."

He spoke jokingly enough, but with a bit of snap in the words, and she pulled away from him in fear—"You'll not want to do me in—" and in the dull watchlight above the door he saw that what he had taken for a smear of makeup on her face was a truly blackened eye.

He kissed her hands, but gently this time. "Sweetheart, I never meant for you to take the knocks." He wished Jacaranda could have had a dab at those clients.

"Go tell me Ned the Pug you've never had a whore and beaten her?"

"Truly I never, I promise—but yes, I've had whores." This was true enough: Jacaranda was only occasionally a whore, and he had beaten her for show; in the arena she had beaten him nearly for good.

Poll seemed to believe him, for she whispered, "Then you can take a bit, 'cause yer better set up than the lot of them."

"And so are you," he breathed into the trace of perfume in her shoulder, a curious clean scent, and then he had her hard and quick in the shadowy doorway, where no passerby paid them attention and no one opened the door because it led to a storehouse shut down for the night.

As he pulled away, she nipped his nose between two strong fingers and twisted it viciously: "That's for the sons y' sent me, y' bastard!" She pulled her zips closed with sounds like teeth grinding.

"Christ, Poll, you're an unforgiver!" He rubbed his nose with one hand and with the other caught at her as she went to dart away. "Here's half my tin, and be satisfied." That was not much more than a few chiggers, and while he was hooking them out of his belt he felt the token from Zamos. Anything he might have hoped to give his GalFed employers in sweat tracks or fingerprints was now drowned in his own sweat, and he offered it to Poll. "Here's a thing I got from the Zamos clown, it's a lag dud but maybe some kava dipper will think it's the fruitful."

"Gold, and such weight? Who'd give you that?" Doll seized and bit it. She spat. "Ptui! by dammy, it's all crumbs and bits! Might be you were meant to eat it, and be poisoned at that—pfah!"

"Oh, let me see, Poll, don't toss it!" Ned grasped the crumbled pieces as she was about to fling them away. Even in the dim light and to his untutored eye they were significant. He hooked more coins from his belt: "Here's all of the cash and good-bye, sweetheart!" And he was off, hearing nothing more from her but a faint cry of "—see you again?"

He stopped in the light of a lamp for two seconds to eye the broken coin, then tossed it in his hand once, where it glittered for an instant, what was left of it, and a few passers roused and flicked their eyes at it; then he dropped it and gritted it under his heel. It was a spytick he had been a fool to take, as much as asking to be followed, worse, betray himself and anyone he spoke to. He had not given himself away by speech, he was sure of it, but the device was a sign that he had been under suspicion, and God knew what information it had already given about his fingerprints, his voiceprints, his sweat. He ran skipping and laughing among the crowds, half-hysterical; his ribs and breastbone ached with terror. *A pimp who is allowed to run from Zamos's back door is safe . . .* Zamos, who owned the brothels, owned half the arenas Ned Gattes fought in.

In another doorway he pulled off his bright clothes and rolled them into a knot in his scarf, then went on in his underwear, a thin shadowsuit. Not much to see of him then, a pale man with a grimy-looking jaw wearing mist-colored cloth.

In spite of his dread, or because of it, he could not stop

himself from crossing the bridge over the drainage channel, and pausing unseen down the cross street beyond the thinning stream of people before the brothel entrance. It was in his mind's eye that among the knots of navvies and tuggers arguing whether to go in, there would be another knot surrounding a body cast out with the trash, flattened in the dirt with her brilliant cloak faded like a dead bird's plumage. But there was none. Spacers were going inside, workers going home, and the street turning quiet. Dead or alive, Jacaranda was in the brothel.

Ned Gattes jeered at himself for the panic attack, and for his show of great bravery in front of Lizard Lady. He took the helibus and alit six streets from his kip, where there was a public comm with scrambler-code access and vid. Manador expected his call, and he particularly wanted to see her face on vid. And therefore she would see his; he paused again and brilliantine-combed his hair.

Manador had thick black hair twined in a bun at the back of her head, and one white lightning streak at her temple. She was wearing black lace and was carefully made up but looked stern, like an old ballerina. She did not ask how things had gone. "I have more work for you." She was his agent, and also owned the franchise of the local gladiator factory; as well, like a weaver, she picked the strands of gossip from Starry Nova and its environs and transformed them to the broadcloth of information for Galactic Federation. She had recommended Ned to GalFed Security because he traveled much and observed wherever he went.

"I've had enough spying, and I need sleep." He watched closely to see that her lip movements synchronized with the sound of her voice.

She smiled briefly, with sharp bracket-shaped creases, and he was sure that this image he was watching was Manador, and not some deceiving artifact. "Send a boy to do Manador's . . . how did things go?" Jacaranda was her latest lover.

Ned Gattes had never been a braggart. "I was scared shit-less—" He told her everything. He had been her lover too, briefly; her arms were like the lions' den.

"You were not scared stupid anyway. You did well. No need to jeer at yourself, my dear. Zamos is just fishing. They give those things out at random to see what they can pull in."

"Why in God's name didn't you tell me?"

"You'd have been hyperconscious of it, wouldn't you? This way you were only in character. Just keep your mouth shut when you're with the ladies."

"Then I will be hyperconscious." He added quickly, be-cause she had pursed her mouth, and her expression brought to mind his picture of Jacaranda dead in a gutter, "You said you had work for me."

She dit-dahed the console beside her with dark red nails. "This is an invitation to try out with the Spartakoi." The Spartakoi were a stable of gladiators that the Zamos Corpo-ration owned and ran in a huge gameplex it ran and owned in a colony on Shen IV that it largely controlled.

"They know about me?"

"Why shouldn't they? You've fought in ten or twelve Zamos arenas."

"Yes." *Fishing.* If they were to twig Jacky, they'd certainly know about him. Not a thing to say to Manador. Ordinar-ily he would have been burning to join the Spartakoi. He had applied to them many times. "When did this invitation come in?"

"A short while ago . . . um." She moistened her lips. "A little job you can do for GalFed there."

He stared at her for a moment. "Oh yeh . . . GalFed set it up for me, didn't they?"

She said, in a little spit, "That's all there is for you. Take it or leave it, damn you, Ned Gattes." She had had no contact with Jacaranda, of course, and would not until the spy got in touch with her. "If you take it I can get you a berth on the *Zarandu* right now, second shuttle hits Shen Four the fifteenth of quarteryear."

"*Zarandu*? Probably along with Lizard Lady."

"Skerow? How did you get on with her?"

"Not to go to bed with, but friendly in an awe-inspiring way . . . what's the GalFed job?"

"It's your basic look-but-don't-touch, evidence of forced employment."

Code for slavery. "Come on, Manador, they've been trying to pin that on the big Zed as long as I've been alive. That's a cold trail."

"They don't talk to me about it. Take it or leave it."

"I suppose I'd better take it."

"I'll book you, then. I'll have the faxpax on the Spartakoi waiting onboard for you with new I.D. and access numbers. Learn and burn. And get a shave before you let any of them see you. You look like a wharf rat."

He did not know what a wharf rat was, but got the drift. "Um, you'll let me know about Jacky?"

"You'll be gone by touch time."

"I guess so. Good luck."

She did not answer, but before she signed off he noticed faint blue spots on her cheeks to either side of her nose, and on her forehead above it. She was sweating in the manner of a blue Pinxid woman made up to look like a Solthree.

Instead of going back to his doss near the helibus station, Ned Gattes took a cab to the Sol3City Athletic Club he usually avoided. There he sat in the steam bath to befog his mind, and finally fell asleep in a stopover bunk among sweaty and familiar pugs who might fight him to the death in the arena, but would not kill him in his bed.

Zamos's Brothel: Jacaranda and Kobai

Yah-ee! That damned white light push and push me down in that water don't belong to my sea! Like waking strange on a shore where the wave wash you farways and you get the Up-there fellow come by you with the zapstick in case you think of going too far. Some thought.

This is what happens: one time after Poor Stupid Om bites the air that dung-clot Nohl Lord Big-One Up-There come down along the home sea with the tin hat he calls Ferrier and a lot more fishbelly faces, put the sting in you like the pinfish, you blink out in a bad dark like bang-the-head, too much like Big Dark Dead, and when you think to wake up, you lucky one, it's this place with more stick-you and big light in the eye and feel like it go through the skin, right out to craziness. There is nowhere to go because it is see-through but not go-through, bang your nose a lot before you learn. Big white bulb faces shove at you from otherside, water wash you around to where they want to get you, big slug hands reach down in, twist your tail. This place is one big bottle with us water-drinkers inside, and outside is even a bigger bottle of air for air-drinkers.

Here in this water they put stuff I don't know what, it smell like what Doctor fellow puts on a hurt. It make the food taste something like, you bet. Not to think I ever get off the feed—at home that is same as saying you will not work and asking to get gutstuck with the Long Knife and hold-me-down with a bog stone till good-bye Kobai. They throw you down chunks to eat like an animal, but the food here is not so bad—I like the *memsa* worms and the halfway-gone oyster meat better than sea-smik from back home. Slave don't get to pick anyway, do we?

Bip-bip! your folk is always in a hurry to hurry Kobai. If you want to work with a slave you can torment till yourself is heartsore and your arm ache, but you go by slave time anyway.

The light. For making you do what they want. And the zapstick, and the needle with doctorstuff to make you go down but not out. Fingers. You want to go big-out when Doctor comes and pinch here and poke down there, say: She'll do.

Some ones here speak by hand like the Folk, and it tell you not much, but you find out what this place is for. It is a bottle where all kind of peoples like you never saw come and give gold to swim around air and water, play *this-here/that-place* with all kinds of other peoples, and hard to figure out all what they think is that game. But by your Big God Upside, I know one downright rule is: the one who gets gold is not one who gives *that-place* or *this-here*. It is the one who own the bottle.

There is up and down here: up is where they grab at you and down is where the bottle goes through a hole in the floor where they walk, and you fall into a place where they get to look at you with all the others and say: Give me that one. Nobody ask for me, yet. No one here even look like me, human. They are all kinds of colors, all kinds of hand, foot and grabbing parts, but none like me, or even Nohl or Tinhat Ferrier.

Only every one time or another—and Peoples, it is very hard to say what this is like—there is a being that comes to sight. First I think I am going crazy like poor Om, and my food wants to come up my throat, and then I think maybe I am only going blind because this Being is in pieces of big blurry colors like if you have three eyes and they don't work all together. Sometimes it comes near where I am in the bottle and *even halfway through* without breaking it or spilling water. I bang my head really good and hard trying to get away from that. Later I get to find out it is only an *image,* like the idea in your mind of something that is not there, and if you have a right type of eye it is not in all the pieces and colors. This *image* has a big round head like Ferrier's, not kind of going back shape like mine, it moves the mouth and others make please to it, like some god or Big Lord Upthere. Maybe the one with the money.

Now here comes another new being. Something like Ferrier that wears the clothes over its skin. It has the big head same as the image that speaks, and teats like the big blue booby that bring the customer in and same like what I have, but has got no tail. It is real, and not an *image.* It is also blue and green. Some kind of monster. For sure is not human.

The Varvani woman's heavy hand led Jacaranda by the shoulder through the Showroom where the plasmix columns ran from floor to ceiling, illuminated from within and filled with the waters of alien seas. There were locking passages between them that drained and empited as the life-forms varied. Some of these glowed or flickered with strange phosphorescence, but Kobai did not; the deep matte red of her skin absorbed light as if it were black—or perhaps it was her mood that absorbed the light—and only her eyes were vivid. Though they were very dark and large-pupiled, and sealed by hairless lids so transparent that the veins in their whites could be seen, they belonged to a Solthree human woman, full of life and no mistaking her; if she did not recognize Jacaranda as a fellow-being in the first glance, it was because she did not know many forms of humanity.

The cylindrical tanks rose up in their columns of light through openings in the ceiling to the floor above, an open set of rooms where the spherical dream-chambers were clustered; where in a cool white light women and men wearing furs and feathers of their own or of other creatures gave gold keys to clients, exchanged money, took bets, dispatched orders for food, unguents, makeup, served kava, whiskey, froths of formic acid, and loaded sterilized needles; where clients lounged on couches or hung in slings waiting to meet those they had chosen.

Every few moments the freestanding hologram image that had frightened Kobai appeared on the floor, quite whole and clear, completely lifelike except for its suddenness: a toga-robed hairless male Solthree speaking words of praise or criticism, keeping an eye to the pleasure of the clients. Jacaranda was familiar with this: it was supposed to be the image of Zamos, though it had no distinguishing marks, and appeared as a trademark in many of his establishments. By an unspoken agreement it was treated as a person and with the same deference as if it had been Zamos himself.

The ceiling of the waiting room rose up into a huge vault divided into three sections, hologram screens that played out the actions of three exhibitions that were taking place on platforms below them: one showed a fat and darkly hairy Solthree man sitting in a tableau rather like a painting on an ancient Greek vase. With a grin on his face he was using one hand to eat *zimb* fruit and with the other playing with the body of the slender pubescent girl who was pouring a jar of perfumed unguent over him and manipulating his penis; a boy was placing a flowering wreath on his head and in turn a second girl played with the boy. The children had sweet slender bodies and wore green wreaths on their fair curls. The grinning man appeared to have narrow hairy legs that ended in hooves, or perhaps his shins were so hairy a trick of the light made them seem so. Once he was anointed the children stepped back; one of the girls produced a lighted taper and touched it to the flowered wreath: immediately a fountain of cool fire cascaded down his glistening body until every hair stood in a tiny blue flame and the aroma of the heated unguent exploded through the room. The other girl leaned over and dipped her head into the fire and the hair to suck him; he laughed and lay back on the green velvet, reaching out his hands for a girl's genitals as the boy straddled his head.

The screens magnified and intensified these acts and showed the pores of the man's skin and the papillae of his tongue, the petaled softnesses of the children as well as the knowing expressions beginning to harden in their faces.

Two screens away, in a double tableau a Varvani couple were arousing each other while they watched two froglike Orpha puffing up toward orgasm. The male Orph was fingering a melody on a nose-flute to coax the female into releasing the egg mass from her womb opening into a bowl between her legs: Orpha sex was a powerful aphrodisiac for Varvani. When the song had reached its climax and the eggs poured into the cup the Orpha clasped hands and licked each other's eyeballs. The seed drenched the eggs and they quivered and twisted with life. Now the Varvani, the slabs of their thick bodies rippling furiously, coupled in a springtime of ecstatic lust, ripping off each other's molting skins with their teeth.

In the last of the tableaux two Solthree women lying on a huge circular bed with a crimson cushion were licking and caressing each other. They were wearing wigs of an antique style, white and powdered, heaped with curls upon curls and decorated with flowers, gold pins, stuffed birds, miniature sailing ships, and jeweled sunbursts. Their faces were powdered and black-patched and their pouting lips very red with rouge. On arms and legs they had sleeves of frilly lace bound with red velvet ribbons, and on their feet little pointed shoes with square buckles and French heels; their waists were looped in gold chains. After they had advanced for a few moments in the course of their erotic dance, gracefully balancing their gigantic headdresses, one of them turned her back and her rosy buttocks to the audience for a moment, and when she faced them again, half-rising, was wearing an artificial penis; smiling, she held her arms out and her frilled legs splayed to draw attention to it and the screen picked it up, in its ivory shape of a jewel-eyed snake's head with gold-edged scales. The other woman opened her legs to receive it, and the first began to bend toward her; then the snake stirred, arched its head, blinked its emerald eyes. Its tri-branched tongue flickered two or three times, then advanced, like a little claw, toward the vulva.

As Jacaranda rode up the helix between the floors Kobai floated up along with her, grasping the tank walls with thickly ridged fingers and peering at her curiously with those deep eyes. The Varvani shepherding the newcomer reached an arm through the lift cage as they went by and flicked at the wall to chase her away, but Kobai made what must have been an obscene gesture among her people and flattened her face grotesquely against the glass.

"One will learn," said the Varvani.

Jacaranda made no sign to her—there was nothing she could say—but let herself be delivered to a Kylkladi woman with purple-dyed feathers and led to a washing room where she removed the wig and paint and used the autobath. Without the thick false lashes and the smile lines she drew under her eyes she was a lean tight woman with cropped red curly hair, white brows and lashes, and eyes the color of slate and just as hard. Only her lips were full, and only when reddened were they sexually expressive rather than contemptuous, promising nothing but war.

The Kylkladi, stupefied on narcaine, did not recognize her from the arena—no one ever did—or interpret her expression, but was lazily amused at her transformation from

Pinxid to Solthree. "Do you really think you will have clients?"

Jacaranda kept in mind that she was only a whore beaten by a pimp; she touched her tongue to the sore where he had bruised her lip, and said meekly, "I hope so. Where am I to stay?"

"A little room in oxygen country three floors up. They are only allowing you in because there are not many of your type here."

"What kind is that one in the tank with the tail?"

"Some Solthree undersea colony, I suppose; I don't know where. Why?"

"I was wondering how they would do it with her."

"Tik-tik!" The purple-feathered woman clicked her beaky mouth in a Kylkladi's laughter. "That is not a professional yet—I imagine someone will teach her! They are likely saving her for an underwater show. Can you swim?"

"A little."

"I'll tell the Keymaster. You will meet him tomorrow after the doctor has seen you."

Jacaranda, a careful observer, was hard put to keep track of where she was taken, and almost lost the way among the narrow corridors, staircases, slides, and elevators that twisted into heights and depths she would never have guessed at from seeing the brothel's exterior. The atmosphere of the windowless place was close and full of perfumes that went deeply into musk and sometimes lingered on scorch or sweat, and she did not know whether she was in the upper-class section or the lower—or if there was any difference. Soft light bloomed from the walls; the hallways were lined by doors with handles and latches of crystal knobs or golden loops. Some entrances rose to the ceiling, or were oddly broad or round: many of these were closed by half a score of locks and labeled with warnings of alien pressures and atmospheres; some that were ajar seemed to lead now into more passages, stairways and bolt-holes; now into storerooms heaped full with garments of bright scales and drifting luminescent tissues, leather and cloth-of-gold, wigs and whips and armor, jars of oils, creams and skin colorings, tanks and cartridges of liquids and atmospheres; and now again they led into unoccupied silk-draped retiring-rooms furnished with chairs and divans contoured to support the passions of seven or eight human species, and machines fitted out in soft leather and polymer appendages to help stir them.

Sound was muffled here, whether of feigned ecstasy or real pain, but Jacaranda thought she saw down one of the shadowy halls a dark creature scuttling on fours, and heard the iron clank of a chain—even that noise might have been part of the music that wafted on the air: wind chimes, harps, a snarling song wailed along with stones rhythmically cracked against each other. A screaming of machine joints.

No image of Zamos appeared to disturb the privacy of clients, but wherever the doors of retiring rooms were open Jacaranda could glimpse the holograms: the old satyr grunting and panting as he writhed with his three sylphs in a Laocoön's knot of passion, the Varvani crooning in their new skins, the two snake-joined women shuddering in orgasm, or seeming to. Through some unguarded doorway she heard along with the performers the Bacchic cries of another many-mouthed group.

None of these displays affected Jacaranda any more than they moved the performers and servitors. She knew brothels, and had seen all the acts, if not the players. She wondered about the children for a brief moment, what made it worthwhile for the brothel-masters to bring fragile young children far from home to dirty their hands and souls on old lechers. For herself, she turned tricks when stranded in ports without arenas, and spied when Galactic Federation's gears meshed with hers. Now, having come to Starry Nova as a pug, she was spying on her own dangerous employer Zamos, and had let Ned Gattes beat her for a cheap whore. She was tired, not from physical exertion but tired of herself; she kept her mind on the turnings and landmarks of her trail, and when she reached the small room that was spare as a nun's cell, did not even hear the final sarcasm of the Kylklad, but lay down on the bed and closed her eyes.

After a moment the image of Zamos sputtered briefly into life and roused her awake: clearly, in the world's most luxurious bordello, there were electronics even in so spare a room, but the image was not quite clear or whole: it mouthed into space and did not look at her, and perhaps had been beamed in by accident. There was not much she would do in this scrubbed white room either to please or disturb Zamos. The bed was narrow, but at this moment it meant safety to her. Jacaranda did not allow her mind to dwell on more than the next move: she fell asleep wondering what she must do to please the Keymaster, and how to communicate with the innocent sea creature. It came into her dreams wearing Manador's face.

The Devil's Wife

Jacaranda had three stads of sleep, and when she opened the door a thick-armed bruiser, cousin to the bouncer who maintained the peace at the common-gate, was waiting for her in the doorway with arms folded and feet crossed. She gaped at him. "How long you been here?"

"As long as I had to. You're going to the doctor." He was chewing something. Betel: his lips were red.

Jacaranda shrugged and ran her fingers through her hair. "What's your name?"

"Barr." He followed after, touching her arm, muttering, almost subvocalizing: *This way. Down here.*

The house doctor worked out of a small lab crammed with computer consoles and diagnostic machines. Barr waited in the hall, crossing his arms and feet.

Jacaranda was relieved to find this doctor no coarse-fingered groper but as in all Zamos brothels, a Lyhhrt in a gold-plated hominid workshell with a sunburst face, a person capable of jacking into any of the instruments that surrounded him. He—or it—was so subtle and neat-handed that Jacaranda did not feel grossly violated delivering blood and urine.

Whatever a Lyhhrt might look like externally, it was really a brain-sized and timid lump of protoplasm working its shell with pseudopods, trembling with desire to be at home on its own world, lying entwined in many layers of its fellows and engaged in Cosmic Thought. If Galactic Federation had not discovered and encouraged the Lyhhrt passion for metal-working they would have deprived themselves, if not the Lyhhrt, of half their surgeons, anatomists, goldsmiths, and professors of these arts. It was a feature of Lyhhrt philosophy to work for the welfare of others, but they hated being separated and were almost fanatical anti-individualists. This avoidance often made them feared and hated. Not by Jacaranda. They treated her with care and respect.

After the examination the Lyhhrt extruded sensors, dipped them into the samples, and read the values into a computer. "You are free from communicable diseases." He took her hand, turned it palm up, and touched her wrist with a burst of cold spray from a plastic bulb. "These are the boosters you need for forty-six viruses endemic in this district. Your breath is a trifle short and you should change oxygen cartridges more frequently." :*It is dangerous to interfere.*:

Jacaranda's reaction time was a little slow after three stads of sleep out of the local twenty-eight; it took her a half second to realize that the Lyhhrt was communicating by esp.

Lyhhrt were very powerful ESPs but held fastidiously to the rules of law and courtesy they had helped to frame. Jacaranda was not an ESP, but kept her mind rigorously to herself and was quick to defend herself against intruders. She glanced at the expressionless gold mask. The Lyhhrt, though they loved ornament, were masters of good taste and did not try to create false expressions: the metal head might be hollow, or filled with computer chips or nutrients; the Lyhhrt itself would be ensconced somewhere in the torso, operating its gleaming shell in the silence and darkness it loved.

Within the space of the half second, she understood that the Lyhhrt was—reservation: claimed to be—the agent of another GalFed department; the object of investigation was unclear, but she was being told: *Do not try to rescue Kobai.* She asked no question, did not give herself away except to show by the stance of her body and mind that she was far from planning to interfere. She was here only to find out if Kobai was inside the establishment, and make sure she was being well treated. She had brought no weapon and never had a thought of rescuing Kobai: it would have taken a traveling circus to do that. "Thanks. I'll take your advice."

The Lyhhrt asked with grave courtesy, "Are there any other problems you wish to discuss, madam?"

"None whatever."

"Remember to renew your oxygen cartridges more often. The lift is down the hall to your right. You will find the Keymaster's office one floor down just opposite."

"I have an escort."

FLESH AND GOLD * 73

"Yes. So I see."

The Keymaster was another Kylklad, a flutterer in dyed green feathers who had sore eyes, and wore thick lenses set in a clamp around his head. "Jacaranda. Is that all of your name?"

"Drummond. Jacaranda Drummond." She had already given that name to the Varvani madam—even though it was not her own—along with references to two other Zamos houses. A self-important man, this.

The Keymaster's office was very small; Barr was forced to wait outside again. The upper half of the wall facing the door was slotted to hold code-card files of employee information, as in other houses where Jacaranda had worked, and the lower was a panel with hundreds of hooks holding little gold locks and keys. A second wall was composed of tiny doors with ostentatious complicated hasp locks, and probably contained client information. Or perhaps not. Perhaps all this was for show and deception. Another wall was lined with screens that looked into hallways, offices, and whatever retiring rooms were in use. There was no day or night in Zamos's brothel.

"Not much flesh to you, is there, dear?"

She said with rouged lips: "I do what I can to make it effective."

"*Tik-tik!* And I am sure you shall!" He ran a black-enameled claw down her arm very lightly. "Here is something to wear around your neck." A little gold lock in the shape of a heart or vulva. "Let me put it on you." The claws circling her neck with a narrow cold line. "Piri'iryk says that you can swim."

Purple feathers given a name. "A little."

"Good. You will go into the tank with the delphine."

"Delphine?"

"We call her that, not having other names for her kind,

whatever they are." No questions please. "In structure she is basically Miry"—an approximate word for Sol III popularized by the Russians—"and the dolphin of your world is an intelligent animal—so there you are."

"Yes, Keymaster."

"Run along now, dear, Piri'iryk will tell you all about it and outfit you. Up two floors and second door on your right."

It is not very easy to see expressions on Kylkladi faces, though there are a thousand fluttering gestures that express what a Kylklad feels. Jacaranda did not know very many of them.

Piri'iryk's office was even smaller than the Keymaster's; it was also lined with slots, but by their symbols these held key-cards to a thousand other closets and cupboards. The Kylklad was waiting for her. "There you are." She plucked a card from its slot: "Come," and with a feather-draped arm led Jacaranda along and through the narrow hallways she had traversed the night before. Lit by artificial light, they looked no different, but Jacaranda felt the brush of a feather across her ribs, the touch of a long silvered claw on the prominent vertebra between her shoulder blades. Barr followed along, silently plodding. "Here." The Kylklad woman seemed less stupid today. Evidently she did not need much sleep. She stopped before a door and slotted the card.

The entrance opened into a vast storeroom of costumes and parts of costumes. Piri'iryk looked at Jacaranda with a beady eye. "Underwater . . ."

Jacaranda waited.

"This one, I think . . . try it."

A tube of blue, green, and silver spangles like fish scales. Jacaranda stepped out of her torn finery and pulled it on. It fitted her quick, not covering anything. "I'll need waterproof Pinxid makeup."

"That will not be necessary."

A diamond light in the bright fixed eye made Jacaranda think of escape routes. "Is the delphine woman a professional?"

"You will teach her whatever she needs to know."

That was it, then. They were not seriously hiring her on for her experience. She had been ticked, and they knew her. And they seemed to be willing to sacrifice Kobai.

All in my mind?

No. She had the dread conviction. She had had friends and lovers who were snuffed . . . The Lyhhrt doctor, maybe, had twigged her, the only one she could think of. But he had tried to warn her: more than tried. He had warned her fair and square. If it was true, Kobai would not need any experience.

The appearance of Barr should have warned her; if she had killed him—there would have been an excuse to snuff her more conventionally and right away.

She sniffed. "I don't work in aquatics or with nonprofessionals," she said firmly. "Even my rotten gentle-Johnny can do better than that for me."

"You do not want work, then."

"Yes I do, but not this kind."

"This is all we have, dems'l. We took you in and sheltered you when you did not want to have much to do with your pimp. And now you want to go back to him! Do you specialize in hurt-sex?"

"You want me to pay you back."

"It seems reasonable. One short act for a well-paying audience . . . don't you agree?"

She doubted she could handle two of them. Piri'iryk's neck was very scrawny, but she bristled with home-grown weaponry: the talons, the horny mouth and ankle-spurs; she had the advantage of home ground.

And it did seem reasonable. "I suppose so," said Jacaranda. She had nowhere to run in this ant-heap of winding tunnels and twisted cul-de-sacs. Alarms would harry her down.

Piri'iryk pulled open a drawer, one of the many set into the wall, and found a wire cage studded with cheap jewels and plated with imitation gold. "Here is your imper helm." Jacaranda put it on and fastened it. "And your oxygen mask." This was in the shape of a white scallop shell worn with the flutes raying upward; it had slanting eyepieces set into it, and inside, nose tubes that curved up inward. The three mini-cartridges together would last half a stad. Crossing her fingers mentally, she fitted the tubes into her nostrils and sniffed. The usual stale smell, nothing to make her dizzy or drop dead; she had a moment's flicker of hope.

"This capsule is a little off." She pointed to a crystal that was slightly discolored. Without a word Piri'iryk opened a tiny drawer and gave her one in an unbroken package.

Barr and the Kylklad followed her down the corridors where she had come last night feeling the momentary false safety. Jacaranda did not claim a vivid imagination, but it seemed to her as if all the office workers and all the professionals not in the retiring rooms were turning in chairs or slings or harnesses to look at her. Kylklad, Solthree, Dabiri, a Tignit in bubble-helmet, a Lyhhrt in brushed silver, the faunish stripling who had played with the satyr, looking as if he had not quite wakened from leafy sleep. In fur, feather, or spangle, they stared at her affectlessly, with flat eyes. Piri'iryk's clogs hammered the floor, her talons and feathers grazed now Jacaranda's shoulder and neck, now her thigh. At no time were the two alone.

The tank had been moved into one of the niches beneath a screen; it was the same fishbowl Skerow had seen in the window. Kobai was floating curled up, clinging to the back wall with her face turned away; the little heart was chained around her neck.

In the arena Jacaranda always fought with dagger, whip, or *chebok*, a kind of mailed fist, and here had nothing like them. She was not enhanced except by a short course of steroids she had discontinued early to avoid being blown up into a parody; the only steel in her was her determination. She could not even see how they might try to kill her, except by poison in the water. Whatever happened, maybe she could find some way to save Kobai, or protect her, or . . .

There was an audience before the showcase, a Miry group accommodated on hammocks and couches, waiting in dreamy attitudes and watching an erotic display of pre-Raphaelite-styled couplings on the Tri-V screen. There were five of them, three men and two women; the men were perfect and empty, the women, the white-blond and the brunette with red highlights, seemed rather too eager. The image of Zamos danced among them, speaking for one moment to them, then turning to address the world.

Piri'iryk guided her, always with the silver talon at neck, shoulder, or armpit, along the walkway behind the scenes, among stages and huge robots that manipulated scaffolding to the hatch that led into the bowl of the tank like the neck of a Florence flask.

"Are you ready?" Piri'iryk asked with no particular tone of voice.

"Yes."

Piri'iryk summoned Barr to pull open the hatch door; a waft of air smelling of salt seas rose from the opening.

Jacaranda did not think then about anything more than the next moment, but fitted on the mask and slipped down the opening. The water flowed around her into the hot creases of her skin; above her head she heard the thud of the hatch closing.

*   *   *

I never feel truly stupid in my life until this monster come into my water and scare me up the wall, and I am just about to give her a two-finger in the eye when I see the eyes are not real but some kind of mask she is wearing that gives bubbles. When I reach for it she hold her both hand together like so: *friend*, and touch my hand.

Then she grab me by the two teats! I don't think she will be my friend. I guess this is the one that ask for me after all the time, but she will not get me. I am going to take her two hands and crack her head open with them like an oyster, and she knows it.

And what happen but I get this smell coming off her skin. It is the smell of one really scared, even if she is not running, and looks like a tough one. Afraid of me? It look to me like there is something about her I know . . . I don't think she is afraid of me . . . I take her hands off me, but not in a bad way, and keep hold of one, to say: *Friend, yes?* And she nod the head, what I guess is yes, so I say to my own self, if this pretend-fuck is what I got to do so nobody get hurt, that's it—

—and next thing, the whole world boil up and go bee-BLOOP!

The fury blazed through the water like an undersea earth-quake, and flung the women against the wall of the tank. There were claws and teeth attached to it, and black flaming hunger. In the half second it paused, disoriented, Jacaranda recognized it: a serpent from the Copper or Cyprian Sea of Thanamar II. It was powerfully telepathic and brutally half-sentient. She pushed Kobai aside and clamped her teeth on the tooth-stay of the mask to withstand the crackling of the savage mind. The helmet, a cheap barrier to low-grade esp, was useless against it. Solthrees called it "devil's wife": it was a hermaphrodite that bred parthenogenetically and used its male function for gene renewal when its numbers diminished. She had watched bouts where the devil's wife was fought by dagger fighters who were willing to risk everything.

At her first dodge a claw caught her down the outside of her thigh and the blood slinked away in a curling trail. She shuddered in the pain, the bubbling fury, with Kobai's jolting terror driving through the beast's esp; dived through marbled water under the hook-toothed jaw, clasped the long neck between her knees and slammed with the heels of her hands hoping to reach a nerve complex. She had fought underwater but never without weapons and could not get enough purchase to do this.

She wanted to push Kobai up into the neck of the bowl where she might have protected her but that was impossible. The devil's wife writhed, the bestial form of hell-broken-loose, and she rode it as the hag rides the nightmare, feet tangled in the laces of its gills. Her own determination hardened to a knife-shape in her spirit, and when the claws raked her back she did not feel anything. She did not let go even when the flimsy helmet broke off and the full force of the black mind hit her inside the arch of her skull. She tasted the iron of her own blood in the water.

Kobai had pulled herself up into the chute as soon as Jacaranda thought of it, but when she saw the helmet falling dived down with a flick of her muscular tail, picked up the helmet, and smashed the devil's wife in the eye.

The fake jewels tearing through the eye's precious layers loosed a cloud of blue-green copper-based blood, a bulge of grey-pink tissue and a psychic shriek that brainburned its way out to the white-noise limits of the brothel. The blue-green and the red blood mixed and blackened into a cloud in which all were blind for one stunned moment.

Jacaranda could not break the serpent's neck. Still gripping the snaking torso with her legs she took one deep breath and tore off the mask, grabbed gill tendrils with both hands, shoved them into her mouth and bit. The devil's wife bent its head against its side and crunched the back of her neck between its jaws. Jacaranda died without a thought.

Kobai smashed out blindly; the twisting serpent's tail slammed the side of her head and the thrust drove her to the tank wall where she flattened gripping the plasmix with palms and soles in the opaque water, stunned, waiting to die. The water darkened further as the devil's wife lost blood, and the mind of the beast began to darken.

She sensed now the blood-thirst of the watchers, the terror of the beast that could act only as nature allowed, the dizziness as she sank into unconsciousness. A voice filtered into what awareness she had left, through the serpent's dying mind:

Who has done this? Get her out of there NOW!

Words she did not understand.

You fool. You absolute bloody fool. You will be smashed. THAT DELPHINE'S A BREEDER AND SHE'S PREGNANT!

Jacaranda was found in much the way Ned Gattes had envisioned, half in the gutter before the brothel door. Her white drowned body was scarred with wounds that had drained pink, her spangles dulled like the scales of any hooked fish. By then Ned was wrapped in sleep aboard the Zarandu's shuttle along with Skerow and twenty-five thousand other souls bound outward across the Galaxy from Galactic Central.

It was a Lyhhrt who told Manador what had happened to Jacaranda; she did not know which one it was among the physicians, surgeons, and lawyers. "How do you come to know this? Who are you, anyway?" Her skin was blue and dewed with sweat.

"I cannot tell you that." The Lyhhrt had taken a Kylklad form and looked like Death's angel in feathers of silver filigree.

"Damn you, was it one of yours who did it?"

The Lyhhrt stood still for a moment in this shape, which it made more graceful than the true one. "I allow for your grief and anger, Madame. You are well aware that such a question is inexcusable."

She was. "There is one of you who works for Zamos. That one knows, and so do you."

"I cannot—"

"You cannot tell. Oh yes," said Manador. "But I will find out."

THREE ✳

Khagodis: *Skerow on Raintree Island*

On Khagodis the Diluvian Continent forces its way up through the belly of the equator between the Greater and the Lesser Archipelagoes and pushes into the Great Spine mountain chain that twists to the north and south. With the mountains running up just east of its center, it looks from space like the body of a sleeping animal covered by a green pelt that stretches whitely over its backbone. From this heaped backbone the Great Equatorial River flows west toward the Greater Archipelagoes and the Isthmuses; in its tangled chains the river islands seem to be sailing upstream.

Every year in the winter season the Organization of Poems and Their Authors holds its conference in the Orchard Gardens of Raintree Island. Poets and other artists come from all over the world to attend it.

One of these was the first public function Skerow attended after returning to her home world; her duties on the Assizes Circuit would not begin for another thirtyday, and though she was fearsomely weary and felt as if her brain was boiling, the government-supported Raintree Conference was one of the few opportunities for her to see authors from her own country, local travel being both slow and expensive.

On this evening there had been a barbecue of fingerclams and water-bracket given by the Island hosts; a group of seventy-five was gathered under the lobe trees licking its collective fingers and watching the sunset. The sky was suffused with rose and mauve, with the fragrance of *sessu* vines, and the moons were huge and creamy over the flickering river and the deep green humps of its islands. One of the host poets was reciting, by esp, for though Khagodi poetry need not be an esp form, people do not vocalize much among themselves. . . .

> *. . . he was moving in the river to his lover*
> *he was moving, moving in the river in his lover, as*
> *their sworn-to-die attackers swarmed around*
> > *them,*
> *swarmed*
> *in the sedge with the reeds above them bending*
> *down toward the currents of the river*
> *Do not leave me! cried*
> *the lovers, crying*
> *in the reeds of the river*
> *while the spears of bloody vengeance*
> *hovered, hovered in shadows among the brambles*
> *and the points of their reflections*
> *quivered in the river's mirror*
> *and lover clasped lover*
> *he in his vital brilliance, she in her awesome power*
> *hers the greatness of power, his the tension of*
> > *brilliance—*

Skerow's mind wandered away from this recital, yet another old-fashioned retelling of the Great River Epic, and she watched as a heavy seed pod dropped from the lobe tree with a thud; its shell split and it extruded four root legs and wandered off crookedly in a vain search for sunshine. Eskat crawled up and down the back of her neck and beat the knob of his tail on her head for attention, but she was thinking of Kobai swimming frantically in another kind of great river.

Every once in a while the poet, a shallow and rather foolish fellow named Fasethi, raised his voice in a series of tremolo squeaks, to illustrate how brilliant, how tense his lovers were.

At the edge of this distraction, Skerow sensed the faint touch of a mind seeking her attention. She had been so preoccupied by recent events that except for a few old friends she had spoken to almost no one in the last day or so; this inquiring mind was that of a stranger, a woman not a poet but the friend and guest of one. *:Skerow . . . ?:*

:Yes, Lady.:

:My name is Thasse.: When Skerow could not bring herself to answer for a moment, she added, *:Thordh was my husband.:*

:I know . . . He mentioned your name.:

:Did he? Not very often, I am sure.: The woman was a form unseen in the darkness. Skerow could not tell what her size or appearance was, or the color of the drapery she wore against the evening breeze blowing off the river's current.

:He . . . never spoke of you. He never spoke of anything but our cases, Thasse.:

:Yet you have seen him more than I throughout our lives. Tell me, did he truly disgrace himself?:

:That is not my business to know. His death was a tragedy,

*and it is being investigated . . . Thasse, would you like to
withdraw aside so that we may speak more freely?:*
*:This is free enough for me. Did you have sexual relations
with him, Skerow?:*
:Never. He did not like me.:
*:Really? I am not surprised. He never cared for me or the
children either. He was impotent except for the first few times
that were necessary to get that brood of seventeen—his Lineage. After that he stopped being a man. I have been burning for forty-seven years.:* She paused, then: *:You have not
much to say to that, I suppose.:*
Skerow was trembling. *:Forgive me, Thasse. I envied you.:*
"Eeyik!" sang Fasethi, sounding very much like Eskat.

> *. . . yes then*
> *lover clung in despair to lover*
> *as the minds above them clouded*
> *darkly in bitter vengeance, dark*
> *as the spears whose black moon-shadows poised*
> *above them in the silence, the red silence*
> *those adversaries*
> *sworn enemies of centuries, of millennia*
> *shot the lightning of their spears, and of their mind*
> > *bolts*
> *on the innocence of lovers, caught*
> *in the greenblack waterweeds*
> *in that one immortal River.*

Skerow joined halfheartedly in the applause for this
poem, which she considered rather silly stuff; small prizes
had been offered for some of the best recitals, and she was
sure this version of the Epic would win one in this Equatorial land. In spite of these feelings Skerow had always admired the River poets for their enthusiasm and vitality, and
indeed the Epics were vastly popular everywhere—mainly,

she thought, because their double-diastolic rhythms echoed so closely the beating of Khagodi hearts.

Tonight Thasse had spoiled her pleasure. When she advanced into the center of the circle to recite her poems she felt so alien, so seized by homeward longing, that she forgot her text and dropped the daybook with her notes in it, and Eskat jumped off her shoulder and onto someone else's head. Desperate and beside herself, she cried out:

> "*O*
> *this desert*
> *I drown in moonlight!*"

She stopped in horror, voice drowned in her own passion, as the audience directed its attention to her in a still moment broken only by the chattering river and the whisper of the fragrant wind. These calmed her, the indigo dusk hid her trembling, and she continued voicelessly with the cycle she had vowed to show no one:

> *where*
> *ice ages*
> *folded the seas under*
>
> *and*
> *wave-crests are*
> *combs of ancient salt . . .*

and, whispering:

> *I*
> *drown and burn*
> *there in its white light*

shocking herself once again, for these words had come out without her conscious intent—and realizing with a satisfaction that came from another part of her mind entirely, that she had both combined two dissonant elements, and played them off against each other, to express the fullness of her spirit.

There was a moment of intensity in which this feeling swept out through and back from her circle of fellow poets, a double beat; then she found her notes and continued with her recital as planned.

When awards were given out, Fasethi was, as expected, winner of the first prize; afterward, the participants snacked on roasted *lekk* pods and sweetcomb nectar in tiny alabaster cups, and engaged in a lively discussion about the next day's main topic: *The Etiology of Fourteenth Era Riparian Metaphor Derived in Terms of Post-Fluvial Ideation.* With her mind too full of her poems, and Thasse as well, to concentrate on this, Skerow let herself be drawn into a less serious conversation going on near her, yet still rather hovered around it than entered into it.

. . . saying good-bye to Thasse? gone home already? no, not home surely, she came from, lives in, moved to, away from, the Isthmuses, to the Deltas, only yesterday, last thirtyday, half a year ago, after that awful thing happened, the Deltas is where she lives, but here she's staying with, very well fixed for herself, playing the great lady with, Fasethi, him? that silly fellow, that minor talent, that never deserved the prize, you voted for, no! certainly not I, no one thinks much of his
    talent with women?
    and after she wears him out, next two off-moons with, with one of the wealthy Nohl families,
    indeed?
    then who voted for Fasethi in the first place?
Skerow had turned very still and cold. Eskat squeaked and crept down under her arm.

When I get hold of that Nohl there is not one scrap left that the dung-fish chew on.

She would never understand what made her mind work so quickly then. "Nohl families? . . . I understood that they lived in the Isthmus provinces near the gold fields. I've never heard the name anywhere else." Not quite a lie.

The gossiper was flustered. "Surely you're joking, Skerow! No one speaks very much of the Isthmus branch of the family . . . they are as good as banished to that estate in the gold fields."

Perceptions still colored by Thord's betrayal and death, Skerow could not tell whether the conversation had become actively malicious or only that it seemed that way to her.

:POETS AND SINGERS!: said a very loud mindvoice. *:IS EVERYTHING OVER WHEN I HAVE ONLY JUST ARRIVED?:*

The group retreated, a last wisp of thought drifted and eddied away: *: . . . eh, yes, there were rumors they'd sold it, with its Titles of Ancestry and everything, to a consortium!:*

Everyone cried aloud, "Threyha! How good to see you!"

Threyha was a newly retired Sector Coordinator who had been based on Fthel IV and V, and was living now on the other side of the world in a West Ocean country.

"Why are you so late, Threyha?"

"I was held up at Port Manganese, where the shuttle could not lift me!"

There was laughter, but Threyha was not joking. She was three meters tall and weighed six hundred kilos: her voice was a well-controlled baritone with a lot of resonance, but it occasionally veered off into the falsetto when she was out of wind. After a few more pleasantries, she turned the beam of her attention. "Hello Skerow, my girl!"

Skerow had not seen her old friend and former colleague

in the flesh for twenty years, but Threyha was strong and hearty. Her topaz eyes still burned in the ancient face that glistened with *kerm* oil. "Not quite a girl, Threyha." She was delighted to have a friend with her.

"Less than half my age, that's a girl to me! Dear child, you left no forwarding address. I had to trace you."

"I needed a few days to myself." Skerow looked away. "I suppose you have heard a deal of gossip."

"I learned the news about Thordh. I know that he was not your friend, but—working so closely—you must have been affected."

"Yes . . ." She longed to tell Threyha everything: *I was nearly murdered, I nearly killed another person, I learned horrible things!* But all of that belonged to a case yet to go through the courts. Yet . . . she had sworn to help Kobai, a woman she had known for hardly one tick of a stad. "Do you know of the Nohl family who have the estate in the Isthmus gold fields?"

"A branch of the Deltas family, you mean?"

"I was told so. I'd never in my life heard of the name before."

"Yes, the gossip. The name's common enough in that district. The Isthmus Nohl is one who married an infertile woman for her wealth: he had none of his own. They sold the estate to the Brokerage Consortium, though they still live on it."

Skerow said, half to herself, "There was someone who needed help when I could not give it, whom I promised . . ."

Threyha watched her shrewdly. "Nohl's disgrace made a huge scandal at the time, and though it was hushed up it is common knowledge in some parts. Not here. You know how often we tell ourselves it is so rare for Khagodi to do such things."

Skerow bowed her head. She had been just so naive.

"And of course we cannot discuss it as a case—but you are not the sitting judge! All this information is available in records and archives: Nohl was accused—but not convicted—of dealings, like giving shelter and laundering money, with major crime figures of several worlds. These people were slave traders, and were murdered before they could come to trial; there was no trial. Nohl faced a lesser charge, but was let off. It happened thirty years ago, and many people who do not live as long as we have forgotten about it."

Skerow felt the same icy stillness that the name *Nohl* had given her earlier. She said to herself, *And I said that she was a gold picker from the Isthmuses. I forgot that machines pick gold for honest dealers, but slaves may pick gold for* . . . And to Threyha, "You did say slavery?"

"I did."

"And have you known about this all along?"

"Only vaguely, that Nohl had been in some trouble. I was working far away from home then, and of course I know everything in the Galaxy except what goes on here in this world. The old memories stirred when I heard of Thordh's death, and I knew he was your workmate, so I looked up the records."

"And Nohl got off."

"Yes. After that fracas he decided he had no head for business. Wisely, I think." Threyha drew down her upper lip in the reptilian smile that had her sweetness of character in it. "You can find the details in any good data base, including the name of the presiding judge."

Good neighbors, Nohl and Thordh. "I don't think that name will surprise me," said Skerow.

The conversations had dissolved around them. The tropic sky was very clear now, very black, and the stars rushed blazing forward out of the flare of the Galaxy. The group fell silent: even with their dim eyes they felt the starlight crashing down on them.

I cannot see them distinctly, Skerow was thinking, *but Fthel and the Twelveworlds are in that group of stars southeast just above the horizon, and just beyond the horizon east of them are the Lesser Archipelagoes and the Isthmuses. Thordh and Nohl, neighbors of a sort. And fellow aristocrats in the shadows. I could not help Kobai, and I was too befogged in myself to see that Thordh was corrupt. No, I am being too harsh on myself. I can think of something to do. Now,*

> *sleep*
> *is waiting under*
> *swooning stars*

—tik! that is bad poetry, but even though slaves exist, and on this world, I am alive, I have a good friend with me, and this is a magnificent night in a beautiful land.

FOUR *

Shen IV: *In Zamos's Palace of Knossos*

Zella raked Sweet down the side of the jaw with the chebok and when he raised his buckler ducked underneath and got him in the belly. She laughed as he backed one foot out of the practice-circle. "You're rashers!"

If the chebok had been a proper one with spikes of steel instead of polythene, he would have been well sliced. He mumbled, "I wasn't really trying," and grinned. His teeth were pearly, ceramyx mother-of-pearl, and one of the front incisors had a diamond set in it. He simply could not see Zella as deadly.

She was a white-blonde with very pale eyes and corn-silk hair tightly braided and wound in spirals on the back of her head; the hair shaded into a darker ash in the depth of the plaits. She had coral lips and milk-white skin: there were pink exertion spots on her cheeks.

The half score of hungover spectators in the small arena applauded halfheartedly as they rose and began to file out; there was no blood at Zella's practice sessions.

Sweet made a complicated performer's bow, and Zella repeated it in parody, then she laughed again, shadow-boxing, zipping around him like a hummingbird, one circle of hopping and grinning before she pulled the weapon off her fist and flung it in the tackle box. Just as it landed a spyhawk whipped out of a pneumatic tube in the wall and fluttered round her head. "*Awk!* Sztoyko," it cawed. "Front Office asap!"

She flapped it away with her arms, always afraid one of them would land on her head. "What could they want? I've never been called down before."

"Gonna give you a fucking promotion."

She made a face. 'Yeah, sure. I've been here one whole half of a year. Got to run." And shrugged a shoulder in annoyance, because asap meant sooner than possible here; no time to change out of the grubby sweats.

Sunlight was lying along the grey scrubbed gym floors in brilliant planes; the huge waterfall windows were deeply tinted, but still the light was intense under the white sun Shen that so passionately kissed its fourth world. As Zella rode the walkway she could see to the left the port of the Palace of Knossos, stretches of whiteness curving around the purple blue aquamarine of the sea; to the right hundreds of cubicles stretched out on the level below the railing snaking under her hand. Some were open practice rings or small arenas where spectators were free to watch and usually made small bets. Others were capped with plasmix bubbles, and under them dark figures armored in bone or metal fought through swirling clouds of their own strange atmospheres, or swam like whips with knives in their world's waters.

There were fights still going on. A group of four young Khagodi men, very low-grade ESPs wearing impervious helmets of steel and bronze were squaring off at four-in-corners; their tails were their weapons: they had chopped off the ends and stimulated the growing buds to split; all of them had three or four tail-tips armed with steel spikes. There were only a few Khagodi fighters, in Zamos's arenas or anywhere else; most Khagodi are not capable of much physical grace, and therefore not much interested in developing it; those who do are rather despised.

Next cubicle to them a pair of Kylkladi in electric blue and poison green feather armor were dueling with long sharp swords, and being watched by two coaches in stripes of the same colors, one of them a Varvani. Kylkladi were extremely punctilious, and in serious battle very cruel fighters, as opposed to Varvani, who fought merely crude and dirty. It seemed odd to Zella that the two peoples got on so well, even that they breathed the same air. The rudest Kylkladi were still only caricatures of the most refined. It seemed less odd that Zamos hired so many of the two species; Zamos chose extremes of everything.

A red-eyed Kylkladi woman whose bleached white feathers were lacquered with pearl met Zella at the reception desk and ushered her into a tiny office lined with slots, key-hooks and minuscule drawers. "My name is Kati'ik," she said. "I believe we've met before."

"Yes ma'am. You registered me when I first came."

"That's right." There was a file displayed on the vid, and Kati'ik tapped the screen with a gold-plated talon. "We've been watching you."

Zella stared at her; her heart did a double beat and she made a swift review of her life and its sins. But the record was there under the gold-taloned hand. The supervisor raised her head. "Keeping an eye out for someone like you."

Zella could not help feeling that these officious Kylkladi were sinister; she wondered sometimes if the Kylkladi did not recognize and exploit these feelings. There were no known ESPs among the pugs except for the few Khagodi, and none admitted among the staff. She said quietly, without enthusiasm, "What did you have in mind for me, ma'am?" She felt sweaty and self-conscious facing the sleekly vicious elegance of this creature.

"We have found you a fighting partner . . ." The gold claw tap-tapped and a new file flicked on the screen; Kati'ik pointed to the holo in the screen's corner.

A step up: perhaps. More money. More safety than being drawn from the pool and paired with an unknown crazy, or worse, a known one. Zella peered at the tiny holo image. The fellow wore his hair too slick, but was not bad-looking except for the red pustules flourishing thickly on his three-day beard growth. "Edmund (Ned) Gattes. I hope he fights better than he looks." *I'd never want to jump into bed with that one.*

"That is nothing, a beard rash. You will find him a good fighter, and I want you to be very good to him."

Zella stared at the woman, who was buffing a claw with a small piece of chamois. "That's not in my contract. There's a clause that says, no whoring."

"That is true, and whoring was not what we had in mind. We believe this man is a spy working for a huge gambling ring, and we want to catch him communicating with them. You will be with him all the time, and tell us if he does. It is very important to us. If you can do that without taking him to bed, so much the better for you, I suppose."

Zella's cheeks were flushed deep red. "I don't know how to do that kind of thing. Aren't there other women who'd be better at it?"

"Perhaps there are. But you are the one we particularly want for this task right now."

"I don't have to do this. I'm not legally bound—"

"You are a very naive young woman, dems'l! You can

ship home if you wish, but *Zarandu*'s shuttle lifted off yesterday and will not return for one year. The fare is expensive, we paid a deal to bring you here. And right now you are very, very far from home."

Zella was sweating hard and terrified; she had reached a point where all she wanted to do was give in and agree. "I've worked seven of every ten days, I've earned my keep and over." She felt the roots of her hair prickling, but she steadied her voice and said, "I'm a free citizen in every place that recognizes Sol Three's worlds and colonies. Just because the *Zarandu*'s gone doesn't mean I've had to give up the protection of interworld law." Her jaw was set like stone.

The Kylklad stood looking at Zella, tapping her flat hooked beak with the restless gold talon. After a long moment, she said, "Let us begin again, Sztoyko. You need a partner, and this man is a good one. We need information about him and feel you are the person who can get it. It's a case of spying. Does that offend you so greatly?"

"No, I suppose not," Zella said. "As long as he's not violent."

"No more than the usual gladiator. You might even like the fellow."

"If I did I might be happy to sleep with him." Zella was grateful to be let off the hook.

"I am glad we are finally in agreement," Kati'ik said dryly. "You will meet him this evening."

Zella went back the way she had come, furious with herself for having been so manipulated, and helpless against the attack strategy the Kylkladi used so well. She was conscious, to the point of self-consciousness, of being unsophisticated. She had been born on one of the many farming communities of New Southsea World, a planet belonging to Sol III that had already shaken off names like New World, Second Chance, Last Chance, and Heaven On Earth. Its colonists were determined non-polluters, and Zella's people were secular fundamentalists who lived on solar energy, avoided electronics more complicated than radio, raised all their own food, and went to bed with the chickens. The energetic young left early and sometimes came back when they were tired. Zella did not repudiate her community's ideals, but wanted excitement. She was getting it.

It seemed to her that the atmosphere, which had seemed no more than coarse, had now become sinister. The ivy-latticed crèche with its garland of gladiators' children playing ring-a-rosy now struck her as perverse; one of the dueling Kylkladi had blood on his breast feathers, and the Brazilian machete fighters conferred darkly with their priestess—a thick woman with bursting black hair and sharp protruding teeth; draped with the bones of small animals, she was stamping to an unheard beat that rattled the tiny skulls.

Ned Gattes had taken all of his worries into deepsleep and woke to them in the long pull out of it descending to Shen IV. For years he had longed to train and fight with the Spartakoi. Now the condition of fulfilling the dream would mean going into more danger than he had ever known in the ring. The spytick he had been given at Zamos's brothel might not have been meant for him particularly, but given that he had just delivered Jacaranda through its doors as a spy, what else dared he think? Manador had not reassured him. Even in deepsleep he could see Jacaranda going through those heavy doors wrapped in the arm of the tattooed Varvani woman.

During the gradual awakening on the shuttle in its long descent, and the regimen of exercise and diet that brought him and seven hundred and eighty other Shen IV-bound passengers back to life, he found himself distracted from his fears; for a long while he felt still wrapped about with hazy sleep, his bones icy from the cold that stretched between the stars. His one satisfaction was that the shuttle's clinic had built him drugs that depilated his rough beard and altered the genetic structure of the follicles so that the hairs grew in straight. The skin still tended to turn red or sallow at strange times, but he had a smooth chin. And he was not thinking of Jacaranda.

Eventually he found himself threading his way with forty-six other new-dogs through the endless halls of the Palace of Knossos, shepherded in a ragged line by a Varvani woman with a clipboard. He had slept both too much and nowhere near enough, and could not fully open or close his eyes in their gritty sockets. Like everyone with him he was wearing thirty-four patches of drugs and stank of disinfectant; he could sense the shielding of noses as the file went by.

He passed the Kylkladi fighters wiping blood off their swords, the crèche whose ivied lattice fenced in the brawling children, the Khagodi fighters pulling the steel spikes off their tails and wrapping them in soft leather thongs, the divided bubble where two devil's wives swirled in trails of their turquoise blood from flinging themselves at the partition to get at each other. In another cubicle three Brazilian machete fighters idly clashed blades together while four others honed theirs with whetstones, and their priestess crouched in a corner and muttered to herself.

The moment Ned stepped off the walkway into the momentary shadow of a less brilliantly lit hallway two figures with daggers leaped at him screaming "Ya-hee-ya!" and the world changed. They had khaki-colored skin, headdresses that looked like heaps of blue blocks and earrings to match, and brass breastplates with symbols in bas-relief. Neither had a left arm.

Ned marked all this without thinking as he came awake: he had no maneuvering room and twisted sideways to avoid the downward swing of the weapons. As he drew back the momentum of the pugs marching behind him pressed him toward the dagger points, and he began to fall forward. Just as he crumpled two golden hands reached out and grasped his attackers by their two right arms and pulled them away.

By then he was on the floor and the woman behind him had tripped over his ankles and fallen to her knees. Her scream of "Shit!" brought the Varvani lumbering to help her up, and the golden hands with mother-of-pearl fingernails caught Ned under the armpits and hoisted him to his feet. "Are you wounded, friend?" the equally golden voice asked.

"I don't know." He could not think to look for wounds. His eyes were compelled by the figure before him.

"I am Spartakos. What is your name?"

Ned stammered something. Perhaps it was his name.

Spartakos was a robot in the shape of a male Solthree. His head, hands, and feet were plated with gold, and his athlete's body chromed. He moved seamlessly and without a sound. Ned's eyes could not take him all in at once, he shone so. "You will report this to the front office."

The line back of him was untangling its knot of traffic and snarling at him to get going; the one ahead was turning to see what had caused the commotion. Nervously, Ned tried to draw away from this awesome figure, but Spartakos drew him aside into the shadow, seeming to realize that he was trying to avoid attention. "You will," said the robot.

"What?"

"Report this."

"No, no! I don't want to stick out as a complainer before I even half got here!"

"But they tried to kill you!"

"Yes they did, and I thank you, Spartakos, for saving my life—but please don't report this to anyone!"

"And you are still my friend?"

Ned could not believe that this voice sounded anxious. "Oh yes, forever!" He pulled away at last and ran to rejoin his gang.

"You will see me in a moment," Spartakos called after him, but he did not turn to answer.

"Ee, chummie, what was that about?" said his companion, a woman with a cybernetic arm.

"I'm damned if I know," Ned said fervently.

"Yer been singled out for special attention," the cyborg said.

Ned shuddered and did not answer.

Presently, armed with a bag full of contraceptives as well as the keys to the lockers and storerooms where he would keep his possessions and fighting tack, he was standing with the others in Common Room #27 while a burly fellow named Gretorix, who looked as if he had fought with every army that ever marched, harangued his captive audience about payday, policing, and prophylaxis. He finished off by saying, "Now, here's Spartakos, who has a few words to say to you," and the robot came into the room and stood among them.

Everyone was taken aback. Most of the pugs had never seen such a robot before, and they could not help drawing away a step. Their desultory muttering stopped. Then curiosity conquered uneasiness and the men, women, and non-sexed of eight species surrounded him at a distance of three meters in a rigid and almost perfect circle that had grown as naturally as an organic cell from the balance of attraction and repulsion he had stimulated in them.

Spartakos said: "Gladiators, I am Spartakos, your guide to the Palace of Knossos, its labyrinths with their pleasures, treasures, and dangers. You will find perhaps love, perhaps death, and some of you will have both, and die beloved."

The Common Room was just easing into the shadow of

evening; its furniture, chosen to fit itself to several kinds of bodies, was comfortable but neutral in color, and the radiant surface of Spartakos was almost an assault on the eye, as if it carried its own light.

"The most experienced among you will be assigned partners here today, and perhaps you will find in them . . ." He raised one gleaming hand toward them in an almost tentative gesture at which the stance of his body shifted at the hip in what seemed thoughtless grace. "Is destiny too heavy a word for the love, or friendship, or even hate it will be so interesting to find? Whatever it is, I invite you to it, gladiators. Now come with me."

Ned Gattes knew of such robots, but the few he had seen were not completely robotic, and had been directed in part by human brain matter. He did not think this was the case with Spartakos. The pug standing beside him, a hairy Solthree with a regrown nose and unmatched ears, sniggered and said, "Wonder if he gets any fucking use out of his equipment."

"He'd smell a lot better than some," said a woman who did not care to be standing next to him. Ned Gattes was to find it characteristic of the pugs that when Spartakos was among them they became uncomfortable and spoke coarsely of the flesh, as if to reaffirm it in themselves and each other. Even cyborgs did this. Especially cyborgs. But they obediently picked up their baggage and let him lead them down the halls, hypnotized by the light that glittered on him from one ceiling lamp to the next, until the hall broadened and became lined with doors. Then he withdrew into a corner and stood as still as if he had been turned off, and Gretorix, who had been worrying the file of pugs like a sheepdog, directed them to their quarters.

Ned sat on his bed with his gear around him, and noticed for the first time that there was a fifteen-centimeter crust of dried blood running from right shoulder to nipple on his taklon knit jersey; one of the knifers had got him, and neither he nor anyone else had noticed the shallow cut because the shirt was dark red. The thin material had been designed to deflect such attacks, but the blade had caught it along the grain when he was twisting away and driven a tiny fold of the fabric into its slash; the shirt was not torn even though the skin was cut. In all the excitement he had not noticed the wound; the moment he noticed it it began to hurt. He softened the crust with cold water, pulled off the fabric, washed and sprayed the cut with picrocin and dermatex. Then stuffed his shelves with underwear and sleepsuits, and arranged toothcleaners and depilatories on the washstand. He did not even try to sort out what had happened, but merely pushed it away; when Gretorix directed him to one of the trestle tables in the huge dining hall and the young woman stood up to greet him, he did not want to look at her face.

Zella had dressed carefully, in a light blue leather doublet, slit at the sides, that showed some thigh but not much, dark blue stirrup-hose and cordovan laced sandals. Everything was mixing itself up in her mind, Ned Gattes and his terminal acne, being demeaned by Kati'ik, Sweet and his diamond and his dead end life as a sparring partner for the Spartakoi, whether she might become one like that or be fired, how lonely and out of things she felt in vast surroundings where the other women seemed so experienced and self-assured— hard, anyway—and she was not quite sure whom to trust among the men, whether she could survive a Bloodfight, how soon the Lottery would come up for it . . . whether Kati'ik had it in for her, everything whirling together—she caught a side glance at herself in the mirror that formed one wall of her small room, braid half-fallen over her shoulder and looking young and naive. But she had fought in thirty arenas, and drawn blood. She stared the image down. And now, hurrying on her way to the dining hall, she knew she was still young and healthy enough to feel a stir of unreasoning hope.

The hope was seriously threatened when she stood up to welcome Ned Gattes. He grimaced when he shook her hand and looked as if he would rather be somewhere else. That look was not the only one that put her off. "You don't look like your holo—oh, maybe I shouldn't have said that."

He grinned. "Yah! The jaw! That got fixed up, at least for now."

"I heard someone saying you'd been attacked."

Ned sobered, and said, deadpan, "Only a flesh wound."

"Couple one-arm bongos," said the woman sitting next to Ned, and he recognized her as the one who had tripped over his ankles. "But you got hoicked up by Spartakos. Never figured a mekko would have them kind of brains."

"Oh, he does," said Zella. "But I don't know of any one-arms among the pugs. Maybe novelty-fighters like Spartakos."

The cries and cheers ringing in the dining hall heralded the first good meal in months to the long-starved travelers, and Ned fell to ravenously and would not take up the conversation.

Zella was becoming worried that she would never be able to find her way into his confidence when, toward the end of the meal, she looked up and found him staring at her. She said, "Something you were meaning to ask me?"

The grimace returned to his face. "You remind me of somebody—a bit."

Zella thought, *Wouldn't want to be that one, whoever.* But she said, "Is that a line?"

He showed teeth. "Only if you bite." He had Jacaranda

on the brain, he knew that. He was being paranoid, but then he often was, lately, and with good reason. But the moment he had first looked at Jaca—no, Zella, the sense of determination in her face and how her features were set by it, the white skin, the way she moved her shoulders and arms, recalled—

Cut that, Ned, or yer a dead 'un! His father was always saying that, with a whack, when his mind wandered.

—reminded him of a younger Jacaranda at the time when they were both being seasoned under the hand of Manador.

The antique pornograph had a room to itself adjacent to Level 3 Common Room #15. Most of the habitants had exhausted its treasures after a year in the Palace of Knossos, but many of the new pugs had never seen such a thing, and thirty-odd were crowded around it, faces flickering in its light.

The machine measured about four meters by three and glittered with the sexual symbols of fourteen human species from twenty-five worlds in a thousand shades of color and intensities of flashing light. It housed six peepshows with touchy-feely and Orpha *dugak* music on the Varvanian *wabu*, eight erotic computer games with sound effects, a two-meter-square screen that played holo cartridges, and a three-dimensional Tri-V that programmed itself with innumerable variations on the same theme.

Ned was standing near the crowd, for safety, but a little apart, to avoid being jostled. He wanted to put an arm around Zella, not just only to make her an unwitting ally, but the part of his mind that equated her with Jacaranda balked: every man who touched Jacaranda paid, one way or another. When he finally did bring himself to circle her waist, she relaxed against him with what seemed to him—relief?

Something had gone wrong with the Tri-V and perhaps

because it was so old no one had bothered to have it repaired. Its colors did not coalesce: each person in its dramas had become a close cluster of three images in red, blue, and green, and each gesture was tripled as three, six, nine hands groped for their shadowy pleasures.

The cyborg woman said, "Shit, even I've seen all this junk and the thing's buggin my eyes out. Where's all the cartridges with the good stuff?"

The man with the bad nose job was digging into a rack of cartridges below the big screen. "These things are so old I can't even read what they say." The fluorescence of the titles had rubbed away.

A Khagodi with a tri-split tail picked a cartridge off the floor. "This one looks new."

"Yeah! *Sisters*, it says. Yeah. Every man should have one. What I—"

"Just cut it out, Smugger, and get going," the cyborg said. Smugger gave her a leer and slotted it in.

Sisters opened with the camera eye looking from above at a woman lying on a bed, lit in dark red, infrared. She woke up, turned on the light. It was . . . not sure yet, but . . . she looked into a mirror, yes, it was Jacaranda. Red curly hair, white skin, small tight build. Ned's heart bumped and he began to sweat very cold.

The woman opened the door; a big man was waiting for her. She went down a hall with him: he stood by while she went into a room where a Lyhhrt in a workshell gave her an injection. There was no sound but the pornograph's crazy music, and the action was tightly edited.

"Ain't they gonna do anything?"

The woman, still shadowed by the bruiser and just as blank-faced as he was, went to a second office, where a Kylkladi man with dyed green feathers, wearing spectacles, put a thin gold chain around her neck. The camera moved along with her but did not shift from its over-the-shoulder point of view.

"Aw, let's get offa this an find somethin with some action!"

"Shaddup," a woman said. "I wanna see what happens to her."

Another man said, "I think this kind of looks like a snuff act. I remember one where they put a chain on her like that."

"Yeah? Then let's get on with it!"

"Sure, you'd say so!" the woman snarled.

Ned was rigid, streaming with sweat. Zella pulled away and whispered, "Are you all right?"

His headshake was the barest of gestures, he raised a hand to be let alone. His eyes were locked on the screen, he could not blink.

Zella was staring at him. Then she said, again in a whisper, "You know her." It was not a question, and he did not answer. She said, in a louder voice, "Why wouldn't she fight?"

"Maybe she didn't know what was happening—or maybe it ain't gonna be that a-tall."

A Kylkladi woman in purple feathers led the red-haired woman to a store-room where she she removed her clothes and put a corset decorated with spangles, gave her an impervious helmet and a mask in the shape of a scallop shell, and led her down even more halls, all the while touching her on neck, shoulder, or thigh with a feather or a silvered talon while they passed between rows of staring people of strange species.

"That's a whorehouse." The others did not answer, and the pornograph fell silent as the gamesters came around to look at the screen.

The scene flicked to a theater with screens, holo receptors, and the camera facing an apron stage where a gigantic Florence flask was waiting; it was filled with liquid, and another tube led into its belly. Swimming inside the flask was a hominid female with a deep red skin, and a tadpole-shaped tail as long as her legs; there was a gold chain around her neck. Her eyes were huge and dark; she stared out for a moment and then retreated to the wall and turned her face away.

"I never see one of them before."

"Some animal they breed for games."

The red-haired woman dropped down the neck beside her; she was wearing the shell mask and the impervious helmet. The water blurred in a flurry of bubbles. When it cleared the two were staring at each other; the red-haired woman raised both hands and grasped the aquatic woman's breasts.

"Yeah! It's about time!"

"Shut up!" Zella hissed, surprising herself. Ned tightened his grasp on her shoulders as if she were his lifeline. He could not bear to watch, nor force himself to turn away.

The aquatic raised her arms in a startle, then without violence plucked the other woman's hands away, and the devil's wife came boiling out of the tube. When the thrash of bubbles settled down the beast had already slashed the woman along the side of her thigh, the screen zoomed close and the ribbon of blood seemed to be splashing the eyes of the viewers.

"I know that! It's a devil's wife."

"And he can keep her too."

"Them things got esp," the cyborg woman said.

Smugger called, "Hey Barley, I bet you never fought one of them!"

The man who had brought up the talk of a snuff act answered, "You can bet your eyeballs, pignose, and I never saw one of them killed either. She don't have much chance with no weapon."

The woman had wrapped herself around the serpent's

neck and was trying to choke it, but could not get a tight hold on it. Clinging under the jaws, she tried with one arm to push the aquatic toward the neck of the flask. The sea-woman did not understand at first, then pulled herself up and away, but when she saw that the claws of the devil's wife had raked the fighter's back, and the helmet had broken away and fallen to the floor of the tank, she dived down from her shelter, snatched up the helmet, and slammed it in the beast's eye.

Then the serpent's blue-green blood mixed with the red and turned the water smoky, but before it was completely obscured the red-haired woman had dropped the mask, shoved her face into the serpent's tangled gills and savagely bitten into them. As its blood billowed again, the devil's wife twisted its head and bit her halfway through the neck. The screen went black.

There was a moment's silence, and Barley said, "Looks like she fought."

Zella murmured, "She was trying to protect the other one. I wonder what happened to her."

"If she'd died they'd'a showed it," Smugger said.

Ned thought that was probably true. He scrubbed the tears from his cheek in a one-handed gesture.

"Hey!" said Barley. "I think I know that woman! Didn't she use to be a pug? I never recognized her without the gear. She used to be one of that blueface woman's string on one of the worlds in Central—that funny name, Starry Nova. She had a funny name too. Like, Jambalaya."

"Hey, Ned, didn't you come from there?"

"Jacaranda," Ned said. "Yeah. I knew her. She was a good fighter."

He walked away blindly, arm still around Zella.

So there just happened to be a holo with Jacaranda getting ripped to death. It was the Khagodi that picked it up off the floor, but all forty-six of them shipped out with me. So this classy armful I got here looks like Jacaranda. If I went to bed with her would she kill me in my sleep? No, I don't think she would. If the Weird Twins had wanted to stick me with those daggers I'd have been dead as soon as they jumped me. They'd have driven them up through my belly. I would've died anyway from everybody pushing me at them if that robot hadn't saved me. A robot! "Are you still my friend?" I sure as hell need one.

That spytick I was dumb enough to take. Means they— THEY—want to know. Something. Something about the delphine, because we were interested in her, and we never found out anything, but they don't know that, whatever we know may be too much. So they don't want to kill me—yet. Just scare me to death. It wasn't GalFed, I bet, that sent me here, they just hooked on, and I don't dare try much spying in this place. But I'll die of a broken neck if I have to keep twisting my head around looking to see who's coming at me next. I can't stay here.

I gotta get outa here, gotta get out. Out.

Fthel V: *Lebedev*

Two days after the body of Jacaranda Drummond was found, the *skambi* dealer of the Gamblar at Zamos's brothel in Starry Nova was offered a much better slot in the Kylkladi GamePlex on the other side of the world. The following day a Miry applied at Zamos's for the vacated place. He was a small compact man wearing a short *zaxwul* pea jacket and a Russian peaked cap with a button on top; his eyes were black and heavy-lidded and his grizzled beard was cut close.

"A.G. Lebedev . . . yes," said the hiring officer, a thin artificially red-headed woman. "Full name, please, spell it."

"A-L-E-K-S-A-N-D-R G-R-I-G-O-R-I-Y-E-V-I-C-H L-E-B-E-D-E-V." He offered his GalFed Working Permit. The holo showed him with his mouth crooked up as if he had something awful in his teeth.

"You got a short form for that label?"

"Lebedev."

The woman looked up from the keypad. She was wearing a big locket that glowed and blinked, saying urgently: I'M SHIRLI!—I'M SHIRLI!—I'M SHIRLI! "Don't lip me, chubby. We already got twenty-three applications for that slot, and it's only one table."

"Excuse my feeble joke, Madame—but none of your bidders seems to be the right one. Your table is shut down, and the table-players are fighting for the machines they usually despise."

She sniffed. "Where was your last job?"

"In the Investigative Bureau of Starry Nova, Miry Division. Police Inspector."

She squinted. "Did you play a lot of skambi there?"

"No. That I did in the Starry Nova Institute of Correction and Rehabilitation, Miry Section. As an inmate." He smiled. "Importing illegal substances. I stole nothing." He added, "There are a lot of skambi players in prison."

She kept squinting at him, the gears meshing in her brain almost as visibly as the locket on her chest shrieked, I'M SHIRLI!—I'M SHIRLI! "You have proof of all this?"

He drew a neat packet from his pocket and displayed his employment termination notice with special condemnation, his prison I.D., his ticket-of-leave dated three thirtydays earlier, and was reaching for a birth certificate when she put up a hand.

"Stop. You really think you can handle a table after playing with bread crumbs or whatever?"

"I have visited here many times in an official capacity before you began working at this desk. Your table has a disk shuffler, a scoring display, and a pair of white gloves—and you need a dealer who is not timid."

She thought for a moment and pushed a button. "Go play a couple rounds on the machines while I check you out. Ai'ia will put away your hat and coat and take you to the Keymaster for tokens. That way." She pointed to a door different from the entrance way. It led farther into Zamos's brothel. Deeper. Lebedev nodded and went through it.

Skambi is not the most popular game in the Galaxy. It does not fire philosophical discussions and seed libraries the way chess, *ip, go, huka* and *bodoko* do, even though it is a game like *Temple of Brahma,* which is a matter of three diamond rods with sixty-four gold rings of different sizes heaped on one of them, and when they are all transferred in the proper order the universe will vanish, *pfft!* That is a puzzle for mathematicians. Skambi is played across the Galaxy because it has few cultural connotations, no requirement but a good mind, and is only a matter of placing a smaller piece on a larger one in a pile; though the rules are complex and constantly being changed, it can be played with tokens, coins or buttons of different sizes and the same shape, disks of steel—even gold—or pieces of leather, cloth, or plastic, or loops of string, chain, or beads, or with playing cards, tarot, mah jongg tiles or any numbered pieces. Or, by the truly obsessed, with slices of food. A dealer's call, like "Number fifty-seven today, gentle-persons!" begins it.

Lebedev went to admire the old-fashioned table, then into the huge hall where he found the skambi machines crowded by moping Bengtvadi whose friends had left for home on their mother ship, *Zarandu.* No one was willing to share a game, but eventually he squeezed in between an emaciated Bengtvad and a thick Varvani who had pulled one of the smoke-cones over his head and was smoking *ge'iin.* Wisps of escaping smoke made Lebedev a bit light-headed, but he did not complain to the hulk beside him. The game's vid was holo, and even looked as if real diamond rods were being eternally ringed by gold disks, with sounds to match over a swelling and dramatic music.

"Didn't know you played, Lev. Thought you just ran us in."

The not-quite-young woman passing with drinks to the table-rooms had straight brown hair cut to the jaw; there were red lights in it beneath the flickering lamps, and it swayed around her face as she balanced. She paused for his answer.

"Hello, Tally dear." Lebedev looked round at her, turning his head like a teddy bear so that the rest of his body did not move. "I have missed your sweetness."

She flushed for a moment under her freckles as she had always done at such remarks, and calmed quickly, knowing that Lebedev truly liked her. "You've come to ruffle us about the dead whore again."

Lebedev smiled. "Your drinks are melting." He dropped a token in a slot beside the game and drew out a very small Polish vodka. "I came to look for work." He tossed off the drink.

"Work?"

"A job."

"That's a very strange joke."

"Have you not noticed I have been away for a year?" She stared at him, as if she were not quite sure she really knew this Lebedev. "Yes. All that time I have been in prison. Far from the sunlamps of the Gymnasion. Disgraced. Abased. Everything."

She gave a hard grin. "I've got to hear that story—how you got on in there with all the poor mumpers you dusted and stowed away." She swept off in a whirl of russet velvet and lace. Lebedev laughed and placed a SayNo wafer under his tongue to dissolve the vapor of alcohol, though it would have been hard to notice through the fumes of ge'iin escaping from the smoke-cone.

"Mister." He turned. The soft voice belonged to the woman Ai'ia, who had led him to the skambi machines. She was slender, grey-beige in skin, hairless and wearing a black silk wiglike headdress woven with pearls: an impervious helm. He had not noticed her, with her strange near-beauty, when she led him to the Keymaster; in the dimness with his eyes on the footing he had only been aware of the floating hem of her caftan, patterned in oriental waves of seafoam and sky.

"You said something, Mister?" this vision asked.

Lebedev became aware that he had been staring. "I am a romantic, dems'l. I was admiring your beauty."

Her smile was not an expression of anything in particular. "I come to tell you that you may try out at the tables."

"Thank you, dear." He rose and followed; she moved before him carefully, with a learned grace, and seemed conscious of being observed.

The skambi table stood in a niche of its own under a bright light; it was star-shaped and had five seats between the points, each with an individual LED display set into the table in front of it. Three brass rods rose from the center, and the thin disks piled in the mixer were centered and rimmed with brass; they were real mother-of-pearl with streaks of blue, cerise, and yellow-brown, and inside every one of the sixty-five was a tiny alarm that shrieked if it left the table's circumference.

There were four people already sitting impatiently at the table. One was a Bengtvadi woman wearing plain working clothes, her long narrow head tattooed with complex clan insignia; her wrist was looped with a cord carrying an un-limited GoldCred disk. The second was a blue-pelted Dabiri man with an elaborately waved tail. The remaining two were a Solthree couple, a businessman in a dark green brocaded zip with fancy epaulets and his company's logo on the breast, and a thin fluffy young woman all mascara and lip rouge.

Lebedev found and pulled on the white dealer's gloves which had been folded in a little drawer beside him, along with a pair of armbands, purple with pink *yeye* flowers; he leaned over the table to wind the crank that traditionally mixed the stacks, and withdrew the first disk to appear in the slot.

"Number twenty-eight today, gentlepersons! Enter credit I.D.s and wagers on your panels. Numbers fourteen, thirty-nine and fifty-one are wild." He punched numbers to light up the displays, gave one more wind of the crank to send the disks into the players' racks, set the clock, and threaded number twenty-eight on the first spindle, belonging to the Bengtvadi woman on his left.

"West plays twenty-five, North twenty-two, East nine-teen, South eighteen," the game went on to fill the first spin-dle with twenty-four disks, the second with twenty, and battled on to the third, where the winner would be the first player who stopped the game with an unbeatable piece or, when all pieces were gone, made a similar move from one disk to the other.

"South passes, West fifteen, North—sir," to the Dabiri, "five is disallowed if you have a higher number in hand that is within minus five of fifteen, Cruxan Standard Game Rules"—the Dabiri snorted, tossed his mane and played twelve—"but that move will not lose you a point on this round, courtesy of the house, sir, East plays eight, South—" he looked hard at South, the businessman, who was offering

3: he was almost certain that this player was holding number 6; he had noticed in his earlier examination that 6 had an odd little dent on its brass edge that was visible only in the bright light. "Sir, do you wish to play three?"

"Question!" the Dabiri and the Bengtvad cried in unison. South flushed deep red. "You calling me cheater?"

Lady East shrank back, and Lebedev spoke quickly before North and West could put in another word: "Oh no, sir. I thought you were intending to play six. The symbols are somewhat alike." His foot was poised over the alarm button.

There were one or two watchers impatient for a game; South swallowed his anger and drank most of a large mauve liqueur garnished with zimbfruit slices. He muttered, "I suppose I did mistake it—I seem to have a six here." North and West wisely did not argue, but settled back into the game and their drinks: the Bengtvadi tossed back her pepper vodka, peppers and all, the Dabiri lapped at straight gin.

South lost the game by one point, whether or not because he had been prevented from playing his three would never be clear. As soon as the game was over he retrieved his credit chip, stood up, and marched off leaving his companion staring at his back. She rose as if to follow, then glanced aside at Lebedev and he shook his head very slightly; she nodded, snatched up her feather boa and left to chat up someone else: she did not want a thick lip.

Tally, pausing to refresh drink orders, murmured, "That's a rough one, but he drops a lot of money, in the house too. He give you any trouble?"

Lebedev, looking across the room, saw that South was lingering near the poker tables. "He might have if we had been alone." The vacated places were already filled by eager players, and the Bengtvad was snapping her fingers for more pepper vodka. Lebedev wound the crank and said in a croupier's voice, "Number forty-three today, gentlepersons!"

It was nearly evening by the time his afternoon shift ended; Lebedev slotted the disks and glared at his gloves in disgust: "Feh. Such beautiful things and all so dirty."

"Mister." He turned to find Ai'ia at his shoulder. "Keymaster says you are in, Mister. You get a tenday's pay, and find cheap room and board next door with other employees."

He stood up stiffly. "Also I would like a little time to pack and move."

"You ask Keymaster for that."

"It is a change of clothing and a soup crock," said Lebedev. The Keymaster's office was up one floor, and he found the rank of chutes; as he stepped in and turned round to find the UP button, the closing door was wrenched back open and the flushed face grinned at him savagely.

"You're gonna get it, you sonofabitch!" said South and pushed inside with his fists clenched. "Last time any fucking ESP screws me!"

Lebedev did not try to explain that like other policemen he was not only not an ESP, but had had an imper circuit tattooed under his scalp. He kicked South in the knee, punched his face as he hunched over in reaction, and sent him a hard blow to the groin with his other fist when his head shot back. The doors closed and the elevator rose with a hiss of pneumatics.

South snarled in pain and his nose ran bloody, but it did not end there: he was a head taller, and for all Lebedev's pudginess, had an advantage of ten kilos in weight. His cupped hands were on their way to breaking Lebedev's eardrums just as Lebedev was aiming the hard edge of his hand at the bridge of South's nose; one hand caught Lebedev a clout on the ear but his own hand in its trajectory knocked South against the door, slamming the buttons. The elevator paused without opening and fell whispering down its shaft.

Lebedev hooked South's leg from under him, both fell, South got his hands around Lebedev's throat and Lebedev gave up his Police Inspector's aim of hurting without doing harm and did his best to tear South's ears off his head. South's grasp loosened a little and Lebedev twisted and bit him hard on the thumb. South yelped at the moment that the elevator cab landed, the doors opened and Lebedev pulled his strength together for a last burst and rolled out.

He lay stunned in a dimlit corridor with his arms and legs splayed, only just aware that his enemy was on hands and knees, reaching out for him. The closing doors caught South's wrist edge on, he yelped again and pulled his hand in quickly. Lebedev heard, through his ringing ear, the muffled cursing and pounding on the doors as the cab rose. Lebedev gasped and could not move for a moment; his other ear caught the ringing of the first as if it were a contagion, he felt South's very fingerprints on his throat, his tongue seemed to want to take leave of his mouth and crawl away. South was a strong and very angry man who must have done hard fighting in some theater of war, and if he had not been very drunk, Lebedev knew he would have found himself dead.

He heard, or thought he heard, the elevator stopping and beginning to descend. South had more fight left, but he did not. He rolled over and got to hands and knees, spent another moment gasping there, and pulled himself up painfully, one hand on the wall. He looked round: there were no other elevators at this level. There must be stairs. He did not want to go up, or in any other direction that South might be going. He could not see anyone and the distances of the corridor were dark. He blundered along trying to look as if he knew what he was doing, searching for a ramp or stairwell.

Around the curve of the elevator housing there was an

opening to a ramp that corkscrewed up and down, as far as he could tell in the dim light from the hall. The landing was unlit and he could hide there for a while. But when he stepped into it a soft light rose from the overhead lightstrip, the same kind as the one that had lit up the corridor. It jolted him, he was still sweaty and gasping, and terrified of drawing attention. He glanced round but could not see any camera; the switch was either a pressure-sensitive one under the floor or an electric eye. He heard noises behind him. There was no hiding place here; he started downward, and the strip lighted ahead of him, he was dizzy, the twist and slant of the ramp disoriented him, the light ran before him: *follow me! follow me!*

He stopped and panted, leaning against the wall, trying to gather his scattered wits. *Lebedev, you are too old for adventures! Nobody is following.* His ears were still ringing, but now he clearly heard voices overhead saying, "No, thought there was some noise from—" and trailing off. He pulled himself straight, staggered down and down, until he finally found an exit where the light did not accuse him. For a moment not knowing where he was did not bother him. Because of the grin, that particular rictus of facial expression, that South had shown him:

Look here, you lags and groaners! Look! Lebedev is here in his prison among us! His law once delivered us into the Pit, and now his law has delivered him to us! The forest of grinning faces and clenched fists had drawn him into its fearful depths. Lebedev, the former Inspector of Police, who had never been required to do more in the way of violence than twist an ear or kick an ankle, had been forced to fight his way through many bruising days. The attack had most unpleasantly reminded him . . .

But Lebedev, he told himself, *you who fought there are hiding here with your hair standing on end and your shirt falling out of your pants.* He pulled out a shirttail to wipe the sweat off his face, tucked himself in and straightened the points of his vest. He was standing in a small square area with three doors; one was slightly open and through the crack he could see deep red light. He had become calm enough so that he thought this was worth exploring, but he was sure there would be someone inside. And by now South would have been found and sent packing by a bouncer; it was safe for Lebedev to go up and collect his money.

As he took his first step on the ramp a loud banging and clattering came from above, wheels hummed, lights whirled and flickered and he shrank back. A cleaning robot was coming down the ramp, spraying and swabbing with disinfectant: the smell of it made Lebedev's eyes water.

He shrank back into his hiding place. The robot paused at the foot of the ramp, and then came forward. There was no way for it to go right or left. Lebedev gently tried the two closed doors; they were locked. By the time the robot reached the doorway, Lebedev had retreated farther, into the room from which the deep red light was coming.

He closed the door silently and flattened himself against it. His nose was itching, and his ears were playing the music of his blood. The place he was in was not quite a room but a square space a little smaller than the one he had come from. Its walls were heavy glass, and red lamps in the walls and ceiling beyond them were illuminating what seemed to be standing frames of hexagonal lattices, row on row, hundreds as far as he could see, perhaps thousands. Their sides were stamped with luminous world-symbols: *Demor V, Kemalan, Sem II.* They were looped with thin clear plastic tubes that looked like vines twining on fences. A score of mantis-shaped robots moved on tracks between the frames, now using a spraying limb to wash down a wall of latticework, now peering into a cell with a red eye. In the center of each hexagon was a tiny dark knot, like an insect in its cocoon, no, not an insect. An embryo just short of becoming a fetus. In human terms.

Lebedev stared.

The sweep of red hexagons ran on forever, like the folded linings of an immense womb, they seemed to pulse with his heart. He pulled himself together once again. He might be mistaken, only think he was seeing embryos. But his eyes were good, and he was not mistaken. It is true that most embryos look alike, whether they are Khagodi or Miry or Varvani—or horses, for that matter, or oppothruxes. He did not think they were Varvani—and certainly not Khagodi. He thought that when they grew up they would most probably be small humanoids with hairless grey-beige skins, and look like the one that Skerow had so painstakingly described, the one who said, *We have always lived on this world,* and the one called Ai'ia, who had evidently risen a little higher than those others, the ones with the fascinatingly good false I.D.s and working permits, whom he had been watching for years as a police officer. A relative to that other one for whose sake he had sent Jacaranda to die in Zamos's brothel. And it was all here. The answer to everything was here, in the brothel.

Why not? he asked himself. Why not in a brothel? But he did not know what he expected himself to answer. He was in the grip of an excitement perilously close to nausea: he had learned more than he wanted, and far too soon. Too soon for him to leave the place without being hunted down, because he had made his cover so conspicuous. He had to wait here, in his sweat, and deal *skambi.*

He was sweating again, the red pulsing was so oppressive. He turned away from the infrared and the slender machines moving among the red folds of the womb. He listened at the door and opened it a crack; no one there, robot gone. He pulled off his shoes to avoid leaving prints and hurried up the ramp in his stocking feet.

Lebedev and Lyhhrt

Lebedev's criminal record was not only part of his cover. For many years he had been engaged, wherever he was stationed, in smuggling rice, barley, dehydrated peas, lima beans, onions, scallions, tomatoes, and various other soup accompaniments as well as thyme and bay leaves. His half year's supply took up no more room than ten Karnoshky flamers, or even twenty Gothenburg stunners, certainly weighed less than one gold ingot—and were camouflaged in similar packagings. Importation of these scarce foods was allowed only to high administration officials and the expensive restaurants where they ate. Lebedev's superiors in the Police Department had known of his smuggling—they had all done it themselves at one time or another—but turned their eyes away, until a malicious informer had pointedly drawn attention to them; examiners had found among the dried packets a half kilo of karynon, the powerful vicious aphrodisiac, derived from yohimbine, that maddened as it aroused: Lebedev had tugged at some giant's beanstalk once too often.

The police had narrowly exonerated him from the charge of transporting a dangerous illegal substance, but could not free him entirely. Skerow herself had been obliged to try him for smuggling and send him to prison; she was furious:

"What an idiot you are, Lebedev," her pronunciation was nearer "Yebiteff"—"and all for some soup nuts, or whatever you call them! If you can bring those goods here so easily it must be easy for real criminals. You have been really too careless."

But though Lebedev dreaded prison, neither he nor the Police were put out at the conviction. They had been working along with Galactic Federation; now GalFed took over as Lebedev's employer, and Lebedev had a cover, bizarre as it was—and another bizarre and promising one at Zamos's brothel.

He had not foreseen Lebedev the skambi dealer crouching in a lavatory cubicle nursing swollen knuckles and a thick ear. They could be not be washed or combed away, and he was expected to present himself for the money he had earned—if he was not fired out of hand. He needed the money, he dared not take any from outside. He straightened his clothes and slipped out; the light was dim along the walls of the game room; the busy gamers and croupiers did not notice him at all. *The wicked flee when no man pursueth*, says the Bible. Roza would say: *The hat burns on the thief's head.* Would have said.

Tally, also off duty now, caught sight of him. "My God, Lev—are you the accident that happened to that bastard?"

He shrank. "Hush Tally! I will lose my job!"

She glanced round and said in a low voice, "Not if the girls have anything to say about it. They're fucking sick of paying for new teeth."

"I am not sorry I missed all the noise."

"Lady Pepper Vodka jumped on him, wanted to finish the job. I guess her breath knocked him out. He's gone."

"Now I must collect my clothing and my soup crock."

"I'll just send one of the O'e for them."

"What is oh-ey?"

"They're the native people of this world! Surely you must know them. Ai'ia is one."

The servant woman at the Residence had told Skerow: *We have always lived on this world.* "I know of them. I never knew there was a name for them. Let one bring my baggage, then."

In the Keymaster's claustrophobic office the light was dim. Lebedev tried to keep the bruised hand in shadow as he offered the chit.

The Keymaster peered at the disk and said, "One tenday." He pushed a button and a pack of tokens dropped into his claw. Another button brought a HouseCard popping out of a slot. "This is your room key." His fixed and staring bird's look showed no more expression than Kylkladi usually did. He said: "Your hand and ear need attention, Dealer."

Lebedev accepted card and packet. "I had intended to visit the doctor in the morning." He had thought he might have to see the doctor for inoculations, but he also knew that the doctor was a Lyhhrt, and he was afraid of Lyhhrt. Next to them Kylkladi were full of bonhomie and conviviality.

"Your hand will be stiff then. It is wiser to do so now if you wish to keep working here." Lebedev nodded submissively. "Take the walkway to the House office and the clerk will direct you."

Now in the pit of the night Lebedev found the halls and walkways of Zamos's brothel as busy as they had been in the surges of noon and evening custom, when he visited them as Police. In one alcove a woman as lustrous in starry blue as the Queen of the Night was smiling while she locked manacles on the wrists of a naked Varvani man three times her size. Through the open doorway of another room, Lebedev could see three business suits in black dominoes grouped around a Pinxid woman in red fringed *blemskin* leggings and a rouged boy in a spiked collar.

The Pinxid looked up and said, "Allo, Dealer," and for a

moment he lost track of himself and thought she might be Jacaranda, but Jacaranda was dead. No one deferred to him; everyone knew that he was not the Police Inspector.

He went on unwillingly, sweating again; he did not even know why he was afraid of Lyhhrt. His ear rang from far away, he was weary both from his fight and the long day of dealing skambi, rather dizzy, becoming claustrophobic. For a moment he thought that he had unwittingly been drugged, then wrenched himself back to awareness and realized that the corridor had narrowed and the walls were writhing with vividly colored images of sexual encounters, while the overhead lights were dimmer now; the place had become at the same time both brighter and darker. The clients staggering along the hall in various states of undress and levels of drugging and drunkenness, the men and women trying to lead them into or kick them out of this paradise, seemed coarser and shabbier.

A woman came out of a door or shadow. She was wrapped in a towel and carried a silver pitcher with a sponge for stopper. She had black hair and eyes and wore no makeup on her strong planed face. Nothing came between her and the eye.

Dizziness rose in Lebedev's head. He said, "Nadezhda?"

She looked at him.

"Your mother is dead. Why could you not come?"

He did not know if he truly heard her say: *I am not Nadezhda,* because the whirling darkness that replaced her twisted and flung him against the wall before he fell into it.

Something shifted under him, accommodating his body like a loving woman. When he opened his eyes he found himself in a contoured chair, and the Lyhhrt doctor was standing beside him, as magnificent as usual; this time arrayed in copper and brilliant as the setting sun.

Lebedev said, "Are you the same one?" It was all he could think of.

"I/we are well acquainted with erstwhile Police Inspector and now skambi dealer Aleksandr Grigoriyevich Lebedev." Probably the Lyhhrt himself did not know if he was the same one whom Lebedev had interviewed in earlier times. His esp was powerful enough to penetrate a police shield, but not without Lebedev knowing. "You received a blow to the ear."

"I am aware of that."

"You had a cyst in that ear. I removed it. You would have died of brain infection if you had kept on neglecting it. The blow quickened its pace. I am surprised that the pain did not alert you."

No one ever hurried to see the prison doctor; Lebedev had pushed pains aside. "I had thought it more likely that the blow would crack my skull. We live and learn."

"Your hand is bruised but no bones are broken."

"Good enough for dealing skambi?"

"Carefully. It will remain in good condition as long as I am caring for it."

Lebedev regarded the sunburst head with its beautifully moving and unfeeling features. Lyhhrt did not chat and rarely volunteered information. "I need not worry then." He did not look for the spy-eye.

"There are no guarantees. Time is pregnant with possibilities. Turn back your sleeve, if you please." He pressed three dermcaps against Lebedev's wrist where the veins pulsed. "For inflammation, infection, and pain. I will see you again in three days."

The accommodating chair delivered Lebedev to his feet, and he lingered standing for a moment, wondering if he actually had been told that Kobai was still in Zamos's brothel, well cared for and—pregnant? "Good night," said the Lyhhrt, though night meant nothing to him.

Lebedev had not even had time to be afraid. He paused again in the doorway long enough to think that the woman had not been his daughter Nadezhda, and that he had pushed her out of his mind, like the earache, since Roza had died.

Lyhhrt and Kobai

When the door irised behind Lebedev, the Lyhhrt pressed a place in his neck and his abdomen opened. He reached in and removed a glastex globe, twenty-five centimeters in diameter, containing his actual self, which he placed on a table top in a gold basket. Holding a tiny remote in one pseudopod he directed his shell to unplug the globe and siphon off the liquid he was swimming in, then replace it with a fresh mixture of food and oxygen from a jar stored in the wall refrigerator.

He splashed around in this for a moment, and pushed a pseudopod through the globe's opening to taste the air. When he withdrew it, the plug was replaced, and he used the remote to open a cupboard door and summon a different hominid shell of dull brushed silver in plain features considered, by Lyhhrt, to be less intimidating than their displays in gold and bronze.

Once nested in it, he connected up the sensors of the seven electrocardiographs, four electroencephalographs, and fifteen sphygmomanometers—all installed in clients—which he had been monitoring by remote. When he was satisfied with their reception he stepped into an almost invisible circle on the floor and stood with his hands at his sides while a plasmix tube descended around him from the ceiling, withdrew its air, sealed itself, dropped him down three levels without a sound. The place where it freed him was alongside the shaft that was wound about by the ramp Lebedev had descended; the tube shut and rose back into its recess.

He went down the ramp and into the anteroom where Lebedev had watched the robots attending the lattices of embryos under the infrareds. He did not look at them but elongated his silver arm to pluck down the spy-eye Lebedev had not noticed, removed the spool recording that showed Lebedev watching, reduced it to an inert pellet in a flash of his personal autoclave, refilled the capsule with a fresh wire and replaced it. His signal opened one of the doors Lebedev had found locked and he went through.

A third of the room beyond was taken up by a tier of bunk beds, one occupied by a snoring Solthree guard. Next to the bunks was an office table with an ordinary medikit opened on it, and beside it a squatting Varvani woman crocheting a long scarflike piece in purple silk with an ivory hook.

All other space in the room was occupied by the cylindrical tank of water bubbling with tiny streams of oxygen where Kobai hunkered at the bottom under the cold white light with her arms folded and her tail curled up like a roll of parchment. Her face was sullen. She grimaced at the Lyhhrt and turned her head away.

He stood with his silver hands and forearms against the glastex wall and regarded her the way he saw things, as an electronic image, for a moment before he engaged the mind back of those furiously sparkling eyes and began to tell her how babies are made.

ME? A BABY? WHAT IS A BABY??? Inside ME?? ALIVE? like the lugworm crawl in the dung-fish belly?

NO! come out of me like SHIT? I want to puke. NO!! NO NO NONO!! Take it away from me, I don't want this BABY!!

From when I let Siko or Pers or Om make the in-out it gives me this THING? *Everybody* makes in-out. I'm the very first? First of whats? Folk that make the New One in the belly! Let me out of here! Why you ask where I think the Folk person come from? Everybody know a New One fall down from Upthere when an Old One die.

I want to die. I am like dead in these walls with this thing inside feed off my meat! All my old Folk in the free water forgot me, you bet. You machine man you don't know what is to be in a cage and no one of the same breath with an arm around you to say Wake up, Kobai, new day, come work with me, come eat, let me kiss you, come make love, come sleep. Not even one friend.

:I am trying to be your friend,: said the Lyhhrt.

:Then let me out! Please, let me go home and pick the gold!:

:I cannot let you out.:

:You gather of all those cold hard pieces, you don't know what is a friend!: Face twisted in a snarl, she was on her knees, fists beating on them and her tail rippling as in a windstorm.

Inside the gathering of machine parts the Lyhhrt was nearly as cold as the salt seas Kobai swam in, and somewhat slimy, not one who would be attractive to her. He considered words carefully; it was rare for him to speak his mind as an independent person. He esped the others: the Varvani with her skein of silk was thinking of home, and the fellow on the bunk was dreaming of being somewhere in the universe that was warmer and sunnier than Fthel V; he made sure they would not esp him.

Finally he said, *:I am a fleshly being who needs these*

metal parts to work in as you need water, and they are a kind of cage.:

He opened his mind to her, as far as he thought she would understand a person who wanted only to be lying in a layer among his fellows with pseudopods entwined under the wet and grey-green skies of his world. *:I know what it is to be alone and lonely far from home.:* He added, *:When you have this baby it will be outside of you and taken care of, you will be free of it.:* He dared not promise her that she would be truly free, or that no one would ever again force her to bear a child.

She pulled herself back and down into a hard knot, with her arms wrapped around her legs and her tail rolled up again. *:Free is not what you want to say to me, Lord Jelly-in-the-Machine. I will die before I have this Baby-thing, and then I will be free.:*

FIVE *

Khagodis: *Skerow and Evarny*

Port Manganese is the star-shaped main feature on the map of Southern Vineland, a desert tract belying its name. Although the Port is as vital to Khagodis as Starry Nova is to Galactic Federation, it is a simple and homely facility, where travelers debark from their shuttle capsules into a huge round stone building to be sorted into conveyances according to their world of origin and local destination.

Khagodi, along with Varvani and other weighty outworld travelers, board railway flatcars shaded by umbrellas and drawn by steam engines; the tracks form the star that shapes the Port. Kylkladi run the airship lines that carry lighter passengers. Their helium balloons are decorated with colorful advertisements in symbol *lingua* for establishments like Ygglar's, in Kylklar's Port Na'at, where discriminating shoppers may buy gifts of fashion and refinement.

Threyha had boarded the transworld shuttle that hooked on to the solar-sailer *Yankee Clipper,* and after saying goodbye, Skerow spent the afternoon waiting for the interconti-

nental train that led to the ferry. She had rented an alcove
with bath, and drowsed there for a while; now, wrapped in
a white flax *aba* against the heat, she was resting on the
balustrade looking down into the great round courtyard;
people of many worlds were buying tickets at the railings
that encircled the communications center built around tow-
ering antennas that rose far above the roof. Every once in a
while some official would dash about with a banner to summon a group for boarding.

A muted roar, like that of a far-off crowd, reverberated
around the stone walls, a comfortable sound, and the sky-
lights were covered with dust that softened the afternoon
glare. But Eskat, who did not like noise, shrank fearfully
against Skerow and sucked his bead. She was not at ease either; her mind was still echoing with the conversations of
the last few days, and she longed above all to do the forbidden: take a side trip to Nohl's estate and pin him to the
wall. She dared not try it for fear of prejudicing any case
against him.

As she watched she sensed something else familiar and
very old: a mind resting along hers, as if someone were shar-
ing a bath with her. Her heartbeats tangled for the moment
in which she found the eyes meeting hers: those of Evarny,
who had been her husband. Who had divorced her when
their daughter had died and they were left childless.

She had not seen him for more than thirty-five years.

:Blessings,: he said. :In spite of your terrible experiences
you seem in good health.:

He was still sharp-colored; she said, :I am. You look as I
remembered you.:

:Perhaps. Will you come down? I want to talk to you.:

:Very well.: She could not think what he would have to
say to her. But he seemed to know more of her than she
knew of him. After she had descended by the lift she waited

near the entrance way because Eskat was trembling so hard in fear of the crowd, and watched Evarny working his way around the knots of people toward her. He stepped briskly, like a true Northern man, but as he came to face her it was strange to find how short he seemed, compared with the big Southerners she had become used to, like Thordh and Commissioner Erha; they were just her height, and Evarny was half a head shorter.

He led her past the lifts and outside through an arcade into a gazebo, where a failed garden was struggling in the hard-baked earth under the hot sun. Eskat had crept under her arm, and clung to a fold of her aba, sleeping. "You still keep that detestable little beast," he said, a remark not meant to be ill-natured.

She did not answer it. "I hope there is no bad news. I trust your family is well?"

"I have one son." She knew that his fertility was as weak as her own, but the new wife with whom he had hoped to strengthen it had evidently not done this. He added quickly, "No bad news, but there is a change of plans."

"What do you mean? Have you been sent here to tell me this?"

"I have been living here. Last year I was appointed Head Galactic Federation Representative for Khagodis. I have tried to reach you ever since I heard of Thordh's death, but you had left no address."

"My sisters have it—but go on."

"I want to ask if you might possibly change your itinerary and take over an important case of Thordh's."

"Thordh! There is no getting away from him! And I have hardly been home!"

"It is an Interworld Trade case. One of the witnesses is ill of poisoning and may die, half the parties are outworlders, and we cannot keep them here forever."

"I knew of that case, I was to sit on it as Thordh's under-study. Poisoning? It must have been brought forward then. But Evarny, I am not qualified."

"You not qualified? You were his understudy—now you are a senior interworld judge."

"Yes, and there are many others at least as competent as I."

"May be, but their appointment books are full, and this case came up too quickly to be put on the quarteryear calendar." He reached into a carryall looped around his neck and shoulder. "Here is the seal of order, and this is your ring of office."

She recognized them both. The heavy silver thumb ring was set with an opal. "This is too sudden for me."

"Frankly, it is far too sudden for the attorneys and clerks. They have only now gathered all the principals together because of this endangered witness. Of course I told them I meant to approach you, but your presence is still something they did not expect."

She grimaced slightly. "I imagine so. This sort of promotion is no favor to me. Thordh died very strangely, and I am sure the *Zarandu* unloaded a heavy freight of gossip and rumor along with the passengers. His friends and well-wishers in court will look at me cross-eyed, believe I coupled with him, the way his wife Thasse did, implicate me in his death, try me in their minds, and find me guilty."

He had raised his hand as if to touch her, and pulled back. "Blessed Skerow, you have reached a powerful depth of cynicism!"

"I have nearly killed and nearly been killed, by one of my own people, who are so deeply respected for justice and morality."

"That does not disqualify you from dispensing justice. You rode circuit with Thordh for over twenty years without being stained by the rumors that clung to him. I have followed your career."

"I still feel too close to Thordh, in an unpleasant way, to want to have much to do with his cases, and I don't care to face a court that is inimical to me—but yes, I am sure I may still dispense justice. I took the minor cases, when I worked with Thordh, but I did not resent it, because he was the senior, and I learned much from my travels. I am simply not feeling very strong."

"You know everything Thordh did and there were never ugly rumors about you."

"There were not. Tell me, Evarny: you say you followed my career, and yet you never once sent me a message. Why?"

"Perhaps I thought you might despise me."

"You were right. Perhaps I did, then. I hope I have got over that."

He was a little taken aback. "Will you stand on this case, then? I confess I have bought you berths on the train and ferry to Burning Mountain in the hope that you would."

"Yes, I will." He had had the grace not to mention that it would go ill with him in the eyes of his government superiors if he failed to persuade her. She was experienced enough to know that.

"The Forest Line train boards at fifteen ticks of twenty. Here are the ring and seal. Give them to the Officer of Court and she will invest you. And thank you, Skerow." He presented his tongue.

"May your one son beget thousands," she said, and bowed her head to touch his tongue with hers.

Burning Mountain was an extinct volcano, but the town built at its base was hotter than Port Manganese and very damp. The Khagodi Division of Interworld Court had been established here through political deals with several worlds, at a time when Khagodis was more innocently impressed with its membership in Galactic Federation than it is now. The courthouse's construction had been financed and its site chosen by Kylkladi, mainly for their own comfort—Khagodi do not like extreme heat—and one of the building's most ridiculed features was the clustering, in the streets around it, of a great many vending machines dispensing antihistamines and remedies for scale-rot and psoriatic fungus—local hot-weather plagues of reptile primates.

Yet Skerow had always found the building graceful, and even pleasant in the temperate winter months. The Kylkladi had built a model of their most common house style, the bower, on a tremendous scale: a circle of reinforced saplings of *ebbeb,* an equatorial tree that was the tallest in the world, with the branches curved to join at the top and the thin trunks interwoven with boughs and rainproofed preserved leaves, layered so that light was let in and rain kept out. Several banks of fans hung beneath the top of the dome, and their whickering leaf-shaped blades dispersed some of the intense heat. Skerow thought it was too graceful a place for men and women to be condemned in.

She had only a half day to listen to recorded accounts of charges and pretrial reports, and spent them resting in the basin of the Court's guest suite. The trial she was to sit on, *Interworld Trade Consortium against Goldyne Incorporated* was only one small part of a huge series of legal actions that involved fraud, market manipulation on several worlds, and insider trading, with theft, extortion, bribery, and sexual scandal on the side. . . .

Skerow's mind lingered on Evarny, a man restless in mind and body. She wondered how he liked the languid South, whether he still lived alongside his none-too-fertile wife, chided herself for making useless conjectures, and made them anyway.

She wished she had not met him, had missed him, gone home; wrenched her mind away, opened the books, and switched on the reports.

Goldyne, a Solthree firm that imported and used gold for manufacturing its instruments, had expanded to lend gold at cheap rates to mines on Sol III and other worlds wherever production might be delayed because of local strikes or other uninsurable conditions. . . .

The subject of gold made Skerow uneasy.

. . . Goldyne was only the newest of a series of names used by a firm eager to shift off a sleazy reputation gathered from earlier shady dealings. In its latest incarnation as a lender of gold it rivaled the Interworld Trade Consortium. Goldyne's services were so popular that they made the price of gold fluctuate and drag that of other ores with it.

Now Goldyne was charged with stealing from the Consortium the gold that it was lending to Federation worlds; because several Khagodi merchants working for the ITC were accused of supplying some of the ore, they were being tried on Khagodis. There would be many other charges and other trials.

Zamos Corporation was an important member of the Consortium, and was listed among the accusers. Skerow did not like the chain of associations that the name set off in her mind: *Zamos, Kobai, Khagodi, Nohl, gold, Isthmuses, Nohl, Consortium, Zamos.* They knotted themselves uneasily into her dreams, twisting and winding under the tropic storms through a night of unsatisfying sleep.

Skerow took her place without formality under the ceiling fans and looked out over the courtroom. The air was still cool, but smelled of the heat to come. The principals were filing in, outworlders settling themselves in chairs, slings, or harnesses, scratching the itching skin around their oxygen capsules; her landsmen easing themselves into whatever tail-resting positions they would find most comfortable during the long morning's work. The dawn was green and mysterious; it muted the men's colors, and darkened the shapes of the women. Light sparked to life in arched tubes of coldlight that ran up the room's walls and met in the center to repeat its lines. Under these arches figures became flat and either garish or dun-colored, the helmets of telepaths glinted dully. Someone behind the scenes hauled a squeaky lever that turned on the electricity, observers and journalists switched on recorders, display screens, and translation machines.

The Bailiff's Clerk came forward and began to read the long list of indictments concerning Khagodis. While this was going on one of the lawyers for the ITC, a Solthree named Blaylock, noticed that a clerk had been beckoning to him from the side entry. He slipped away, and after a moment of conferring signaled to his team that he was leaving. When he returned the reader had reached an item concerning the three Goldyne representatives based on the world: Walton Chong, Joseph Ferrier, and Jennifer Halet, all of whom were included in a charge of paying Khagodi to obtain gold.

After a whispering consultation with his colleagues, Blaylock raised a hand and said, "I beg your pardon, Madame Skerow, but an important matter has come up and I must discuss it with you."

"Will you come forward and tell what it is, sir?"

The man had turned quite red in the face, and his upper lip glistened with sweat. He said in a near whisper that Skerow had to turn her head to hear: "An essential witness, who is in danger of dying, has refused to testify and says— Madame, it concerns you, and I can't say any more here, would you come with me and speak to the Court Officer?"

"Counselor, have you given any thought to what you have said already?"

"Madame, you wouldn't believe how much thought I have been forced to give these few words."

"One moment," Skerow said. "Members of the audience, there will be a recess of one stad." The members grumbled, because even that short a fall of the clockweights would take them much further into the heat of the day. The young woman representing Goldyne tapped the floor with her tail, but before she could speak Skerow said, "If it is warranted, you will learn everything."

From behind the judge's rostrum a ramp led underground to the administration offices; it was cooler here, but damper. Following Blaylock and followed in turn by two more of his lawyers and the clerk, Skerow, used to leading the way in these situations, felt disoriented and almost like a prisoner.

The Court Officer, Ossta, a sharp old Northern woman with mauve glints to her scales, called from her archway, "Hullo, Skerow! What are you doing here now?"

Blaylock said quickly, "Madame Ossta, I have an urgent matter to discuss with the judge in your presence."

"Indeed, Counselor? Do we need all these other fellows?"

"Yes, Madame. The clerk may stand off, but my law-brothers should know what I know." He stood clasping his hands, flanked by two slightly shorter associates and facing two very tall Khagodi.

"Then tell us, sir!" Skerow cried.

"One of our witnesses, a man named Sta Farre Samfa, is in hospital in this city after a murder attempt against him. He was to have been brought here today, but now claims that you were one of those who hired him, Your Honor."

Skerow's mind closed down in shock and for one instant she could not swallow air. "To obtain gold? That is a damned lie."

Blaylock did not quail. "It was not I who spoke it, and it will become a rumor that cannot be put down."

Ossta said, "When did your witness say this, and to whom?"

"After waking he told it to the peace officer who was to bring him. His statement was recorded."

"What do you have in mind, Counselor, a declaration of mistrial over this sick man's rumor?" Ossta asked.

"He seems likely to die before a new trial date is set," Skerow said before he could answer. "Counselor, this statement is worthless. Your witness may have been threatened further—I cannot think with what, further than the death already upon him—but most likely he is in pain, or has been having nightmares. If he wishes to bring these baseless charges against me formally, I must see about getting myself a lawyer. In any case, I am standing aside. I will tell the audience that the trial has been voided."

"Just wait a moment, Skerow my dear," Ossta said.

"Yes, please." Blaylock had become calmer, and took a deep breath. "I beg your pardon, Madame. I was taken aback and misjudged in haste; it has cost so much effort and expense to bring this case to court. Of course I must ask for an adjournment until tomorrow so I can question the witness."

Skerow said, "Do so. You disturbed me very deeply when you said that your witness's false statement will become a rumor impossible to put down. Make sure you have not made a prophecy that will fulfill itself."

The feeling of dread that weighted her as she left the Court Offices and climbed the ramp was deepened when she removed her helmet at the doorway of her guest chamber: she had not felt such an intensity of silence for half her life. As she stepped through the archway she could see the wicker cage floating on the water. It had been flattened, and Eskat's body was splayed inside it. As if someone had flung down the cage, tramped on it, and tossed it in the bath.

She waded down the ramp and fetched out the cage. The water had been warm, and so was the body. When she freed it she thought there were flickers of life in his heart and eye, enough to ask, *Eskat's One, here?* before they folded into emptiness.

She unfastened the chain and bead from his neck and clasped him against her belly. So stupid to kill this frail chained beast; her eyes were blind with the tears she would not shed. She climbed the ramp and wrapped him in a towel, sent the bundle down the disposal and followed it with the broken cage; she stayed there crouching by the pool.

A black river of thought rose up against her. She could not think of anyone on this world who wanted her harmed or dead; most of the men and women she had judged on other worlds had been involved in civil suits that had nothing to do with violence. What happened on Starry Nova had seemed to her a dreadful aberration.

Her thoughts blackened more deeply. *That detestable little beast,* Evarny called him. Evarny had urged this case on her: *You rode circuit with Thordh for over twenty years without being stained by the rumors . . .* had he involved her to repel stain from himself?

No. She had been married to Evarny for as many years as she had ridden circuit with Thordh; she had never known the Thordh beneath the impervious helmet, but she had lived in Evarny's mind. She knew that the blackness was in herself.

There was half a day to waste and all of a dreadful night to get through.

Brains Storm

Skerow had not visited the Hall of Ancestors since her divorce. Stripped of daughter and husband then, she could not bear the presence of the Saints. They had never been a comfort.

The day was full of mist, and the shrine seemed to have an aura it would not claim for itself. It stood in the center of the Courts and Administrations Complex, but was so unpretentious and modestly recessed under the low-branched *beq*-trees that it was often mistaken by tourists for a public lavatory. It had been set half-underground for coolness, and flowing airstreams running down from ventilators on its low dome roof shielded it from the damp. The dehumidifiers hummed intermittently, and the coldlight strips in its ceiling were dusky yellow.

The walkways between the pillars seemed black with darkness from where Skerow stood looking at them on the thick green sward of moss at the edge of the downward ramp. She stepped down and inward.

:Skerow? Is it truly you?: The thoughts eddied around her like the currents of wind that gathered in the early afternoon.

Another step and another until she was immersed in the sickly aura of the yellow-flickering lights and the swarm of ancient minds.

:Yes, Blessed Ones, Skerow it is:

:Wake up, you damned souls of the Unblessed! Skerow is bringing us eyes!:

One more step and the light strips brightened. Another noise reached Skerow. The almost silent throbbing of scores of pumps.

:And ears!:

The Hall of Ancestors on Khagodis was the last of its kind; sometimes it was referred to as a Memorial Garden, Hall of Elders, or Knowledge Park. Never a Cemetery.

But it was a hall of the dead whose brains had outlived them in the years when a misguided technology had kept them "alive" in globes of nutrient liquid. The practice had long been stopped, but because the Khagodi were the longest-lived of known sentients, there were still these few in existence.

The spheres of dark green glastex stood on veined green-marble pedestals among their skeins of tubing, in no particular order, as if they were galls on the underground root systems of the surrounding trees. There were more than a hundred and twenty of them, and the youngest was nearly two hundred years old. No Governor dared stop the pumps of These Last Ones no matter how the Ancestors or their families pleaded, and no one loved them either.

There was a musty smell here; Skerow felt the membranes of her gill-slits thickening in reaction to the molds that flourished no matter how well the place was cleaned and ventilated. :*Hello, Aunt Hrufa!*:

:*Skerow, dear!*:

:*Uncle Lokh, are you there?*:

Lokh was Hrufa's uncle, but he answered sharply, :*Yes, yes I am! What have you got for us, Skerow?*:

The minds clamored: :*Give us! Give us!*: They were more than half mad.

There was a vending machine in a pillar to the left of the entrance; Skerow dropped a two-*pista* coin into its slot, and the machine gave her a bubble filled with colored pellets. She half turned toward the green moss and the red stone buildings outside. :*I can give you eyes and fresh memories . . . I want something in return.*: She turned back. "Who killed the tethumekh?"

She spoke this aloud, and the sound bounced off roof, floor, and pillars. She was absolutely certain that even now their combined minds, fused and focused, would be fifty times more powerful than her own.

There was a sullen emptiness. She broke the bubble and it collapsed into a filmy sac, plucked out a red pellet, and dropped it into her mouth. It gave off a warm and redolent spice.

:That's good . . . : Hrufa's thought was a curl of smoke. *:You haven't forgotten how you brought me the* sesshi *pods, even as a child.:*

"I remember it very well." She manipulated the pellet on her tongue as if she were a seducer perfuming her mouth.

:You never loved the tethumekh.:

:I treated it as if I did. I truly loved you, when my mother died and we all felt lost because my father insisted on living so far away . . . I am sorry I never had the heart to come here when I became lost again.:

:Skerow! Skerow!: the minds swarmed around her. She did not know anyone else among them, and for a moment resented their intrusion into the private moment, but took another pellet. This was a cool blue one, tasting of menthol. *:Give us more!:* They encircled her, their texture hardened, like a headache. A draft of wind puckered the protective windstreams, and she smelled the afternoon rain. "The storm is coming."

:What is lightning when we want life and blood? Why did you not have lovers after you left him? You have nothing to tell us!: Skerow did not know any of these who were so greedy for her life.

"What must I do or give for you to tell me who killed my tethumekh?"

:How to do that? Everyone wears the damned helmets nowadays.:

"I believe you know how."

:You say yourself you did not love the beast.:

"The one who killed it is more than willing to kill me," Skerow said. *:I would never bring you lovers even if I could. Do you need to know of all my fearful experiences, all the torments I have seen and felt, to do me this one favor?:* She noticed that even with ventilators the moss was encroaching on the stone, and realized that she was speaking aloud to distance herself from these minds. She was near tears for them now because they had lost, all of them, their self-images, and become so shameless.

They were almost abashed, but they did not answer.

:I will give five thousand pistaba *for someone to come and drink the nectars, eat the foods, listen to the music for you until you are ready to sleep.:*

One old man, once hearty and gracious, struggled to free his self from the formless group. *:Die, you mean, not sleep. Do not undignify our scraps of life with euphemism.:*

:And will that surrogate have lovers too?: Lokh, quite undignified, asked slyly; he had always been sly.

:I cannot force a person to do that.:

:That was my joke. I am not too old and crazy to make a joke.:

:You are not too helpless to make one, grandfather.:

She heard a spatter of rain at that moment, and then a lightning bolt. Thunder broke, the rain fell in sheets; she would find more relief from her frustration in letting it storm around her than in waiting among these Saints. She thought of how often the heroes in the River Epics descended into the vaults of the dead to take counsel of the spirits, and how difficult it was to make them give it. She tucked the little package of pellets into her sling-bag and stood watching the rain. It would clear in a few moments, and likely start again in a few more, until sunset.

Eskat had trembled so fearfully at every disturbance . . .

She cast the net of her thought out over the city, but her sorrow removed her so far from the purity of contemplation that she caught nothing but the knucklebone-tossing games of children playing in the rain. No other mind gave back the resonance she was searching for.

The Ancestors gathered round her and watched.

:Truly, Skerow, we cannot find—:

Were they so old and powerless? Individually they were, yes. She realized that none had real power, and not one would admit it.

"Together—" *:Together you make one powerful mind, and I will not die, damn you, until I have done what I promised myself. You know you have the power, don't you? Don't you?:*

Lightning-flash, thunderclap! children running for home, now.

:See there—: She did not know who spoke.

A spark. *:It's a mind somebody knows.:*

:It is the Solthree.:

:He has static in his helmet—:

:You can't see him!:

:The helmet is defective—he—:

:—crushed the little beast. But nobody's eye saw him.:

"Who is he?"

:Won't tell his name to himself, will he?:

:He's the voice in the street that says:—AND I'LL KILL YOU FOR THIS! *And the voice in the hall that says:*—WHERE'S THORDH, JUDGE SKEROW? *and on the comm:* IS HE DEAD, JUDGE? WOULD YOU LIKE TO BECOME A SENIOR MAGISTRATE, SKEROW DEAR? *He kills and says:* BE MUCH MORE OF A PLEASURE KILLING THE BIG ONE. *He would have*

killed you, yes. He crushed the tethumekh only because he could not reach you.:

Skerow stood pressed on one side by the rain and on the other by the green spheres. "You did not believe me."

:What would you have given us then?:

Skerow's mind closed and refused to answer.

:Are you angry? You were asking us to break through another person's defenses.:

:I ought to have given without asking for anything. I am not angry, I feel ill. Who would have thought that man, that demon, would be on this world?:

:The police have got hold of him.:

:I daren't look—they would know me.:

:The Crazy Ancestors may look. The police are trying to shoo us away!:

No one shoos away twenty-five thousand years' worth of Ancients. Skerow smiled. She felt herself smiling, but she did not try to join the group mind. She was grateful that the demon had fallen beyond her reach before she did him violence.

:That one's name is Ferrier. Hears the Law say, "Ferrier, come with us!":

The rain had stopped, and a wind was picking up the clouds.

Skerow said, *:He is one of those charged with paying our people to steal gold.:* She dropped one of the pellets into her mouth; it had gone suddenly dry.

:Yes,: said Hrufa, *:Nohl was one of those who worked for him.:*

:You know that Nohl,: said the hundred and twenty Ancients, *:the one that left the Deltas to look for his fortune and married her in the Isthmuses—:*

"Stop!" cried Skerow. "That cannot be the same Nohl."

:You have been out of the River for a long time, Skerow.

Your Nohl is not simply Mister Nobody,: said Uncle Lokh.

"Ancestors," Skerow whispered, "could it be? In court the poisoned witness was called Sta Farre Samfa."

:In back-country Vinelands dialect that is "Citizen Unknown".:

It seemed to Skerow then that all that had happened, everything, since she had first seen Kobai in Zamos's window, had been leading to this moment.

:Who is this one coming now?: Hrufa asked, and Skerow realized how sharply she and the Ancients had excluded strangers from the Hall; no one had ventured in, even for shelter from the rain.

Skerow recognized this one. *:It is the Bailiff's Clerk.:* She stepped forward to meet the fellow as he approached; he had taken off his robe to hurry through the rain, and was twitching the drops off his skin.

"Have you come to arrest me now, Clerk?" Skerow managed to ask this harsh question mildly.

"No, no, Madame! I have come to beg you to speak to the witness. He will testify to no one but you!"

Nohl

Skerow had wanted to bring Nohl to justice, but Justice had come to him first.

She could not tell his age; he seemed ancient. He was crouching on a huge waterbed that crowded the small hospital room, wrapped in a tangle of instruments and tubing, shrunken and twisted with pain, belly swollen with poison; his left eye was invisible in a heap of inflamed flesh. Breath hissed in his gill slits, he opened and closed his mouth continually in his efforts to talk; his tongue was pale and thin.

"You expected me to die," he said. "They all expected me to die."

"I very much want you to live, Nohl," Skerow said, "but you must be careful what you say now, to protect your rights." Now that she had found him she was afraid that he might speak outside the boundaries of the case where his words would be lost in legal jungles and the case damaged so badly that no justice could be done. "I will present your testimony to the legal teams of both sides when you have given it, but you must answer their questions afterward if you are able."

"If the poison and all these tangled procedures don't kill me first, they may ask away," Nohl said with a sneer.

"You must explain why you are accusing me, but you need not incriminate yourself."

Nohl swallowed air chokingly and cried out, "I will speak! I will! What will you do to me, kill me again with stronger poison? Blind my other eye with another red-hot iron?" His only eye was swelling with blood, like Thordh he sweated bloody tears. "I am no longer accusing you, and I will explain."

"You must take an oath."

"Damn you, I will swear by anything you like, only quickly, before the poison kills me!"

"Let Madame Ossta bring in the Court Recorder. You need swear only by your God."

"No one is likely to put much faith in my honor," Nohl said bitterly.

Let me begin at the beginning, it is not all that long a story. My marriage was not as rich as everyone believed. Earthquakes and volcanoes had shifted the terrain the estate was on, and by the time I came to share in it, it was half-sunk in swampland, and the beautiful parks and gardens were ruined from flooding. My wife had no better a name in her family than I did in mine, and no other inheritance than the land. We hadn't the means to keep it up, and no one wanted to rent it. We were so poor that when my wife's house collapsed there was no money to repair it, and we were forced to live under one roof. She had some sort of female disease in her parts and we could not even have children.

Yes, yes, I am getting to it! I have put it together so in my mind, all these horrible clockfalls, let me tell it as well as I can!

Nothing I ever did would work out for me, except to come near putting me in prison. There was nothing for it but to try to sell the estate, anything to get some money out of it, to keep the roof over our heads, to buy food. I went to one of my cousins in the Deltas to find a buyer, those misers would never lend me a half-pista though God demand it, and when they were done ridiculing me, they sent me to the Consortium.

Now I tell you I sold it cheap, and there were faceless men of twenty worlds who plowed it with their feet before they gave me a seal to bloody my thumb on for the money. I kept the house and a hundred siguu of land each side around it. I shored it up, and fought off my wife as best I could with her ailments and whining, and with doctors and lawyers and stonemasons there was little more than enough left to buy a pisspot.

And damn me, no, I'm double-damned already, but by the Unhatched Egg no more did I know what was going on in those swamps and shores until someone comes to me that the Consortium sent and says, Nohl, you know the land and shoreline so well, we'll pay to have you oversee our crew taking care of a stock of aquarium animals we're storing in the bay.

I agreed to this as readily as you'd think, and they sent me a crew of rough fellows with good esp and long prods, one was a countryman and the rest some outland bullies. We arranged nets to keep them in one area, and they dropped in a load of their creatures.

The beasts were good-natured enough, but—my belly! my eye! let me have something to ease me!

. . . That's better. What was I saying? Yes—good-natured enough, but I'd never seen aquarium animals like them, I tell you. They had no fins or flippers but hands and feet, yes, hands. Real hands like yours or mine. They made nests to sleep in out of the sprigweed, and filled puffbladders with seastars to light themselves. They made nets to catch fish, and used shells for knives. They would have killed us if they could.

It was they who found the vein of gold. One day when one of them got angry at something we did or said, one of the females reached up and flung a lump of it at us, and we realized there was a bloody fountain of it coming up with the hot currents, pure and worn down by the sea until it shone. Gold! All that gold! Coming out from under the skin of what used to be my land! Would you have told the Consortium about it? Why do I ask? Of course you would! But you do not need, the Consortium did not need gold as I did!

Well, I had all those fellows with me and they did not care to waste all that gold any more than I, though I give credit to my Khagodi landsman that he took some persuading. We set those undersea creatures to gathering the gold. They were willing enough, it kept them busy and the stuff was only a plaything to them.

Of course even up in the Isthmuses you cannot just spend lumps of gold, we needed someone to handle it for us. One of my crew found that brute Ferrier. We knew he was an agent of Goldyne. And I knew that Judge Thordh was involved with Goldyne. Ferrier used him to get me off the slavery charge, but he was no friend of mine and we were not any kind of associates, we were both only stupid dupes and conveniences for the agents of great financial empires we never knew anything about.

I was earning good money, and happy enough to have it, but every two or three thirtydays the Consortium would come in airflight cars to drop new batches of the undersea folk and cull the old, and those Folk were becoming restless. They had a signaling language that they spoke with their hands, and when we came to feed them they would rise up half out of the water and speak with us. We taught them how to swallow air and speak with their mouths as we do. This is as true as it is that my head is bare and my mind unguarded.

What we were afraid of was that the Folk would tell the Consortium about the gold. Teaching them the language had been a game, and I admired their passion to learn, but that was before they found the gold. Especially there was one female who began to look like a ringleader. So we guarded them more closely, until they became as edgy as we, and one day when Ferrier came to pick up a gold shipment I found my knife gone—one of the Folk had stolen it—and I called them out about it.

One of the males got angry and flung a lump of gold. It hit Ferrier, and he shot the poor fellow dead. I nearly killed him then. I wish I had.

There was enough money to live on by that time, I'd been doing the work for over twenty years. I began to think of getting out of it all. I had to. There were only thirty-five or forty of these Folk, and I didn't know how to explain to their owners that one of them was missing. And I realized that one of them was pregnant, their female ringleader who had made Ferrier so uneasy. It had never happened before, and it made me wonder. I was anxious for her. It was fixed in my mind that Ferrier would try to do her harm.

There was nothing I could do for her without breaking up our whole scheme. I thought I might be able to move her into some undersea exhibit, or some scientific collection, one of the tens of the tens of institutions that Zamos itself runs—but by the time I had made some arrangements I found that Ferrier had used a contact on Fthel Five to put her into a brothel!—dear Saints, a Zamos brothel!—where they were prepared to split whatever income she made! Of course I was helpless after that.

I felt myself forced to tell the Consortium representatives when they came. I was afraid my crew would betray me, even though they were taking up the gold along with me. There was no way, no way I could tell them, without, without making, them angry—no, no, I don't want water!

But I never thought—never thought—they would go so far as to make my own crew lay hold of me while they heated an iron bar red hot—three who called themselves civilized, and one of them a woman!—fired it red hot—and—and—oh my eye! Augh! I am going to be sick!

Yes, thank you, somewhat better, I suppose . . .

I never saw any one of them but Ferrier again, crew, Folk, Consortium. My shock was so deep I found myself in a hospital when I came back to consciousness. They did not harm my wife. She had brought me to the hospital, and now she is living in one room in the city here, she's a faithful woman, I owe her that much. And waiting. For me, poor fool!

About Ferrier, yes. As soon as I woke I swore to accuse them—I mean all of them, whoever they were working for, and I offered myself to the police when I heard that Ferrier was arrested.

On the second night in that hospital at home I woke in my bed and esped Ferrier himself, I swear it!—in a doctor's greycoat, come to attack me with a needle, and no matter how I tried I was too weak to call out before it was too late and the poison seized me. You may tell me it was a dream but I am a poisoned man.

The doctors did their best to save me and sent me here under guard to be safe, but I had become afraid to testify, I was so full of pain, and because you had worked with Thordh I made up that stupid story while I dithered.

At last it came to me that instead of being my enemy you might become my greatest friend, and so I have told you this story.

"Thank you," Skerow said. "I would like to know a few things more, and then we will let you rest. Are you sure the Consortium asked you to care for the undersea Folk, as you call them? Did they pay you with drafts, and if so was there any Consortium crest on them?"

Nohl lay breathing heavily with his eyelids half lowered.

"I never thought much about it I was so pleased to see the money, but I'm damned if I'm sure of the Consortium. I heard them talk of Zamos, that I'm sure. And they paid me in old silver *pistabat.*"

Skerow's heart sank. She believed everything Nohl had said, and his story had explained nearly everything, but except that it would put Ferrier out of circulation his testimony left her no nearer saving Kobai.

Nohl stirred himself and swallowed air. "If I had found that gold before I sold the land this would never have happened."

Skerow could not fault his greedy logic.

* * *

Evening shadows were folding themselves over in the park when Skerow went back to where the swollen brains pressed their lobes against the half-translucent glastex,

> *where*
> *the moss grows*
> *over burning heads . . .*

:*Surely we are not quite so buried,*: said Hrufa.

"My poem is meant to tell you that you are not," Skerow said. "Your help meant a lot to me, and I came to thank you for it."

The thoughts of the Ancestors gathered around her, and the old man who had once been dignified said, :*It took us some while to come to it, but we were able to prove to ourselves that we could be useful. Good-bye, then, Skerow. Send us our taster of life, and hope that we are gone before you need our help again.*:

The too-bright lights had been turned down for the night, and Skerow stepped out of the dimness into the dark. The faint throbbing of pumps was the only sound she could hear, and she stood for a moment, unwilling to break by her leaving a link that joined the Ancestors to the world. But they had already fallen into a dream, and she moved away in peace.

SIX *

Fthel V: *Manador and Lebedev*

The sequence appeared on the monitor of Manador's terminal, silent but looking very much like the commercial streamers that trailed half her messages because she did not want to pay to keep them off. At first she thought it was only a soft-porn ad for something harder, but when she realized that its central figure was Jacaranda Drummond she crushed the butt of her dopestick and turned up the ventilators to clear the air and her mind.

The scenes were as tightly edited as if they had been filmed for a commercial: woman being herded, examined like cattle for signs of disease by Lyrhht doctor, decorated like a sacrificial animal to please the bloodthirsty, touched on shoulder, hip, neck by death's angel the Kylklad, dropped into a place she could not escape from, attacked by the devil—

As the scene was flickering off at the crunch of death, Manador hit *stop, rewind, replay.* Nothing came on the screen but static. A copy-proof transmission. She stared at the screen while it flickered with calls from old pugs saying hello, new ones needing jobs, impressarios wanting new blood. She clawed the off switch with a red nail and sat listening to ventilators whirring, the suck of drains, the grinding of the disposal unit, and the deep throb of the recycler.

She got up and took seven steps to her private quarters. Discarded her ballerina's black wig, washed down the pale makeup, wiped the red nail enamel, and colored her white chopped hair *tziguat* yellow. Her skin was a deep clear blue, not slate-colored like a Varvani's, and she laid on lotion to give it a bloom, then lined her mouth and lips with green pearl essence; she left her brows and lashes white as frost. She coated her nails with adhesive and dipped them in gold dust, dressed in a straight-cut trouser suit of midnight blue velvet that matched her eyes, its V-neck edged in yellow satin.

Her image in the long mirror gave back the bracket-creased smile that showed her small sharp teeth.

In the Gamblar at Zamos's brothel Lebedev, fighting terror and boredom equally, dealt skambi with his aching hand. He had never found the game interesting; it killed time in prison, that was all. *Here you are sitting on your arse doing nothing, Lebedev.* His sore ear droned with the words. *You have not even seen the mermaid.* He dared not try. He was grudgingly grateful to be alive playing skambi rather than dead being recycled somewhere.

But he was tired of "Number forty-three today, gentlepersons! Enter credit I.D. numbers and wagers on your panels!" Bored with civil servants drowning their own boredom in vodka with peppers and gold flakes, and the five-seed wines of Kemalan IV. As a Police Inspector he had already seen too many of the highroller wearing the lady in red on his arm, the woman in black with her tumbler of whiskey, and the ingenuous new Bimandan ambassador staggering drunk with an alien world's wonders as well as its new ambrosias. Even the image of Zamos wandering about in his gold and purple toga had lost its novelty.

"Numbers nineteen, seven and fifty-one are wild!" he called, and switched on displays, gave a wind of the crank, and set the clock. The light burned down on him, and his fingers were sweating in the white gloves that wore out so quickly.

As he raised his hand to thread disk number forty-three on the first spindle he froze and stopped being bored. Manador was standing in the doorway near the poker tables, drawing darkness into herself and looking like a photographic negative.

He dropped the disk on the table, picked it up and placed it on the spindle. He could feel his eyes darting in their sockets searching for escape routes. Manador had lost her lover and wanted somebody's skin. She came forward to lean on the mahogany shoulder of the *concello* playing a Bengtvad hymn, *Hail to the Heavenly Yeih,* transcribed for the Orpha *dugak.*

"West plays forty-one, eh"—he swallowed on a dry throat, while Manador's eyes, those disks that burned blue flames, moved without hurry to settle on him—"North passes, first of three allowed"—he noted it on his panel—"East . . ."

Her eyes caught his. The bracket-creases of her mouth widened, but not in a smile.

His intermission came up after the game; he pulled off his gloves and armbands, slipped away in the press of people to the hall where the machines were. He wanted time and space to think, but they were not here among the elbows of the Bengtvadi, Dabiri, Bimanda. He found an empty seat and dropped a token. A porn game flared on the screen; he punched buttons randomly and it gave him a razz for bad play. Another token brought him slivovitz when he expected vodka, and he drank it anyway. He was sure she would betray him.

A soft voice said, "Are you all right, Mister Dealer?"

Ai'la was standing beside him wearing a robe of big gently colored tropical flowers and a headdress to match; she was collecting tumblers and goblets for the cycler. Some show of feeling had come into her face during the last few days in which she had watched him with mildly curious eyes; it was as if she had sensed that he too was not quite a citizen, and for him she had stopped displaying her careful poise. She whispered, in a child's conspiratorial manner, "Can I get you some drink that is not like that cheap stuff you took?"

He whispered back, "I would love to have it, dear miss, but save it for a better day." He would not trust her yet, but maybe . . .

There were holstered bullies at every door, and he was too well known for his fight with South to dare trying to escape. Nothing for it but to brazen it out. When he returned through the doorway he found Manador sitting at the skambi table, in South position. She did not look up.

"Number fifty-seven today . . ."

The disks hissed against each other. Manador had pulled down her smoke-cone so that Lebedev could see only the tip of her nose over her green pearl mouth with the dopestick that was giving off its over-sweet fragrance. Her teeth clicked on the onyx holder and her nails tapped the disk as she played it. She murmured, "What are you doing here, Lebedev?"

"Didn't you know I had been in prison? I learned to deal skambi there."

She smiled thinly and hissed, "You will be sorry they let you out, Lebedev."

One or two other players, thinking she was bantering, smiled as well. Then Lebedev had the fearful thought that everyone else in the room, in the brothel, was smiling at him, with pink, green, or thin grey lips, with horned beak or lifted snout, waiting greedily for some fist to crash against him. He licked his own lips. "East plays ten and South plays . . . four?"

It was an illegal move. The other players might have let it pass, but he knew Manador had the dented six that the other dangerous South had held, and her four would have won the game. She lifted the cone and her eyes challenged him. Her whole body seemed aimed at him.

He said softly but very clearly, "That move is not allowed until the last round, Madame. Would you like to play another disk?"

The thin smile again. "I'll play another disk." She put down the six, and a few moments later the three that won the pot.

He swept the disks from the table. "Another game, Madame?"

She dipped her card into its slot to collect the payoff as she rose. "Not yet. I will see you, Lebedev." She disappeared into the smoke among the gamblers.

While he sat waiting for another South and breathing hard, Tally Hawes came by with her tray of fancy drinks and nudged his shoulder with her hip. "Friend of yours, Lev?"

"I hope not," Lebedev said. "It's bad enough having her for an enemy."

The moment he opened the door to his room he smelled her cool sharp essence: ozone and lavender.

She was lying in his hammock with her legs crossed, swinging slowly, fitting a dopestick into the carved holder.

She drew in on it sharply, it flared and lit. "Why are you really here, Lebedev?"

"I told you. I was in prison and I cannot afford a ticket on the *Zarandu.* Who else would appreciate someone like me but Zamos?"

She sat up and touched one of the pasteboard walls. Two of them were within reach. Looked about at the small chest where he stood his soup crock, the open niche with its sink and water-closet, neither bigger than two cupped hands. There was no more air in the room than two persons could breathe. "You have come far down."

He thought there was satisfaction in her voice. Plenty of times as Inspector of Police he had ruffled Manador about some of the odd clients who wanted to hire her pugs privately.

"What have *you* come here for, Manador?"

"Today on my monitor there was a vidsnap showing how she died. She was made to fight a devil's wife underwater. It bit through her neck and killed her. Did you see that, Lebedev?"

"No."

"There was a pretense of having a doctor examine her, a Lyhhrt."

"The doctors in Zamos's brothels are always Lyhhrt."

"The day after she died a Lyhhrt came round to tell me. I don't know if it was the same, but they are all the same. He knows who did it, who gave the order, and I think you do too, Lebedev."

The image of Zamos appeared from nowhere and swept his purple-draped arm through both their bodies. "Enjoy yourselves! Do all you ever longed to do!" he cried. "You're here to live your lives to the full!" He disappeared.

Manador stared at the place where it had been. "What was that?"

"A kind of mascot, I suppose. A signature at Zamos's, supposed to be the founder. Have you never been here before?"

She turned her look on him and said, "I don't gamble for pleasure. Why did that holo come in here?"

"Officially, because something is wrong with the circuits. Actually, I believe, to let us all know we are under surveillance, a warning that all we do is known. The eye is—don't look—up in the corner behind you, among the water pipes. A very small one, hard to see."

"Is there an ear?"

"None that I have been able to find."

She stood up flicking her dopestick in the basin and said in her cold deep voice, "Then you are still looking, still working, aren't you? Was it you who sent her in here, Lebedev?" She reached out a hand and dug her fingers into the ruffle of lace at his throat.

"I—" He grabbed at her wrist but it was hard as steel. His inhibition about harming a woman made her stronger than South, who had been drunk and enraged. "Someone will come here and you'll be the one that's in trouble."

"They'll think we're screwing." Her eyes were like midnight, and her green mouth, full like Jacaranda's in a narrow face, was close to his. It smelled of fresh mint, as if her lips were leaves and her sharp green tongue a growing point. "Don't they do that here?"

A snake's head, that tongue. It touched the hairs at the corner of his lip. He shuddered and pulled roughly out of her grasp. "Stop that!"

She did not back away. "Do I offend you, Lebedev?"

He shook his head as if he had been freed of a spell and straightened his shirt. "I am not a Pinxid man."

She grinned. "There are no Pinxid men. Now, what about her, Lebedev?"

"You were her handler. Didn't you know everything she did? Didn't you warn her?"

"I didn't send her here to die. I hope you get to see that, Lebedev, how she died. Maybe they'll show you, before they kill you."

Lebedev did not believe an ear had been planted in his room, but he was not sure and he dared not shut her up. "You should have called the police and shown them the vid-snap."

"Police! I've seen enough of the police. And I couldn't have let them set their filthy eyes on it if I'd wanted to because it wouldn't record."

The words struck him a blow. He whispered, "The murderers have sent you a message and you've led them straight to me!"

"Have I?"

"You did it deliberately. You came here, showed yourself, bribed the housekeeper, and drew a line from Jacaranda to me."

"You should have let me play that four, Lebedev." She shrugged. "I didn't come here to betray you. I came to find out who really killed Jacaranda, what the Lyhhrt has to do with it, why Lyhhrt know all about this. Anybody wants to know what's between you and me tell them I want to hire you for a bodyguard, because I love your hairy body, Lebedev." She sniggered. "Nobody will bother me, I have six of my good pugs outside playing *ogga-dippa* on the machines. It's a game that's even stupider than skambi."

Lebedev said, "I know nothing."

"You'll find out, because I'll be back to learn. And if you can't tell me then I will betray you." She turned back with her hand on the door latch. "I truly loved her, Lebedev."

"Yes." Lebedev nodded and looked for the love in her

face. "You truly loved Ned Gattes for a while, but you were not overly scrupulous about sending him to Zamos's Spartakoi."

She said in her cold voice as she pushed the door aside, "Ned's a good lad. A little clumsy but lands on his feet." She paused. Stuttering a bit she said, "Trying to save some animal—some damned animal—that's how she died, Lebedev!" and was gone.

"Wait!" But by the time he hauled the door open she had disappeared into branching corridors, or perhaps the nearest shadow.

He was long getting to sleep and dreamed that his wife Roza was sitting in front of a mirror putting blue Pinxid coloring on her face, green on her lips, and leering up at his reflection. He woke startled with a spilling erection and tears in his eyes.

After that the sleep he sank into was a depth of sadness.

Next day he woke gritty-eyed; while he was brushing his teeth the key-jingling Housekeeper hammered a fist on his door.

"Your doctor's appointment, stad oh-ten! Visitors forbidden in rooms, next time you get fined!"

He snarled, "Didn't she pay you enough?" He had forgotten the appointment. The Lyhhrt had saved his life, but he did not like Lyhhrt better on that account; he recalled what Manador had said about Jacaranda being examined by a doctor, but thinking about it made him none the wiser.

In the basement between the dormitories and the main building, coldstrips in the ceilings lit the hallways with diffuse white light, and down the length of the uncolored, discolored composition walls and floor there were no pictures or carpets; Lebedev did not miss them. He felt at every step that there would be someone coming up behind him to hook a claw into his collar or lay a heavy Varvani arm across his shoulder.

As he pushed into Employees' Bath, the door hit an obstruction and he heard a cry. He peered around it and found Ai'ia cowering between the door and the shower-stall curtain. She was wearing a wire mesh helm and a coarse robe with no more color than the walls; her face was darkly bruised on one side, her eye swollen. When she recognized him she clapped both hands over her mouth and squeezed herself farther into the corner; she had dropped an armful of towels and a net bag of crude soap-balls and did not try to pick them up.

Lebedev realized that he could not possibly have hurt her so badly by opening the door. He held his hands up and out, and whispered, "What is it, Miss? Who has hurt you?" He stayed in the shadow behind the open door so that neither of the spy-eyes directed at the ranks of showers could spot him.

"Oh—" Ai'ia stammered, "Oh mister, please let me go!" Her normal skin seemed near bruise-colored and vulnerable.

He bent to pick up the towels and soap. "Ai'ia—"

"Don't talk to me, Mister!" Her whisper was painfully urgent. "They have been beating me up for talking with you, they will make me fight in dirt and fuck with beasts if they catch me again!"

Lebedev felt the particular helplessness of one who has had authority and lost it. He gave her the towels and soap and stepped aside.

After his bath he stopped at one of the stand-up tables in the cafeteria and gulped a cup of chicory that had probably been delivered from the *Zarandu* along with the coffee shipments for clients. He wondered what the O'e were given to eat.

The labyrinth of narrow service alleys that ran alongside the deeply carpeted and gold-lit halls, and which Lebedev as an employee was expected to learn, led into obscure branches that were often poorly marked; some of them were lit by dusty and flickering electric lights.

Lebedev stumbled here, seized by one of the intermittent fits of dizziness caused by his unbalanced inner ear, and intensified by the oppressiveness of the air. In the trembling light of one of these corridors a door was pulled open abruptly in the moment that he was about to pass it. He glimpsed something metallic grasping its edge and then heard the thump as the door rebounded in its socket and was pulled back again. The vibrations it caused sparked the light into a moment of brightness that lit up the figure in the doorway for one moment and subsided.

Lebedev saw a tall being that sparkled inversely with darkness and gave off black spatters with painful bursts of intensely white and spectrum lights deep within them. It crackled with static, it was as if lightning were black, and the universe split.

Yet this creature was physical, and wore a lattice of platinum joined with jewels that repeated its own deep sparkings; through openings it extended or, even, broadcast its six limbs like jolts of electricity. Lebedev could not tell its features because every spark of it seemed an eye.

His mind went quite blank and for an instant he stood locked with the apparition in an alphonse-gaston stance. The ceiling light went dim again, but he could see that the brilliant shadow with its spears of light was reaching out its central arms as if to caliper his head.

The hairs of Lebedev's head and beard rose and crackled with static; he thought of the tip of Manador's green tongue, but could not pull himself away. Whether or not this alien being was satisfied with what it found in Lebedev, it withdrew its points of darkness and shrank back behind the doorway.

Lebedev smelled a sharp tang of ozone, and was briefly dizzy again. Another figure came forward from the dark room; he saw that it was the Lyhhrt doctor, now filling the doorway, who had pulled the door back for the chimera.

The Lyhhrt was wearing what Lebedev recognized as his workaday shell, an unadorned casing with features only suggested; he looked at Lebedev and said, "Please go to my office. I will see you in one moment."

Lebedev went past the doorway without looking back and found his way to the office. He felt as if part of his mind had been burnt out.

It seemed a very long moment that he spent trying to pull his consciousness together. He sat down in the fitted chair and stared at the cabinets. They were as solid as cheap foamplast could be, and their lines did not waver.

When the Lyhhrt came in Lebedev said, "That person is of a species I have never seen. Is it a member of Galactic Federation?"

"No."

Lebedev thought he might push a little bit. "It does not seem quite . . . physical."

"You think so?" The Lyhhrt fitted an instrument to one of its fingers and a light to another, and began to probe the recesses of Lebedev's ear. "Nevertheless it is an egg-layer." When he saw the way Lebedev pulled away and turned his head to look at him, the Lyhhrt repeated, "An egg-layer. Truly."

Lebedev felt as if he had been given gifts by the Greeks. Information from the Lyhhrt, who rarely gave any, and of the wrong sort. He wondered if the Lyhhrt was not out of kilter in some way, and hoped the way did not involve what was being done to his ear.

"Your ear is healing well," the Lyhhrt said.

Lebedev said, "I get dizzy." He saw in his mind the Lyhhrt's attitude, standing in the doorway behind the chimera, head bent forward, with something intimate—no, deferential—in it. *Attitude? Idiot! A machine with a lump of slime in it!*

"That will pass." The Lyhhrt reached out both hands to him and Lebedev went rigid with a jerk, because the unbelievable egg-layer had made a similar gesture. "I want to look at your other ear, Lebedev, that is all. Please do not be so skittish." *What would that nightmare have been measuring me for? What would those two have to talk about?* He knew it was a common belief, sometimes substantiated, that Lyhhrt too long isolated from their fellows in those metal carapaces went off balance. The silver finger poked at his mastoid bone. "Your oxygen capsule socket is very poorly installed."

"In the police force they don't give you fancy."

The Lyhhrt pinched his earlobe, and he jumped.

"I want a blood sample," the Lyhhrt said.

There was something odd and unmodulated in the Lyhhrt's voice, and two words that came together in Lebedev's mind: *blood/egg-layer.* Once again he pulled away and turned to face the silver man-shape with its beautiful articulating features. "Why? Why do you need blood when my ear is nearly better?"

What insects need blood to make eggs fertile?? Woman of the sea, blood red like a fetus, herself a kind of fetus, pregnant with a . . . too damned many pregnancies. Either one or both of us is crazy.

"I," said the Lyhhrt. "We." The lights went out and Lebedev knew that the Lyhhrt was crazy. Before panic could sweep him he felt the pressure of the Lyhhrt mind penetrating his impervious net, saying: :*Neither one of us is crazy. I am angry.:* The lights came on again, and the Lyhhrt regained control of his voice and said, "We are operating now on my personal emergency electrical system. No one else can reach us until I restore the main one. I am not angry at you."

Lebedev wondered if the door was locked.

"The door is not locked. If you are so exceedingly fearful of me you may leave."

"I'm going. Thank you for your care." Lebedev stood up, took thought for an instant and added, "Thank you for saving my life."

The Lyhhrt did not move. "If you should wish to repay me in any way for saving your life, you might choose to stay and hear me out for a moment."

Lebedev wavered on one leg and sat down again.

"Thank you. You do not trust me, but you must know that I warned the woman, Jacaranda Drummond. I knew what she came here for, but not what was to happen to her, I never betrayed her. The ones who recognized her and arranged her murder are no longer here." *Dead,* the tone of voice said. "Her life was not thrown away but used very well to save someone else's—for a while, at least. Now you may go. I am running out of time."

"Tell me about that someone else."

"Is it safe to trust you, Lebedev?"

"You must judge that."

"I must trust someone and I have no one else."

Lebedev waited.

"If I do this now I have never taken such risks in all that I/we remember of time. You must promise to give me your life."

"I'm damned if I'll die for you, fellow," Lebedev said.

"I did not mean for me. Someone else—two of them. I meant that you must risk your life for them."

"If you mean the swimmer—I don't understand you. Aren't you working for Zamos?"

"For and against. Hurry, I have only a few moments before the techs discover I have turned off their power. Will you risk your life for the swimmer?"

"I have been risking it since the moment I stepped through Zamos's doorway."

"Is that a yes? I suppose so." He paused, and his imaging eyes rested on Lebedev for a long moment.

"Look here, then." The emergency lights turned down but did not go out, and the section of wall above the work table slid aside to display a vid screen showing the interior of the tank.

For the first and only time, Lebedev saw Kobai. She was floating listlessly in the center of the tank, making only enough motion with hands and tail to keep from sinking to the bottom. She could not see either of the watchers, but turned to face the camera as the Lyhhrt engaged her mind.

"Is that what Zamos has been calling an animal?" Lebedev heard the thud as Kobai thumped a fist against the screen with such eye-sparking fury that she pushed herself backward half way to the other wall.

"She doesn't think she is."

"What is she then, Lyhhrt?"

"Pregnant. The summit of Zamos's creation and the first of her kind: a fertile clone." It seemed to Lebedev that the Lyhhrt said this with as much pride as if he had created her himself. "Mother of slave nations, perhaps, Lebedev. In herself as an individual quite useless: the need for aquatic workers is very small. But what can be learned when she and the baby are . . . examined, you might say, can be applied to others. Strong body, matures in three-fifths of the time your species does, life expectancy—not much perhaps for this one, but will likely be a good for whatever new type may be developed. Gestation period five thirtydays—she is beginning to show a little."

"She does not seem to have slave mentality."

"That can be built in. Yes. Zamos has all he needs, but we do not have much time, no more than a thirtyday."

"For what?"

"To take her and us out of here."

Lebedev swallowed and stared. He whispered, "How can you be working for and against Zamos? What has all this to do with the egg-layer and the blood sample?"

"I will tell you everything eventually, but now I must reconnect the power, it is the point of noon, and your games table is about to open. I will protect you, Lebedev, but if you are to help me you must remain here and deal skambi, Lebedev. You must deal skambi."

:You Iron Man Out-there, what do you do to feed this Baby that's swimming in my sea? Do you give it more rotten dead-oyster and dried-up sea-smik that you pay for and bring here? That little tiny One? I hope it got to be tiny to come out of me. Tell me, Iron Man, do I get to die so it can feed off me? Is that what you are keeping me for, to make a meal for that One? Is that why you call me an animal?:

:By the Great Ideator, is that what you truly believe, Kobai?:

:I got nobody here to tell me different.:

:You have me! I would never call you an animal I was making it clear to someone else that you are not. If we needed more food we would bring it in, but it's not necessary yet. You make food in your body to give the baby when it's small.:

:I do?:

:It is called milk, and comes out of your teats, through the nipples, those pointed things on them.:

:Is that what they're for? I thought they were just something for men to hold on to.:

:Whatever men may think to do, giving food is what your teats are made for. You can see that your breasts are beginning to swell and your nipples too, and soon they will run a little.:

:That will hurt a lot when that New One bites my teats with his teeth!:

:It may hurt from being sucked but not from biting. The baby is born without teeth. They grow inside his mouth the way he is growing in you.:

:You say that is a him I have growing in here.:

:Yes, it is.:

:And who does he get to make the in-out with? Is that supposed to be me? There is no one else like me here.:

:No, that is unhealthy both for you and your future children. I can't be sure what will happen.:

:I don't think it looks too healthy for me and him right now, Iron Man.:

:Kobai, I am your friend and you are alive today.:

SEVEN *

Shen IV: *Ned Zella and the O'e*

Ned Gattes pushed the foam plugs into his nostrils and let the tech press his face into the mold; the plastrine was soft and warm, like a smothering pillow. Ned liked a little fear, there was a spice to it, a bright flavor: the first pop of blood in the arena, a moving shadow in an alleyway when he knew just where the knife was coming from, going to bed with Manador. Not the kind lodged under his breastbone among the Spartakoi, in the Palace of Knossos on Shen IV. He did not know who was holding the knife here, what cloak the smiler was hiding it under.

The pillow pulled away, the flick of a tentacle dismissed him and while he threw the plugs down the disposal the next gladiator took the step that tugged at the line drawing forty others into the Mask Room.

Through the polarized window the afternoon sky of Shen's fourth world still hit three walls of masks with a blue-white glare. Outside it Knossos lay half sunk in rock on the edge of the sea along five kilometers of stone jetties; the sea heaved and tossed beside them, thick with salt, and all of the buildings' towers and crenellations hid water stills and rain basins; beneath the endless maze of malls in the depths of the Palace there were a thousand artesian wells. There was nothing but lichenous vegetation in the rocks and beyond them a desert covered with vast stretches of tough ground-trees that grew ankle-thick and tangling, and could not be crossed except with huge treaded vehicles. The Palace was a haven of deeply guarded privacy. Too guarded for Ned Gattes.

The sun beat down demoniacally; the air refrigerators thudded like monsters' hearts under the shields of thick polarized glastex and could never make the atmosphere quite comfortable in this upper level where the fighters practiced in public for small bettors. Even so, Ned would have been content here under the high ceilings and their hanging fans, in all the noise of machetes clashing, children screaming, and fighters yelping in pain or triumph if he had been allowed to enjoy it in peace.

He paused to stare at the masks while he wiped bits of plastrine from his hairline. Whores, pugs, and bouncers, many long dead, stared back at him eyelessly. The newest masks taken from the young and living were pale ivory, and as they aged rising in their rows toward the ceiling they yellowed like old bones; it seemed to Ned that their features hardened and twisted with time. Most of the actual faces had been reconstructed before their impressions were taken, some not for the better, and others had gone to their deaths much worse. Jacaranda, who cared little for her looks except to please Manador, had never been so much as blemished.

In one of the lowest rows he recognized Zella's young rounded face, a softer one than Jacky's, and thought his own scarred mug would look odd beside it. Zella was sitting on a bench in the corridor outside waiting to lead him to set-ups. She had been waiting at his door when he woke, and sitting near him at breakfast and noon dinner.

Now she was beside him, putting a hand through his arm. Four cold fingers in the crook of his elbow.

She had been watching him, how he moved. He was really nervous, really working to stay calm. But he'd been hardly half awake when he was attacked, then knocked down in the melee, and after that discovered the fearful death of a friend on that pornopic. It was because of the flurry of new-dog arrivals that all those events hadn't been given much attention; not many people had seen them, and he wasn't in a hurry to report them, either. That woman who had been killed, Jacaranda, was she another spy? She didn't look like somebody caught up in a gambling ring . . . if she was, the Kylkladi had certainly taken care of her.

No more did Ned look like a spy for gamblers, with his grafted jaw and the scar running from his left ear around to the first vertebra below the nape of his neck. And he was too wide awake now, and shy of her. Wary. Not one to jump into her bed and make himself familiar. It looked to her as if he was trying to get away rather than worm himself in. She wondered what he did know. She wondered if that death scene, with its Kylkladi, had not taken place in a Zamos brothel . . . the thought gave her a shiver.

Ned was giving her a curious glance that was chilling in its own way.

With an effort Ned twisted his mind away from danger and set at Zella with the sham chebok. He did not really like the chebok; it was too easy to imagine the spikes slashing him. No other weapon, except for the outlawed morning-star, affected him this way, and he had worked to use it with skill only because it was Jacaranda's specialty.

Zella's style was different from Jacaranda's, her attitude something of an enthusiast's, fresh and a little unwary. He had known pugs like that, both men and women, and a few whores too, young ones; some had even been wise enough to get out of the business before they got old and twisted.

Perhaps she found it just possible to read his mind as he was thinking this. One pass when he did not follow through as hard as he should her eyes sparked, and she fetched him a clout with the buckler that rang changes in his head. On the rebound he caught her with her chebok injudiciously positioned like a burr between her body and her own buckler; he gave her a light tap that did not hurt her, but her fury at herself drew blood to her face. *God damn you Ned Gattes, I was living my life here working at what I do best and you come and everything is turned over in one day!*

They exchanged speculative looks.

"Yer too damn polite, Ned." The coach reached up to whack his shoulder hard with a broad palm. Gobo was very short, long-armed, and hairy; he looked like the result of an only too-successful mating of ape and human.

"Not up to full strength," Ned said, doing a little shadow-box-dance to show he was trying.

"Not good 'nough," Gobo was saying, when the clogs came rattling across the floor, and Ned saw Zella freeze. He thought he could feel the prickling at the nape of her neck.

The clogs paused, and she and Kati'ik, the personnel manager, caught eyes for a sharp moment. *Those claws scratching, scratching down my body like that murderer was doing with her!*

For that moment he thought he could read her mind in her eyes. *Whatever you want, no! I haven't screwed it out of him! He was upset, just left me and went to his room! Did you want me to rape him the first night? Leave me alone, alone!*

The *klok-klok* receded and Gobo sniggered. "Guess y' wouldn' wanner be in a ring with that'n."

Zella said in a strangled voice, "Let's keep going."

"Yar," said Gobo, taking the buckler from Zella. "Get some English on that 'bok, Ned." Without warning he knocked Ned's buckler aside and swung his armored fist outward at the side of Ned's head.

Zella without thinking sent her chebok up his armpit to deflect his aim. He said, "Uh," almost inaudibly and stepped back.

"Not on the first day, Gobo," Zella said, and gave him a grin that did not reach her ice-blue eyes.

After the noon meal the siesta broke the long hot day, and its deserted quietness was profound. Ned was lying on his cot with his hands folded in back of his head, watching the shadows as the sunbeam swung in his round window like a searchlight. Every once in a while he heard a snore from Smugger next door, or a ringing from far off: the robot Spartakos, untiring, a gold-edged guardian with a surface rippling like satin as he moved, stalked the corridors; his feet were padded, but not thickly enough to keep his steps from resonating.

Ned wondered if Zella would come. He was expecting her—whether to seduce him or give him another crack on the head he was not sure. She'd been quick enough with Gobo. The memory made him snigger.

He did not hear any steps at all before the tap on his door. When he called out, "Yeh?" it opened and she came in and sat down on the bed, calmly and looking rather determined.

Her eyes were on him, and she rested her hand lightly just above his navel as if it were the center of the universe and very, very far away. "I'm here," she said. "You want me?"

Ned thought her eyes were a bit smoky. He seemed to hear his father's voice saying, *Better not go blindside to that one, Ned. When her kind rankle up it's devil take the hindermost.* His father would have known, had married one, among others. He had still a way to go in the arena with this one.

He breathed deeply, put his hand over hers, and said, "Any time you want to do it. Right now somebody else wants you to do it."

She took her hand away and looked at him, fathoming him from a new point of view. "Who are you, Ned Gattes?" Her whisper seemed very loud in the silence punctuated by Smugger's snores.

"What'd they tell you? Your people think I know too much about something I never even got to find out until last night!"

"My people?"

"Whoever paired you with me because you look so much like Jacaranda."

Zella recoiled. "Me? Jacaranda?"

"You have the same body shape and movement. Determination."

She shivered. "I'm nothing like, nowhere near like her!"

"I thought you were, the moment I saw you, and they must think so, whoever they are."

"That's terrible. I don't even want to think of it."

"But they wanted you to stick to me?"

"Stay close to you. Sleep with you . . . anything so you'd talk. I was told you were a spy for a gambling ring."

"I thought it was something like that."

"That's why I banged you on the head. I was peeved at being maneuvered into agreeing . . . did you love her very much? Jacaranda?"

"As a friend. She wasn't ever my lover . . . they didn't realize, they never thought . . . she went with men for money, sometimes, but she never cared for any man—the closest we got was that we shared a lover, and Jacky was the one that was loved, not me. They made a mistake, whoever 'they' are."

"My 'they' is Kati'ik. She's the Personnel Supervisor on this level."

"I noticed, when she came by, the way you were looking at each other."

"One thing she's not is 'my people.' " She looked at him directly, daring him. "Why did you come? She'll keep pushing at me, I need something to tell her."

"I applied to join the Spartakoi for seven Standard years before they gave me the call. It doesn't look as if I'm going to enjoy my membership now I've got it. But I had really wanted to come here."

Her eyes were doubtful and searching. "That isn't all, though?"

"It's all I can say."

She stood up. "I hope . . . she'll believe me."

"I was stupid to jump straight into a trap, but what I've told you is true." He took her hand. "You do believe me . . . you wouldn't let Gobo flatten me."

But her mind was on Kati'ik and she forced a smile to cover her fearful thoughts. "Maybe I need a friend here as much as you do."

"Can't I be more than than only a friend?"

Zella slipped out without answering yes or no, and he did not hear her light step beyond the door. There was nothing else then but to sit on the edge of the bed and think of her.

I don't know why I even said that, there's no time for it

now. I've got to keep telling lies and trying to stay alive long enough to get out of here . . . yes, I guess I know why I said that. It's dangerous to trust her, but I want more than a friendly machine, or a good fighting partner, or a whore who lets herself get beaten up for me and makes me feel like a shit.

Ned's first match was one of the many free round-the-clock fights that took place in the lobbies of casinos, brothels, and amusement parks: a game of *blitz*, a simple contest in which two fighters squatted like sumo wrestlers in a circle and tried to shove each other out of it. The arena was a little theater of marble, a miniature Greek odeon with velvet cushions.

Blitz was an old time-waster for spacers and the children who imitated them—and for Ned who had been an alley-boyo; his opponent was Sweet, Zella's sparring partner. It occurred to Ned that he was just being put through the motions until he could be easily disposed of—unless Front Office expected Sweet to do it.

Crouching in this circle that reminded him very much of a target, he was wary; he watched, hands up and out with fingers rigid, like knives; no fists were allowed. Sweet's diamond tooth glinted in the arc lamp.

After dodging a couple of feints Ned realized that all Sweet wanted was the thrill of being in competition rather than sparring. After that he found his rhythm, knocked aside a jab with his shoulder and got under Sweet's arm to whack him on the side of his head with the edge of a hand and push him out of the ring. The members of the audience, mush-mouthed with free drinks and cheap drugs, gave him a few halfhearted yelps of approval and tossed some scant handfuls of brass tokens and sweetdrift petals.

The next day passed without combat or any other incident. Ned worked out in the gyms among the pugs who had landed with him.

Zella kept him within sight most of the time, but she had become untouchable—he had freed her to refuse him and thought she would as long she felt that making love to him was following orders; he was certain she was not his enemy. But he had no lover either.

One more night, and the next afternoon he and Zella fought a double with buckler and chebok for charged admission with a pair named Hammer Head and Knuckle Duster, sisters who usually fought each other or did an act. The arena was bigger and so was the audience. The women were better fighters than Sweet, and the fighting rhythm needed to be more intense and dramatic to give the watchers their money's worth. Zella was used to the techniques of their opponents, but Ned took some scratches and earned his money hard: each of the sisters weighed half again as much as he. All four came back together down endless corridors on the service rideways, Zella weary enough to lean on Ned's shoulder. She murmured, "I told Kati'ik what you told me, that you'd trying to come here for years. All she said was, to stay with you . . . do you think she believed me?"

Ned, much as he wanted to reassure her, could say only, "I don't know. I hope so."

Zella shivered. "She just wants me to be a whore."

"You aren't, you'll never be a whore."

She said nothing.

When he opened the door of his room he found a woman— he thought it was a woman—waiting for him. A beige-skinned, hairless person of a species he had seen many times without noticing or recognizing as a people he knew. He thought she was a servant who brought his towels and laundry. She stirred the memory of the pair who had jumped him on his first evening here; they had had the same color of skin.

She had been sitting on the bed in the dark and as he came in and flicked light on she stood up. Her impervious helmet glittered with fake jewels. He stared at her without thinking very much of anything; she was slender and narrow-shouldered, and her mouth was lightly rouged. "Yes?" A question he forced past his lips. Of course he knew the answer.

"I am at your service, Mister," she said in a soft voice, and began to pull down the tag of her zip. Underneath she was wearing something red with the glint of gold spangles, and a gold chain with a pendant that hung down between her tiny breasts. He reached to touch and examine it and she flinched, just observably. The little heart with the keyhole that Jacaranda had worn.

He felt as if he had been kicked. She stood before him in her flesh almost the color of dust and darker around her eyes and creases, almost asking to be abused, with little lightning forks of fear flickering in her eyes.

"Thank you, Miss," he said. "Not this evening. Maybe another time," and stepped aside to let her go.

But she shrank back into a corner of the room. "Mister, please don't push me out. You don't have to pay me anything."

"I'm tired and hungry, lady!"

She whispered, "They'll beat me."

He sat down on the bed and said wearily, "Sit down. Who are 'they'?"

"The ones that pay me. That run this place."

"What do they want of me?" He put his hand on her shoulder.

"Don't ask me, mister! Please don't ask me."

He lifted his hand. "Don't be frightened! I won't touch you and they won't beat you either." He opened the door, stood up and pulled her toward him; standing at the doorway in full view, he kissed her on the mouth; she flinched a little as if it had been the first time ever. "Tell 'em I like you very much and want to see you again." He kissed her again. "You go tell 'em, darling-o."

He stood staring after her, licking her rouge off his mouth, as she disappeared in the shadows of doorways or among clumps of people gathering families or lovers for a pub drink before dinner. He wondered who she was, surely not a citizen of any nations he had learned of at school in the history book about his ancestral Earth. She seemed to be a Solthree woman . . . *Anyway, it looks as if they've given up trying to make a spy out of Zella* . . . The unease settled into him more deeply.

While he was bathing and changing he noticed that one of his cuts was uglier than he had thought and was seeping so badly that he could not stop it. He dressed quickly and hurried down to the clinic. Though he was not afraid of the Ly-hhrt doctors, the one available to him was a medmech and in a few moments he was absorbing an antiseptic dermcap and being patched.

In the Clinic waiting room there was a cylindrical tank of fish, and Ned paused to watched them for a moment. He wondered if they had developed in the brackish seas beyond the docks; they looked truly alien and not restful. A few were twisted monsters in splattered colors that made him think of the swimming creature who had set the whole train of events in motion by calling out to Skerow, the Lizard Lady.

He asked the robot doctor, "Do those come from here?"

"A few. We breed them. The others are clones that we make here."

"Really?"

"We clone zoo animals too, some for research. We are known throughout Galactic Federation for our Research

Foundation. Have you not heard of it? Tours every tenday."

"Thanks for telling me," Ned said. He did not think he wanted a tour.

The medmech did not quite nod, and its metal face of course did not change expression.

Ned went away bemused. Tanks, swimmer, slaves. *We breed them.* He had wondered first why he and Jacaranda had been assigned to that swimmer and afterward whether that had anything to do with slaves. He realized that the two assignments were bound together in a way he did not understand.

Manador knew nothing about the swimmer and Lebedev had not told Ned much when he was sent out, but Jacky had died for her, he himself had been hunted, nearly killed without knowing what her importance was; innocent Zella was a counter tossed and spinning in a game she knew nothing about.

As he threaded his way back through the level of practice arenas, he heard Spartakos's resonant voice declaiming; the words were blurred by baffles and echoing. He followed the sound to a tiny amphitheater where twenty-odd people had gathered to listen. These were not pugs but the patrons who usually hung about the small arena to gamble.

Ned thought the robot might have been repeating the same spiel he had given to the incoming gladiators earlier, but it seemed he had more than one. "Members of the audience," he was saying, "I have been given the name of a slave." While he spoke he was polishing himself with a chamois, wiping his limbs unaffectedly like a bather, but quite unlike any known bather of his shape, turning his head by a hundred and eighty degrees and bending his arms backward to make sure he had not missed a spot. Sometimes he paused to emphasize a point with a gesture.

"I am sure you have been told by your tour guides that

Spartacus was a Roman slave thousands of years ago who re-
belled, and ultimately led an army of rebels, only because he
wanted to go home to Thrace. Only to go home. I have no
other home than this, so I am home, and I have the freedom
to stand here waving my arms and entertaining you. Therefore I have been given the name of a slave. This shows that
though you are called a slave you need not be one. I am your
example."

While Ned was wondering who had programmed these
strange words, he noticed that not all the members of the audience were patrons; a small cluster to one side was made up
of more hairless dun-colored people like the woman who
had tried to seduce him. There were only five or six of them,
dressed neatly in inconspicuous zips, mesh impervious helmets on their heads, but he thought he remembered one or
two who were supervisors of working machines. They were
not strongly differentiated sexually, but there seemed to be
more females than males. A short distance away from the
group a robot cleaner had stopped as if it had paused and
hunched down to listen. Ned shook himself like a dog
against his imaginings and moved on.

Along the hallway another odd thing caught his attention, a dark corner where none had been before. A recess
where transworld common booths were lined up, usually
well-lit, had gone dark, and while he was turning his head to
look he got a hard nudge from his side and a shove from the
back, so that he stumbled into the corner knocking against
the booths. He did not know either of the two shadow-grey
figures that were rumbling him. One was a Varvani with
limbs like oaks, the other a course-haired Solthree woman
just as broad. The Varvani caught his upper arms from behind and the woman whispered hoarsely, "What do we need
to do to make you talk, Gattes?" and thumped his belly
hard. "Let's take a trip to Front Office."

Ned retched but managed a kick in the knee that sent her staggering, kicked back into the Varvani's shin, stamped on his foot and when his arms were freed slammed the heel of his hand into the woman's nose. Neither of the attackers was more than merely dented, and he had no time to catch his breath before they grabbed him again, but the light came on suddenly and a beautiful voice said, "Hello?"

The Varvani and his mate turned their attention from Ned and gaped at Spartakos, gleaming in fresh and blessed light. His arms reached out, longer than arms ought to, and the pair shuddered away from the threat of his touch. "You get out, now," he said pleasantly enough, and they scrambled away.

Ned tried to make sense out of all this. "What are you doing here, Spartakos? You making a specialty of saving me?"

"Once I was a slave in Rome and in spite of that I broke my chains!" the robot declared ringingly, then dropped his style to a less dramatic mode and said, "You are not hurt badly, are you, my-friend-Ned-Gattes? You will be sure to report this time, won't you? Now I must go before I draw more attention. If I seem to have distressed anyone I will be shut down."

Ned called after him, "Who were those thugs, Spartakos! Is this whole goddam place after me? Who were they, God damn you?"

Like a stream of mercury Spartakos twisted to face him. "Don't curse me, Ned. They are bouncers from a whore-house down in the Labyrinths." And he was gone.

Ned hurried back, half-limping, to put ice on his belly-ache. Zella was dressed and waiting at his door, and he pulled himself up and smoothed his face for her.

She touched his mouth. "Who've you been kissing, Ned Gattes?"

"Do I still have that stuff on my mouth? It wasn't anybody I slept with." He forced a grin. "Don't wait for me, I'll be down for supper."

He gulped a painkiller and sat trying to think. Tanks, swimmer, slaves.

He thought those dun-colored people must be slaves. In all his years as a gladiator he had never seen—or never noticed—them except once he now vaguely recalled in Starry Nova, and maybe in one more Zamos arena. He knew he could not prove that they were not cheap immigrant labor of the kind long frowned on but never completely outlawed. But it was not his burden to prove, only to observe and report. He thought he must be like a great many other people who were not aware enough to realize that they were being served by slaves. Or did not care.

The ideas kept pushing at him. The warped fish, the slaves, swimmers, tanks.

Clones that we make here. The swimmer, the woman, was it possible? All those labs, cloned zoo animals, clones for research. Why not?

Is that what they think I know? . . . now maybe I know it. Time to get out.

He dressed quickly in the best clothes he owned; all of his money and credit were in his belt, nothing in the company safe. His weight allowance coming out here had been very small, and he was a traveler, always had been. He thought of Zella, with a flash of desire, and his bruise throbbed. She would be waiting to go to dinner and he did not know what to tell her. He closed the door behind him.

"Your shadow ain't stickin' to you anymore, Ned," Barley called, going down the hall with Smugger and the cyborg woman Ching Yi. "She got buzzed by one of them robot bird things to go to the office."

"I told her I'd see her at supper—"

"Looks like you won't. You coming to the boozer with us?"

"I'll be along in a while."

"Dunno what she did that made them call her at dinner-time," Barley said.

Smugger was ready with a suggestion, but Ned did not rise. It was possible that Zella had been called down for some minor infraction. Just possible.

He ran.

Labyrinths

It was cool down in executive country but Zella was sweating, waiting for Kati'ik to turn her head one hundred degrees and direct her bird's hard stare over her slant shoulder.

"So, Sztoyko, you cannot fill a simple request." She shifted to align her body with her head.

"What do you mean? I told you everything I knew, everything Ned Gattes told me." She hugged herself to hide her trembling.

"He did not tell you very much. I asked you to continue watching him because I expected you to bring me more information, and he must have been sufficiently frightened by the attacks on him to confide in you. You have brought me nothing—"

"What did you expect of me? There was nothing to br—"

"—because we know there is good reason to be suspicious of him!" Kati'ik's claws rattled a tattoo on the inclined screen of her terminal. "And you are of the same species, are you not? It should have been as easy to draw the secret from his mouth as it is to pull the *yayu* grub from its hole in the *ouil* tree. Someone is telling lies, Sztoyko." She drew closer. "I know your lover is, and I wonder if you are. Perhaps you have not been sufficiently frightened."

"I don't know anything about your grubs and trees." Zella held herself tighter to gather strength. "I told you everything I got from him, I did. I can't tell for sure when a person's lying, I'm not an ESP. But Ned Gattes is a real pug who's all scarred up and does nothing but fight in arenas, he can't be a spy for gamblers when he has no more money to bet with than I have, never goes near a greenboard to see how the money's running, and he never uses a comm line to talk to anybody. I think that story's just a lot of shit—"

"Take care!"

"—and what would you do if you found he was a spy?" She was really angry now, recklessly angry she knew, and couldn't pull back. "You've already knocked him down and beaten him up, what else would there be left to do but kill hi—"

The gold-clawed hand shot up and encompassed her jaw, and the shrill voice came down a dangerous octave. "You are talking too much, dems'l." The talons closed in, she raised her arm to push them away, but they had pierced her skin and she felt the little streams of blood running down. "You have the richness of this world to benefit you and you do not know how to take advantage of it." Kati'ik's feathers were erect and quivering, Zella sensed the thudding heat of the bird body, its smells of flesh and dust.

She grabbed hold of the pearl-feathered arm but her hands were clawed away, she tried to scream through teeth that had been forced to clench. The flat beaked face, like deeply yellowed ivory, was close to hers, the eyes pierced like claws. "There are some who never learn . . . perhaps it is time to hold the Lottery for a Bloodfight. We can still find some use for so froward and ungrateful a person as yourself! Now get out of here!"

Zella pulled away, gasping, but did not run; she could feel herself turning red and then white. Her anger was so pure that she did not feel the pain in her jaw or her deeply scratched hands.

Kati'ik forestalled her words. "Any story you may tell anyone will be treated as just that, a story. Keep that in mind!"

Zella whispered, "Now I know you're a liar," and turned away past the door; its iris hissed behind her. The moment her eyes left Kati'ik's the pain hit her; it was all she could do to keep her hands from her face or from touching them with each other, just walk along as if everything was normal. Most of her own kind had gone to dinner, and there were not many about and no one who noticed, but she supposed she was not the first one to come from that office with a scratched face. She gritted her teeth, she could feel her eyes hot with fury.

Oh Zella, how did you ever get into this? You've let her do it again, you damned fool! She can manipulate you into saying or doing anything! Christ, I'm bleeding! What am I to do now? Try to think, Zella! In her blind haste she slammed into a shape, a man, arms came round her, Ned crying: "God's sake, Zella, what happened to you!"

The terror swamped her. "What are you doing here? Are you after me too?"

"Oh Zella! I just came to see if you were all right. You scared me running off like that. Christ, look at your face! What happened? Who did that?"

"She wouldn't believe anything I said, just went crazy and ripped into me! What am I going to do, Ned? I can't go back there, she's setting me up for the Lottery and a Bloodfight! I have nowhere to go and no money—what'll I do?"

"You'll come with me and we'll do something about it!"

"Come where? Where are you going?"

"To the other side of the world if I can find it, I don't have anything worth going back for and I'm not hanging around here to get beat up again and let you get clawed to pieces."

"No, no! What are you saying? You mustn't let me pull you away. As long as I'm not there you'll be all right, and they'll . . ." It struck her that there was something not quite right in what she was saying, that her mind was stunned with fear and anger. "They'll think of something else, won't they?"

"They already have." He was walking her down branching corridors, hurrying her a bit. "Come on, Zel, got to find you a place to clean up in—looks like one over there, yeh."

"All right. I see it." Her eyelids were heavy, in spite of the pain—or maybe it was because it was so wearying. She whispered, "I didn't give you away."

"I knew you wouldn't." He pushed away at the guilt for the harm he had not done her and could not have prevented. "I'll be waiting here for you."

The blood came off her clothing easily, but there were those four claw marks, one to the right of her jaw, three to the left; they would leave scars she would not have minded so much if she had been able to fight. And her hands hurt worse because she had to move them.

Is that you in the mirror, Zella, all bloody and inflamed? The one that just a couple of days ago was content to live and work here?

You have the richness of this world to benefit you, and you do not know how to take advantage of it . . .

She paused at the door to steel herself against a vision that there would be no Ned, that he would have run from her tormented face. But he was there.

"Come on now Zel, we've got to look for food, even if you might not be hungry after—"

"But I am hungry!" she said, astonishing herself. "But how do we pay? I have a little money, but I won't show a cashcard."

"We'll get some money out of those cards later. I have enough of the fruitful for now, just tell me where."

"There's an escalator."

Ned took his last look down the long high-ceilinged corridors, at the country of the Spartakoi he had tried so hard to join. A few fast eaters who had finished early were coming out of the dining room at the end of the hall. The old sergeant, Gretorix, was trudging along with head bent, earnestly listening to some point Gobo the coach was making, head turned up and long arms waving. Farther back three Khagodi were arguing with each other in silence, also with gestures, their forked tails swinging and thudding, the breaths whistling in their oxygen filters. Near them a cluster of children who had eaten earlier were scuffling and thumping each other with toy cheboks and yelling, "You're blee-eeding!" in ringing voices. Beyond them the halls were empty.

He stepped on the moving ramp and Zella followed. On this floor the air was cooler, there were restaurants, theaters, lounges, museums, boutiques, open arenas, luxury apartments and suites, pools of a thousand sea creatures, and botanical gardens. In the rose-gold light of the evening sun through stained-glass windows three thousand people from nine worlds were thronging the arcades on their way from dinner to theater, gallery, or party, and not even the servants wore the clothing of working gladiators.

But Ned and Zella did not stop at this floor, and some of the party-goers joined them on the walkway down. Zella resisted the impulse to try to curl herself up and shrink into Ned's shadow; Ned put his arm around her gently and not like a pimp who had just beaten his whore. Their travel companions were too absorbed or too googoo-eyed to notice.

No one got off at the next floor, a second-class tourist's version of the one above, with smaller apartments, parks and fish pools, fountains not so arching or rainbowed, and less expensive stores. The ramp wound down, past floors reachable only by service elevators, into the Labyrinths.

There was nothing dark or mysterious about the Labyrinths. The entrance was a maze of screens and baffles, but beyond them the sound flamed out from a vast market filled with milling crowds, splashing fountains, bars, casino lobbies, mariachi bands, strolling singers, and merchants hawking souvenir balloons, nose filters, and seashell necklaces. The walls above all these establishments were lined with screens of news clips, advertisements in flashing lights, coldlight stills, maps that said YOU ARE HERE in twenty-seven languages, and, just below the ceiling, streamers giving the stock quotations of ninety-three exchanges as well as betting odds, point spreads, and last-minute results from a hundred and seventy-five kinds of games, fights, and races halfway across the Galaxy.

Zella had come down here six or seven times; Ned had known places like this on three worlds. "Somewhere to dodge in," he said, and gave Zella a hug. "That's a chemmy over there, let's eat and get some stuff to fix your face."

A score of carts served kebabs of grilled meat and seafood from flaming braziers. Ned and Zella bought and ate them on foot surrounded by porn shops, sex parlors, and antique markets selling genuine fake Mickey Mouse watches and pre-Columbian pottery, as well as phony Khagodi gold nuggets and suits of imitation feather armor from Kylklar.

At one of the parlors a thick Varvani woman spieling on

a bally backed by blinking fluorescents leaned down to leer into Zella's face.

"Gentle-johnny blaggering ye, lovey? Hook on with us!"

Zella stared up at this apparition wearing a black top hat, a clown's mouth of orange lip rouge, and a spread of gold sequins on her huge double-teated breast.

"Johnny's treatin' her good," Ned snapped and hustled Zella away to buy ointment and cover-ups for her face.

Zella was yawning, too weary to feel insulted. "If you didn't have to put out in there, it might be a good place to get some sleep."

"When Security wants you they'll always figure you'll hole up in a whorehouse or a cheap kip. They ruffle those places first."

Zella closed her eyes and leaned on Ned's shoulder, letting him guide her. "What are we going to do, Ned? We can't just keep running."

He sat down with her on a public bench. His mind was trying to sort out the pieces of the kaleidoscope surrounding them: loud-voiced strollers, singers twanging their lutolins, flickering neons, kebobs sizzling over reeking braziers; pushing at the problems inside his head, whether there were really created slaves or he had made it all up in his head and where to find a cheap—or preferably free—doss for the night; finally he shoved it all away. Whether Zamos was creating or enslaving people, where they had come from, what it might have to do with the job he had done for GalFed delivering Jacaranda into Zamos's brothel, who the swimming woman was, the significance of Spartakos, what those thugs thought he could have told them, everything twisting in his mind until it felt full of wormholes—

What do I know? I did a job for Galactic Federation before I came here, the Zamos people want to know what

GalFed knows, and I don't know . . . only that I've got to keep dodging.

"We have to find a comm-line to the outside," he said. "Come on, Zel, we're going to get run over or run in if we sit here long enough. Look—open your eyes and look over there—there's a bar, not very high-toned. We'll go in there, order a drink, not the cheapest, pay for it, and after a while sidle around the back where all the cans are. There ought to be a door leading to a service alley for cleaning machines. If I'm right, we can find an old closet to hunker in just for the night, and if I'm not, we're out of luck and gotta start over."

She let him pull her up and fend off the crowd for her to slip through. He was right, but she hoped she would never come to like sitting in thick sweet dope-smoke drinking brackish ale, or threading her way in the dimness past solitary drinkers wrapping themselves around their mugs, and pushing through a room where a whirring machine spewed lavender perfume to counter the smells of the urinals, thrones, and gratings in the floor.

The alley was cool and dark; a few old bulbs cast yellow stains on the shadows. Ned paused at one narrow door and pulled at its latch gently, but it would not stir. After a moment he heard grunting and giggling. He shrugged and moved on. Behind other doors he listened to rattling dishes, fistfights, and an Orpha chorus singing to kettledrums before he found an entrance he dared try.

He winkled a fingernail into the latch and the door slid open with a scream of runners that made him glance about quickly, but no fleck of dust stirred in the long corridor to either side of him. "What is it?" Zella whispered.

"I think it used to be a lav," Ned said. "Looks like it's been here about three hundred years and long before Zamos." He was exaggerating, but not by much. A dusty bulb, switched on and off by a pull-string, showed an irregular-shaped room with odd angles butting into it. It had not been cleaned recently, but did not have the filth of centuries. The cracked terrazzo floor was grimy but dry, and a large oval basin of imitation marble was sunk into it; there were two sinks of different heights, a wash-tub and a doorless cubicle with two urinals, also of different heights.

Ned warned Zella back, stepped over the lintel and peered about; nothing jumped out at him. He crossed his fingers and pushed the tap button; with a fearful squeal it gave out a stream of rusty liquid that began to clear after a moment. He turned to beckon to her: "Your chamber waits, m'lady, your bath is drawn—not quite, I don't think you'd want to wash your face in that stuff just yet, but if it keeps running it might be useful. Look, here's a tarp folded up in the washtub, it might be clean enough inside to keep us from the dirt. Where do you want it?"

She pointed to the sunken basin and before he had finished smoothing out the tarp had slipped down and arranged herself in its cradling shape. The moment she stopped moving she was asleep. He looked down at her, neatly angled in the rumpled slate-blue pants and jacket, one hand beneath her face and the other curled alongside. The wounds on her cheek had dried and under the covering makeup were dull pink spots. Now that he knew her she seemed so utterly different from Jacaranda that he could not at all find the similarities that had struck him so deeply when he first met her. The look of her dissolved, if only for the moment, the fears and worries crowding his mind; he pulled the lamp string, folded himself down beside her in the darkness, circled her with his arm, and slept.

Zella woke with a start from a dream of a clawed bird dropping shrieking from the sky, not only an image of Kati'ik attacking but an omen of every danger she had ever feared.

Her hands and face throbbed, but not fiercely; the dermatex she had painted them with dulled the soreness.

She became aware of Ned's arm resting on her and the whisper of his breath stirring her hair. There was nothing familiar about waking here; thumps and stirring from the walls around her, the still and dusty air, and the hard basin beneath the rough tarp she was lying on. All of them emblems of the danger she still did not know the nature of, the unnamed peril she had been drawn into because she looked something like—only something like!—the friend of Ned Gattes named Jacaranda, who had died so horribly.

The door squeaked, and Ned startled but did not waken. Zella began to tremble and tried to shrink down farther into the basin. Her heart was churning like a milk separator.

Something bearing a light—an arm?—reached in through the open doorway, and paused suspended. She shaded her eyes with her hand but could not see what was beyond it.

A very heavy moment passed. The light dimmed and withdrew. From the backlighting in the alleyway she saw that the intruder was a servicing robot, who had sensed life and left it undisturbed. The door drew closed on its shrieking casters. Her heart was still jumping and she felt the sweat on her face like a sheen of ice. She could not move for a moment.

The danger of wanting excitement, like a narcotic, she knew it now, everything her family on New Southsea had warned her about. She grinned into the darkness and raised her hand to pull down Ned's zippers.

EIGHT * *Exits*

Khagodis: *Skerow and Evarny*

On Khagodis, in the hot heart of the Diluvian Continent, International Trade Consortium and Goldyne fought each other slowly through the long demanding trial. The crucial witness Nohl—who had lost his knife to Kobai's people the gold-gathers, his eye to the gold-buyers, and most of his life to the sellers—poisoned and wounded though he was, did not die, but stubbornly clung to his terrible existence. Since he had sworn three times to his testimony, and each time more cantankerously, he was left alone; there was nothing more to be gained either by prosecuting or by murdering him.

Nohl had insisted on speaking unprotected by counsel or helmet, and an ESP notary had confirmed that his statement was the truth as he saw it; the confirmation bore no more weight than any other lie-detector test but was there if only to say that he was telling the truth when he claimed to be guilty. His evidence was haggled over by the opposing forces with as much emotional as climatic heat, for its implications, and its hints of accusation.

Skerow was sharply on the alert for any suggestion that she had been remiss, or that Nohl's accusation against her had become a rumor or implication of corruption. There was none; the testimony was being treated like any other.

But Skerow was forced to declare Nohl's account of Kobai and her people inadmissible. There was no evidence whatever to show that the Consortium was actually kidnapping intelligent persons or that Nohl was enslaving them. It was not part of the charges against Goldyne's theft and selling of gold. Her consolation was that there were world and interworld authorities who would be deeply interested in it, particularly on Fthel V in Starry Nova, where the story as she knew it had begun.

Nohl was only one of a sleazy group of would-be crooks engaged in stealing gold and making its owners pay to borrow it. In that limited perspective the matter was clear enough to the court. If Skerow had been younger and less experienced, they would have seemed to her a crew of rogue Khagodi disgracing themselves and their world for the Federation to jeer at. Now she accepted that there would always be such rogues on the fringes. It was the knavery of a powerful judge like Thordh that she found so painful still.

As this excitement was ebbing, one of the three chief lawyers for the Consortium, an ancient Khagodi woman, did not return from the midday break, and was found dead in her quarters. An eddy of fear rippled through the court, but Skerow had known the old woman in a formal way for many years, and for just as long had heard the rumors of her struggle with a rare form of leukemia.

To give the lawyers time to regroup, she declared the afternoon session adjourned, and called out over the whispers of the congregation: "We shall recess for next after tomorrow," grave and sober as ever, though she shared the irritation of the whole Court over a day and a half of doing not much in the tropic city of Burning Mountain at the nadir of its summer.

If Nohl had not been poisoned, the trial would not have been brought forward into the hot season, she was thinking—and he would not have confessed either.

But all that she had learned from Nohl told her nothing of Kobai, who in her mind was still suspended, helpless, in the window of Zamos's brothel, burning in her imagination out of a night of rainfall in Starry Nova.

While she was hanging up her robe in her office and delivering her daybook to a clerk for downloading into Files, Ossta the Court Officer popped her head through the doorway and said, "Skerow my friend, would you like a good hot supper at my rooms in town? They're not far away from here and I have a fresh crock-bull shank and a good jug of white-thorn essence."

"Thank you so much, Ossta, that sounds delightful."

"Meet me about sundown, then, in the front courtyard here, and we can walk over together. There is a roasting spit on the roof of my building and the sunset is so pretty from there."

Skerow had an unpleasant flashback of Hathe saying: *Share the evening meal with me,* Hathe who had nearly killed her, whom she had so nearly killed, and pushed it from her mind. She had known Ossta as a girl, back a number of years it was better not to count, when they had both studied Law. "I'm sure I will enjoy it, Ossta! Now I am going to Central Telegraphy and try to make contact with my sisters. I have not even had an opportunity to tell them I am staying on. Will you leave an answering message for me?" She knew that she would be truly grateful to avoid the Court Refectory, which served food far too much like the sea-smik, myth-ox, and preserved kappyx bulbs her digestion had been burdened with in Starry Nova.

The communications center of Burning Mountain was inside the station where Skerow had disembarked from the ferry. It was not within walking distance of the courthouse, and Skerow was obliged to take the flatbed omnibus, pulled by a pair of massive and foaming *thumbokh,* that bounced roughly on the cobbled road; there was a Standard hour of heavy riding on this in deeply oppressive heat, but she was relieved to be free of the close atmosphere of the Court, to watch persons leading ordinary lives in workshops and at market stalls.

The Hall of Telegraphy was a smaller sister of the one in Port Manganese, a round stone building centered with a tower of antennas; most of the outworlders using it here were attached to the Interworld Court, and half the rest were journalists who observed them. Arches in the thick walls led to small dingy shops where travelers could drink tea or wine, finger tired-looking souvenirs or order take-away food for the journey.

Skerow found her place in line at the railing, composing in her mind the message she would send, watching while the whickering fans stirred the hot dusty air under the dome, and two non-ESP outworlders at her elbow quarreled over who had come first. She pulled off her helmet because her skin felt as if it were writhing with sweat beneath it, and after a moment felt a mental touch, then became aware of someone approaching her.

"Yes?"

A tall young Khagodi man she did not know, wearing a helmet and a messenger's badge on a swag of leather, was standing beside her. "Madame, there is a gentleman who would like to speak to you on an urgent matter. He is waiting in that tearoom."

Skerow glanced along the fellow's pointing arm, noted the darkness of the archway leading to the tea shop, and was instantly suspicious. She said firmly, "I am not going to lose my place in this line, carrier. If your gentleman's concern is so urgent, he may come to me and speak."

"Madame, he cannot."

"Then, fellow, he must do without my advice." Skerow stepped forward in line, and the messenger took a step to keep abreast of her. "It is no use staying with me. I am not coming." One of the non-ESPs was looking at her oddly, but she turned away to glare at the carrier.

What happened went quickly then. She realized that she was going to be touched physically, but her reflexes did not move her soon enough to dodge the pressure that came on the inside of her wrist, of something cool and moist. After one twitch of repulsion she turned her hand out wonderingly and saw the dermcap melting on the thin skin, diffusing into the throbbing veins beneath. *I have been drugged,* she told herself, as if the *I* were somebody else.

She watched the half-crushed globe for a blurred moment, and looked into his eyes; he was her height. "You must come, Madame," he said.

She nodded, and went along with him toward the arch. Now it was full of light. *My pupils have expanded.* Inside there were three small eating tables suitable for her height and five or six others at lower heights, with chairs to match, for squatters. Shadowy figures were crouching at them. The hard center of her being fought to see clearly, but the languor swept her, not unpleasantly, not unpleasantly enough.

There was a bowl of liquid on the table in front of her; its surface seemed to ripple like moving lips. *No, Skerow, no!*

The mindvoice was not quite her own. She shuddered inwardly and drank.

"You must come now," said the young man once more. He had changed his shape imperceptibly, and now he seemed to be writhing like the priest representing the Endless River Serpent at the spring dances of Southern Vineland. With an arm around her shoulder he led her willingly, lovingly, to a portal where she took one step into another dimension, a universe that was the inside of a bubble, colors and music flowing over its glassy surface, whose lights above her came from a thousand stars, whose floor was a pool of pretty blue water. She stood on the ceramic edge, waiting for the one she knew would rise from the water, her dead daughter Bathetto. They would look into each other's eyes and talk together forever.

The love rose swelling in her spirit, it drummed against her forehead and pressed out the tears. So many years of sorrow in alien places far away from even her desert and its moons . . .

Skerow!

The hard daily self that called to her was encapsulated in a bubble of its own, sealed away from her dream.

The being rose from the blue center of the water with massive head turned toward her and heavy jaws grinning. His eyes gleamed bright topaz, and the prismatic colors played over him so that he seemed almost to be part of the bubble's diaphanous wall. The air was full of perfumes.

"It is good to see you, Skerow!" Thordh cried.

Skerow's love collapsed in folds like a struck tent. Even so, she was not surprised. The quarter-century acquaintanceship with Thordh was an unshapely, unfinished part of her life's experience, something she always knew that she must face—but never so pleasantly! "I am glad to find you in good health, Thordh. Even though you are dead." She was laughing and crying. A needle of half-conscious and never-acknowledged feeling pierced her between the hearts: a terrible relief that what she was facing was not Bathetto. She was free.

"Death is not so bad when you get used to it," said Thordh.

She found herself chuckling. She would never before have accused Thordh of being a witty fellow. She warmed to him. "How pleased I am to be with you!" Free.

Skerow!

He stood up in the water so that his serpentine tail rode the ripples of its surface. His upper lip folded over his beautiful teeth in a rictus of desire. "I have always loved you, Skerow, even though I have never spoken my love." The colors flowed over him as if they had a life of their own, and she could feel her passion uncoiling in long swaths that followed the lines of his body. *Free.*

His body swam the air so that it twined about hers without touching. "You are the woman with whom I truly longed to share my Lineage."

"Yes, Thordh . . ."

"How I wish you were the mother of my children!"

Antidote!

She was swimming off the edge and into the depth: the depth not of freedom but of nothingness. *My children.* The words tasted like iron, and her passion, so deeply sexual, subsumed itself into those other and even deeper passions of mother-love, wife-love, that had burned in her unrelieved for thirty-five years. The sore of her being burst and flared its poison into her longing; it set her afire with fury from bone to skin. With infinite slowness and all her strength, before she sank forever, she shook herself free, pulled away the hand with which she had been about to caress Thordh, drew air into her constricted chest and hissed, "That is damned nonsense!"

—damn you, the antidote!

The fading light of her mind sharpened for a moment: before shame at even the thought of delivering her private self to Thordh had time to flood her, she realized that she had been not only drugged, but poisoned. Then her field of vision darkened with a blue-grey stain, the iron burned in her throat, the cramp hit her, she twisted and involuntarily swept Thordh with her tail. She felt a sting and thought it was death. The stain blackened all of the light.

"Skerow, wake up! You must wake, Skerow!"

I am awake. She was just dimly aware of lying in the basin in that strange place where she had found Thordh. Thordh was—not speaking to her but lying beside her on the ledge . . . no, it was not Thordh but someone vaguely reptilian and green-grey, wearing a suit of cloth or leather colored like a Khagodi man's skin. Not a Khagodi even . . .

"You must rouse and stir yourself, move about and circulate the antidote! Do wake up, Skerow!"

I have never been free.

"No one is," said Evarny. "Now—"

Evarny?

"Yes, yes! Try to rise up, get a good breath of air. The Security people are here now, and there will be an ambulance in just a moment."

"Security? Ambulance? Whatever for?" She noticed several more shadowy figures, these quite recognizable as Burning Mountain Security forces. "What has happened, Evarny?"

"You were so near, so near death! I was calling and calling you!"

"I thought it was my own self calling me. What are you here for?" She asked this of the ambulance crew, who were pushing in a proper wheeled stretcher, well padded and broad as a barn door, not like the makeshift cobbled together when she had collapsed in Starry Nova. She felt quite cheerful and lively.

"You are going to the hospital right away to make sure the antidote has worked properly, and they will probably want to keep you a day or two for observation."

"I'm damned if they will! I am going to Ossta's to eat crock-bull shank and drink white-thorn!"

"No, Skerow. Ossta will put her crock-bull shank into the cool-safe and save her white-thorn for one or two days more. You have been poisoned with karynon and must be watched."

"Karynon—the aphrodisiac—ugh! I had to try poor Lebedev for smuggling that."

"Poor! I hope you gave him life in prison!"

"No no! He was quite innocent." The attendants were lifting her up in slings; water poured off her. To herself she seemed heavy as lead now. She had one more side glance at the creature who had pretended to be Thordh. "I had to send him to prison for a year, a heavy punishment for smuggling a few *trogga* of contraband barley and." She had meant to add, "chickpeas," but fell asleep on the word, and knew nothing for a day.

She woke lying on a waterbed like the one Nohl had been on when she heard his deposition; her ears were ringing, she felt dim and nauseated, grateful to see the IV connected to her arm so that she did not need to eat. When she remembered karynon and Thordh she was doubly nauseated, and by the time Evarny appeared in her doorway her first impulse was to cry out, "Don't say anything!"

But his first words were, "Your doctor tells me that you are doing well and may leave here tomorrow."

"It does not matter now. You must find another judge. I am resigning, I am afraid in disgrace."

"You are not in disgrace. You have been attacked, and I feel deeply guilty for pushing you to sit on this trial. Everyone wishes you well, and Ossta will visit you soon to tell you so."

"I am sorry you feel guilty, because I would never blame you. You saved my life. What happened, Evarny?"

"As well as I can gather, it was very much like what happened with Thordh, except, of course, that the aim was to discredit you, not kill you. No one seems certain of the criminal—but I think there are some guesses. Of course they would have preferred to buy you—"

"They had already tried."

"Yes, and given up. One of Ossta's clerks had been tampered with and set to watch you. When you announced to the world that you were going to the comm center, she called ahead to the brothel—yes, a quite legal brothel, no others in the city, where the trap was waiting for you. If you had not gone to the Station then, the plotters would have found another way to bring you to them. You were given a hypnotic to make you suggestible—also quite legal but only if done on the premises—and a dose of karynon, definitely a banned substance and a criminal offense. It is a poison that will kill unless it is taken with a timed antidote. The fellow who impersonated Thordh—"

"Tik! Please do spare me—"

"Your behavior was perfectly decorous and unexceptional—quite exceptional for someone poisoned with karynon! That fellow impersonating Thordh was found to be an illegal immigrant of a source and species not yet determined—"

"I can guess," Skerow murmured, remembering the beige-grey woman who had sweetened her bath in Starry Nova. "Even on Khagodis . . ."

"Hm? At any rate the place is closed and its proprietors arrested."

"Was it a Zamos brothel?"

"It did not advertise itself as one, but I would not be surprised."

"That bubble I was in was very much like . . ."

"It was a dream chamber, where a customer may legally take hypnotics and have assisted dreams."

"If I was not meant to be killed, why did I nearly die?"

"Because things go wrong. Your tormentors forgot to take into account that you are a Northern woman of small build, and gave you an overdose for one your size, and the antidote is not meant to work immediately."

"And how did you come to be on hand at the right time?"

"I had come here to see you and called the court to find out if you were still there. I was told you were at the Station, and I was staying at the Station Hostel, so I looked about, and—and—I was sufficiently familiar with your mind, I tried and tried to reach you before—before—"

"All right, Evarny," she said gently. "I have been saved. Just one more question. What did you come to see me about?"

"Ossta is coming now, and my wits have strayed. Let me tell you tomorrow. I hope you will not mind that Ossta has invited me to share your dinner."

"Not at all, I will look forward to it. Good-bye then, Evarny."

He paused and turned at the doorway before he left. "Thordh was such a fool not to have made himself your friend."

* * *

The sunset was as fine as Ossta had promised, and Skerow stood in its red light drinking the white-thorn out of a thick glass cup and listening to the tapping of the goldbeaters' mallets from the jewelsmith's across the way. "Now tell me why you came here, Evarny." She had a tiny irritating chip of discomfort in her mind at having accepted his presence with perhaps too great an ease after all the years of separation. Even as if their minds were swimmers lying alongside each other in some ocean depth alone. Even as if they were married still, when they were not, not. Ossta had moved away to speak to others cooking at the communal fires, almost, it seemed to her mind now grown doubly suspicious, more deeply cynical, by prearrangement.

Evarny said, in regard to nothing in particular, "My wife and I have been separated for quite a few years. She had had nine children of her own when I married her, four of them are still alive, and later she wanted to move back to Eastern Sealand to be near them. I mention this—I will say why later. Your sister Nesskow called me because your family has not been able to reach you. Communications are poor ... because ... Skerow, it is hard to tell you this, not many know it yet, but the whole world will think of nothing else in a few days. There has been a quake, a land-splitting in the fossil sea some ten thousand *tikka-siguu* from your house in Pearlstone Hills, not a great and terrible one, only a half score injured, your house is safe ... But the quake has cast up a huge mass of metal that your provincial authorities believe to be an artifact, very ancient, possibly alien, they think perhaps a ship, perhaps even a key to the mystery of our civilization. The area has been cordoned off and evacuated, including Pearlstone Hills, because there is a fear of contamination as well as curiosity-seekers tramping all over the place. Until they excavate and open it—I don't know when you will be able to go back."

"Not go back . . ." Skerow murmured. "And what about my sisters? They don't live far away."

"They are not on the fault line, and quite safe. Tikrow is within the cordon, and says she is thinking of moving in with her sister-in-law in Broad Plains, and of course Nesskow invites you to stay with her."

"Yes . . . I see." The food and liquor had lost their flavor. She wet her lips, and said faintly, "Perhaps it is only an old shipwreck."

"I am afraid that does not matter, it is so ancient. There will be a great deal of excitement over it no matter what it is. People are always looking for Gods. I had all of this arranged in my mind to tell you, but I never thought it would be in the light of what you have had to endure already."

"No matter what it is I guess I must face it."

my
desert has
exploded with stars . . .

"There will be religious reformations," she added, feeling an edge of hysteria in her voice. "Our Diggers and Inheritors will discover that there was indeed a right place to dig, the Watchers and Hatchlings will be satisfied that we have indeed been delivered by burning Gods in an enormous Egg."

"Perhaps," said Evarny, watching her with a sympathy she felt a stab of anger at. "Have you definitely decided to step down from the Lectern?"

"I have sent a message to the Court to tell them that. Tomorrow I will make the formal announcement. I suppose after that I must decide what place to stay."

"That was why I brought up my separation from my wife. My wife-house here is unoccupied and I hope you will take it in good part if I offer it to you . . . It would be a base when you are not traveling and I don't believe that at our stage of life the two of us would be subject to much gossip."

"Thank you, Evarny. I couldn't possibly be insulted at such a generous offer—but my head is quite whirling—from everything—and I must have time to think."

"Of course. Then let us have another cup of white-thorn and one more slice of that delicious meat. The air is cooling and the colors in the sky are still beautiful."

"Yes." *In Starry Nova they are probably overcast grey with rain, and the only bright colors will be in Zamos's windows . . . I wonder if my swimmer will be saved, if ever I will come to see her again . . . if I will see my desert again.*

Evarny said, "Now that you are leaving the trial I may also mention some rumors that will probably be obscured by news of the Egg, of a very suspicious linkage between Zamos and Goldyne."

"I am not surprised at that, somehow," Skerow said.

"There will be a much more serious and powerful investigation of Zamos and its doings—and your steadfastness has had much to do with that. The trial, for all its trouble and expense, may yet be declared a mistrial."

I did nothing. She called out to me for justice. It does not matter to me what they do about that trial now. It was not the important one.

I am an exile and my coming here was worth nothing except that I learned something from Nohl, poor fool. If I had not come, Eskat would be alive, I would not have been nearly killed, I would not have had to deal with Evarny, or my feelings about Thordh . . . but if I had not come, I would have felt the quake and strangers would have come to tell me I must leave . . . I would have been driven away from my

home like Sainted Skaathe in the Legend of the Ungrateful Daughter.
   Evarny offers me a slice of meat. No, he offers his house . . . he has kept it vacant all these years. Tikrow will take her wealth to her sister-in-law, and Nesskow's cold slice will come grudgingly from her husband. My hearts are striking at each other and I can hardly breathe from tiredness. It is too late that he cares for me, but for now, I think I will stay with him.

Fthel V: *Zamos's Brothel and Cleopatra's Rug*

It is your old friend Kobai here, that has been telling you this story, swimming and dreaming the long times without day or night, no lantern light to bring me home. In my belly is growing a little fluttery thing like a fish wriggle when it come between my hands, in the waters where I live, where I used to live. Iron Man tell me it is my baby that move and swim in me. But he don't tell me when I get to go home. When we get to go, we two sure don't go swimming home from here . . .
   :Iron Man, tell me we will swim at home and be free, even if it is not so!:
   :I have never told a lie in my life. Kobai, you will swim and be free on your home world. By the Soul of the Cosmos, I will make it so.:
   :I love you, Iron Man.:
   "And I love you, Kobai," said the Lyhhrt.

"Lebedev, I think I am going mad. I truly love that woman. I have sunk into depravity and individualism. I am a pervert."
   "You are lonely," Lebedev said. "There is no shame or

crime in that. I'm sure I am nearer insanity from endless days of dealing skambi than you will ever be."

"From only twenty-five days?" The Lyhhrt stood for a moment like a stopped robot. "Are you making one of those incongruous remarks, Lebedev? A 'joke'?"

"It will be no joke if your masters discover that I am faking a blood disease to be able to come and speak with you. Either I will be fired because they are worried that my medical expenses cost too much or they will simply find out and kill us both—alternatively I will become really sick because you are taking so much blood from me, and then they will fire me, if I do not die first."

"You will not grow ill or die, and you will not be discharged until I arrange it so. All three of us—four to include the unborn—are leaving in one tenday at three stads and fourteen minims past the point of midnight."

It was just two tendays since the Lyhhrt had mentioned leaving, and Lebedev had hoped that the idea was a mere brainstorm, a mad whim. He had not cared much for the talk of blood and egg-layers, after his encounter in the corridor with the strange being the Lyhhrt had been speaking to; he did not trust the Lyhhrt to save Kobai, and his mind had been prickling with plan after discarded plan.

His hope of making an ally of the O'e woman, Ai'ia, had been blasted; her being demoted and degraded was a bad sign for him as well: he was careful to avoid her, and in a few days she reappeared in the Gamblar, but looking fearful and sparkless. He had managed to get out of the brothel with a coveted employees' pass to the black market and spend half his earnings on fresh hydroponic fruit and vegetables; even contrived to pass a message to his contact, but no new instructions had come for him. He had cooked and feasted grandly, but nervously.

He thought of the Lyhhrt spiriting Kobai away in her

tank, as if it were a package to be smuggled away under a jacket. "You have a witching hour, and will roll her up in a blanket, I suppose, like Cleopatra."

"I know nothing of a cleopatra or any hours but Galactic Standard. Sarcasm is something I know well." The Lyhhrt started a centrifuge by some invisible signal. "I am sure you are not an ignorant man but I doubt you know much about the Ix."

"Nothing."

"You saw me talking to one of them and asked if they were Neutrals."

"Ah." Sparkles and flashes. He felt his mind trying to twist away at the thought. "Egg-layers."

"Also they emit a pheromone very much like nerve gas, a sense-disrupting drug. I, of course, in my workshell, am not affected."

Lebedev did not ask what the Ix looked like to the Lyhhrt. "Blood," he said.

"They do not lay eggs in blood. They would like to lay them in Lyhhrt." He stopped the centrifuge and directed the computer to steady a pacemaker in one of Zamos's clients. "Many years ago when the Ix discovered Lyhhr, we were peaceful Neutrals with no defenses except the powers of our minds. Unfortunately I'yax is our nearest living neighbor. Its people came from their dark fouled world to invade our caves and marshes, and discovered that they could rejuvenate themselves in our bodies.

"We fought them with all of our mental powers, but those were not enough to drive them off more than once. Even with all our crafts we could not armor millions, and we had radio, but no space flight. We looked for help from Galactic Federation. Because we were not members and at the time were not doing work for them, they gave us none.

"I do not blame them in a way. My people, like those

snobs the Khagodi, would not even speak to those they considered lesser mortals then, and the category included all outworlders and especially non-telepaths. It is only within the last hundred and fifty years that we—like the Khagodi—learned to do so. Also, of course, other species did not find us attractive. They felt about us much the same as you do, Lebedev, and were just as frightened."

Lebedev shrugged. He could not say that he had changed his mind.

"Galactic Federation did, however, recommend our problem to Zamos—not the brothel-keepers' division, but the scientific one, the Zamos Foundation in Surgical Techniques, which was always working on new materials and practices, manufacturing blood and flesh to heal bodies destroyed in wars that worlds and nations should not fight. They provided an artificial organic medium for the Ix to lay eggs in, and after that they left us alone.

"We swore an oath and signed a contract selling our souls to Zamos for one Cosmic Cycle—one hundred and twenty-nine of our years—and agreed to serve them in whatever capacity they chose. We learned to be physicians and surgeons, lawyers, metalworkers, and philosophers, then at last joined Galactic Federation and served their worlds—but Zamos came first. Even when we learned how to build ships and arm them we did ugly things because our world was saved and we swore that oath. Zamos had made us whatever we are.

"The Cosmic Cycle ends in ten days on that hour I named for you. Zamos's people refuse to let us go, they say we are too valuable to them and know too many secrets. They have been sending the Ix to us as a warning. They have broken their part of the oath completely."

"It usually happens with those soul-selling deals," Lebedev said.

"But we are leaving. I might have stayed longer, but they are planning to move her two days later. Their plan calls for a private yacht to take her to Shen Four, to the Headquarters of the Zamos Foundation.

"Lebedev, I do not interfere in Zamos's business in providing what men believe is pleasure, in a place that conducts a legal business, and even if I had wanted to I have been powerless because of my oath. But now that the oath is broken and both of us know what is going on it is time to move out. You will demonstrate the proofs to your superiors, and I will help you deliver the evidence." He gestured toward the wall behind which Kobai was swimming. "Before you came I made the mistake of persuading her keepers to put her in the window, to attract people like you and Skerow. That was naive—how many such people are there who pass by a brothel?—and it was difficult convincing her captors that she was not suitable as a brothel toy. She is lucky to be alive. If I could not save your friend Jacaranda Drummond I saw how she was revenged, and I will save this one."

Lebedev was less interested than Manador in revenge. "How will you bring her out?"

"You do not really want to know yet. I have sworn to deliver her to her home waters and keep her available to the World Court on Khagodis."

"That's well and good, but I also need evidence to build the case against Zamos here."

"You have Ai'ia."

Lebedev stopped to think. His mind had been so full of everything else about the Lyhhrt's wild schemes that he had not thought of her as an actor in them. "If I can get her out of this place she must have shelter . . . I suppose I could arrange for that."

"Good." The Lyhhrt took a tube from his centrifuge and

poured a drop of liquid on a blotting paper. It looked like blood.

"Yes," said Lebedev. "One more question." Lebedev felt a dizziness and a dart of pain in his ear that he knew were not merely physical: dread underlay them.

"Yes," said the Lyhhrt. He picked up the blotting paper and held it up in his bronze hand as if it were a passport to the world of Lyhhr. His sundisk head turned toward Lebedev. "How I get myself out of here. Cleopatra in the rug. Not in all these beautiful casings you have seen me in all these days, that everyone knows from forty *evvu* distance. That is something you do want to know."

Lebedev could not bring himself to say that he wanted to know it.

"I will leave inside you, Lebedev. In your stomach pouch or between the muscle layers of your belly or back. I believe your digestive acids would be harmful even to my reinforced integument, and since I have satisfied myself with samples of your blood and the tissue of the cyst in your ear that they are compatible—most likely the latter. Small opening, no pain, scarless mending."

He watched Lebedev throwing up into his spotless sink and said, "I cannot understand why you are so distressed, Lebedev. I am the one who is taking all the risk. Whatever happens, I am going to inhibit you from telling anyone of this—something I have done only once before in my singular existence. It is a grave matter to me. Speak up now if you cannot bear it. I have sworn to free her, and if necessary I will stay and die here—a life spent here is not worth living—but if I died Zamos's minions would not learn the lesson you and I both feel they need so badly. Say now, Lebedev." He offered a square of white linen.

Lebedev took it with an infinitely slow hand, spat into it, wiped his mouth and said, "Yes."

* * *

Tally Hawes bumped into him at an intersection of the grey corridors he traveled to reach his room. "Whose ghost have you seen, Lev? Your hair is on end and you look scared shitless."

"Someone has been walking on my grave," Lebedev said. He felt rather as if someone had been doing it on his body.

"I've got no vodka but I can find you some good dope mixed with real tobacco if you want to walk me there."

"Why not?" said Lebedev, even though he wanted nothing more than to disappear behind a wall hanging or under a carpet. He looked at his watch and saw that it was past midnight. "What more is there to lose?" He would do anything to turn his mind from the swimmer Kobai, the ranked red lattices of embryos, the Lyhhrt as embryo, the wrath of Manador, and the deadly empty game of skambi.

Tally was a veteran employee and lived in oxygen country with the more expensive women, even though she had not been one of them as long as Lebedev knew her. Her windowless room was small and neat as the china shepherdess spreading her skirts on the tiny shelf which matched the ormolu mirror above it. As neat as Tally, herself very much like the china figurine in her swirling skirts and flounces. The chest of drawers was of old dark wood carved with vines and serpents; a red and black Spanish shawl with lustrous fringes was hanging from a hook on the back of the door, but the room smelled of innocence, of talcum powder, like a baby.

Lebedev thought that these possessions looked, if not antique, as if they had been burnished by use and care in many countries on more than one world, and could not be spoiled beside a hard bed or shabby sofa. They made him think of his soup crock, and of the tiny disgusting tethumekh Skerow loved.

"Well, Lev, I can offer you some cheap brandy or tea along with the Zephyrelles." She offered a silver box filled with cigarettes, took and lit one for herself.

He sat down on the sofa. "I have not seen those for years." Through the papery walls he could hear the sounds of lives around him, a woman singing to one side, a couple of others talking, toward the back.

"They still mix a good Turkish tobacco with the dope. The house gives them away—to customers, but the rest of us get them anyhow."

He took one in memory of his youth, though he had lost most of his taste for them, and smiled at the mauve paper and gold tip.

She poured brandy and asked abruptly: "You really were in prison, weren't you? I thought at first you were having me on."

"Yes, I was in prison."

"You must have done extra hard time, being a rozzer and all."

"Hard enough." Right now he wished he were back there. "It put me off a life of crime."

Tally laughed. "I think you're full of it, Lev. But you were always a decent sort. I don't think you ever came within a light-year of being bent, I think you're still something of a rozzer."

Lebedev did not look around for the spy-eye. The Ly-hhrt had said: *I will protect you,* and Lebedev would let him do it. "Too bad you never had the opportunity to see the beautiful bruises I collected." He spoke the words more sharply than he meant them.

Someone yelled at the singing woman to shut up, and the two who had been talking began to fight. There were curses and the thump of a head or shoulder knocking against the wall. The same sort of noises Lebedev heard in his own quarters. He very much wanted to be out of the room, this little capsule of stifling homeliness, loneliness inside Zamos's brothel, and at the same time he wanted something more, much more, than the prospect of being caught and killed stealing Zamos's slaves and dying with the Lyhhrt writhing inside him.

Tally said, "Sorry, Lev, never meant to rattle your skeletons."

"We are old friends, Tally, and I am not offended." She seemed to him just a little drunk, and he thought perhaps she had always seemed that way to him. He looked into her eyes and stopped believing that Zamos's people had sent her to entrap him, or the Lyhhrt, to console him. He took her hand. After a moment she disengaged it and opened the clasps of her dress; she took it off and hung it carefully on a padded hanger in her closet, then wrapped herself in the Spanish shawl over her thin silk shift, smoking until he finished his drink and let her undo his buttons.

He came down toward morning at a time when there was not much business and the few remaining customers were being helped or prodded to exits. A shortcut took him through plushier districts along softly lit corridors. The silky notes of lute and violin, and a beam of light spilling into the hall, drew his attention to an arched opening into a round thick-carpeted vestibule with wall hangings and gilt chairs. The heavy door, standing ajar, opened into a perfumed grotto of sunset rose and mauve, of divans and sunken bath fringed with exotic ferns and fleshy blossoms.

He paused for a moment to look inside. There were three fair-haired naked children lounging on the bath's edge, two girls and a boy. They turned their heads to look at him with insolent eyes.

Suddenly they jumped up laughing, joined hands in a little circle to dance three or four steps to the melody, and draped themselves around the pool again, hands on mouths to muffle their giggles.

Looking sharply he saw that they were not pink and gold, but darker and greyer in the creases of their skin, and not young either. They were a form of the O'e, and in this instant he envisioned them forever trapped in their thin false childhood. He could not see how he might save them.

Shen IV: *The Minotaur*

"Hey!" Ned Gattes woke up in a closet, a former lavatory, in the Labyrinths of Zamos's Palace of Knossos, on Shen IV. Zella was breathing into his ear and her cold hand was rapidly warming in his hot creases. He relaxed; Zamos's people would not have awakened him that way. "Oh. I like that." He twisted to look at his chronometer. "Not time to get up . . ."

"There was a cleaner mech came in here."

"What? Why didn't you tell me? Those machines can report us."

"This one won't. It came to fill up on water for its scrubber. When it smelt us it just went away quietly. I've seen it happen before, it won't bother us."

"Um . . ." He thought of the robot cleaner crouching nearby when he was listening to Spartakos's declamation, and pushed the thought from his mind again.

"Ned?" Zella kissed him.

She cared for him, trusted him, had waited for the peak of her right moment to make love to him. Ned Gattes stretched a little to ease the sore point where his shoulder blade was grinding into the granite basin; then nudged his mind toward youthful excitement and sex at midnight, and rolled over into her open thighs.

"That's better . . ."

They were out of there before dawn, mixing with the fogged-up stragglers trying to wake into energetic life by stuffing themselves with seed cakes and bitter chicory, squeezing fingers in their ears against late-razzing bugle-bands that echoed fearfully in the vast lengths of the halls.

Signifying the break of dawn, the cooling systems beneath the floor began to whine, at first, and then roar before they settled into the steady vibration that made the floor seem almost alive. News of treaties and wars and new worlds to fight them over flickered on the walls. The beggars, whose presence had been masked by the evening crowds, were yawning and stirring, ready to play on the guilt of penitents with updowns and hangovers. Robotechs in antiqued silver, fancier than the one Zella had seen, rolled inconspicuously along the walls and entrances laying down liquid films of cleaner that they wiped up after themselves.

"We look too much like mechanics down here," Ned said. "We gotta flame these scrags we're wearing and get something that fits."

"I don't know where to find scrip in these places," Zella said. "You want my cashcard?" She dug for it in her belt pouch.

He hesitated. The thought had lingered in his mind that Zella's defection did not need to be permanent, tempers would cool, Kati'ik would be displaced sooner or later and if he himself was caught Zella did not have to be involved and could safely return to her work. This idea was his way of trying to protect her, the only way he could think of.

"Not yet," he said at last. "Let's save it."

"Where we going?"

He was looking about, in a relaxed way, not staring or curious. Not desperate. "I want to find a GoldMine office . . . you probably know where they are better than I do."

"I've never done anything but fight down here. They're usually around the boozers and brothels."

"We went by a lot of those last night, but I don't want to go back."

"I'm sure there's more than one GoldMine, this place goes on long after you want to stop. Down that way there's a branch of The Pig and The Peppercorn that caters to New and Old Earthers, where new-dogs hang around. But I'm not going in there. Some pug off a night shift might know me."

"No, we won't even go close to it." They had been moving cautiously near the walls behind the path of a robomech, and now Ned took Zella's hand and slipped into the ever-growing stream.

Restaurants and drugsters set their sound systems going, spielers unfolded their ballies and players tuned viols and lutolins. The sound level rose, but still kept its separate filaments of percussion and melody; Ned and Zella could hear above their heads a troubadour clearing his throat and singing in a warm baritone, as if to himself:

> *Rain falls softly on the city . . .*

They paused to listen while the dull roar of the ventilators hit the backs of their heads, and thought of the upper stories where the sun beat down so hard.

> *Rain falls softly on the city . . .*
> *Rain falls gently in the country*
> *Sweetly it falls in the wilderness—*
> *And savage the rain behind my eyes . . .*
> *Savage rain, O savage rain . . .*

"It used to rain like that in my country when I was young and growing up savage." Zella said.

"The rain in Starry Nova wasn't anything you'd much want to remember . . . where I grew up was savage." Ned thought for a moment. "I guess I can see you as a fierce person." Although he spoke seriously he was careful to smile when he said this.

She clasped his hand tighter. "I grew up in a farm commune, I'd been engineered strong. I was heavier then, a chubby teener. My mother's side-husband got too interested in me. I knocked him out. He calmed down, everything went on well enough, but I was afraid of how angry I got, of enjoying it. The place got stifling. I had to get out."

The Pig and the Peppercorn was a small bar faced with little smoked-glass window panes, beyond them a basic low boozer full of smoke and ugly customers. Ned stared through the windows and then at Zella. "You've really been inside there? I sure wouldn't hurry into that place."

"Why not? I just wanted to see everything. I do know how to discourage attention I don't want."

"Yeh." Ned laughed. "I guess now I'm with you I could go in."

Next door there was a Bettor's Parlor, and past that the GoldMine, an Interworld public office where all comers could borrow money on their working cards. Ned did not go in but stood hand on hip a few paces away from the door, tapping the brass-colored cashcard disk against his teeth.

A thin dark reptilian detached him?self from the pillar of which he had seemed to be part of the carving and sidled up to him. "Cashing in a card, you-boy?"

Ned considered him: one of a species he had not personally met, he thought he recognized a Sziis from his shadowy way of moving; he seemed to be going sideways no matter where he was heading. "Are you paying?"

"I'll get you one third more, same cost," said the Sziis.

"I'll take it." Zella pulled at his sleeve, but Ned had always used private agents for getting money, and took her hand to reassure her. He had been tumbled by Security only once, and then talked his way free. He and Zella followed the Sziis, who was wearing what looked like a tube of silver scales and was zigzagging along like a lightning bolt, to a hole-in-the-wall advertising duty-free cigarettes; it had a tiny square window filled with gold-tipped Zephyrelle dopesticks in pink, blue, and mauve papers, but sold none.

Stepping inside Ned found an office with just enough floor space to accommodate four squatters of various species playing skambi with cashcard disks and smoking something that made Ned dizzy and was not Zephyrelles. The Sziis handed over a cashbook and while Ned was counting the leaves said, in an offhand way, "I can get you anything. Anything you like."

"No, thanks," Ned said, "I think I have enough!"

The Sziis stared at him with black bead eyes, and licked his mouth with a pink tongue thin as paper. "I can get you work. Nice work for a good healthy boy."

"I bet you can," Ned said, grinning and skipping away. "Wake up in an alley in my skin—if I get to keep it? That kind of work?"

He found Zella waiting outside, split the cashbook in two, and pushed half into Zella's hands.

"Oh no, Ned, I don't need all that."

"Oh yes you do! We might get separated, and there's all kinds of bad luck you can only get out of with hard cash. Like this stuff we're wearing, that says: 'Casino Pugs on the loose.' Now we can find some new feathers."

"Feathers are the last thing I want," Zella said grimly.

"Silks, then. You can show me the best stores."

"Down that way there's a good one I remember, but I don't like the women's clothes they have. I'll look around."

"Don't go too far."

"No. Let's meet under that balcony." She pointed to a balustrade at the top of an escalator leading to the floor above. She put an arm around him and he kissed her. "I don't want to be far from you, Ned. I hope I never do." Her face shone on him like the sun, and for a moment he almost forgot the hostility hidden among the moving people around him like snakes in a thicket.

Ned parted from her at a boutique where he clothed himself in nuvopunque hypersuede and cylon, then had his hair cut butch and gold-dusted, and his chin depilated by a barber who was high-toned enough not to remark on the strange texture of the skin over his jaw.

When he came out from under the flickering lights of this establishment he had to look hard into the shadows under the balcony through the dazzles in his eyes. Zella was not there.

He thought, She went to have her hair done, probably, and was comforted by the very banality of this idea. He slipped through the streams of workers and early revelers toward the escalator, hands in pockets and plastering a look of foolish enjoyment across his face. A movement up on the balcony made him look there and he saw two Security men, a uniformed Solthree and a Dabiri in a leather tabard, standing with hands on the railing. Staring at him.

One bolt of terror hit him and he could feel his jaw tingling, whether to flash white or red he could not tell; two pairs of eyes locked with his, the uniform raised a hand with pointing finger extended like a gun about to fire, and as it came down, Ned saw Zella five steps away from them. She was wearing a little hat on her blond-white hair, a flurry of black lace or feathers that came down her forehead, and dressed in something long, tight, and sequined black with a froufrou around the shoulders. She was rushing toward them, her red mouth smiling and speaking, her cheeks flushed or rouged, her red-gloved hands—her arms so white—reaching out as if to embrace them, embracing them, fingers touching lightly on the back of the man's neck (Ned felt the touch, its twinge of nerve running up into his scalp and down his spine). How could they not give her their attention?

"Zella!" he yelled or thought he yelled, but the sound was caught and dissipated in a screaming rush of second-class tourists on the down escalator, and he was gathered and swept up in it, no one looked his way, not Zella or Security, and by the time he fought his way up to the balcony they were all gone.

He stood in shock with his hands frozen to the carved serpents on the railing. He could not tell whether she had been saving or betraying him, with that light touch, as she had touched him in the darkness. His mind was awry, he knew that, but he could not set it straight. A man with diamond rings, a head taller than he and wearing purple velvet, was cooing in his ear, but his arm was firm over the thickness of his money belt. Ned blew him a kiss and danced away, shucked off the arms of a woman, a Kylklad or another kind of woman wearing a suit of feathers, yes, buying fancy feathers was a mistake, getting gold-dusted had been wrong, meant nothing, with Zella gone.

It was the smoke dulling his eyes, it was not Zella he had seen with the men, she would be waiting for him down there. No. He had seen Zella and no one else; she was not down there.

She had her I.D. and cashcard, no one would harm her. The Kylklad woman had harmed her already.

She had gone with those Security men in order to save him. She had gone with them because . . .

But she had not given him away. Because she had not seen him.

Ned shook himself out of these riotous thoughts. Unless Zella had taken those men somewhere else he could not find her except by going back to the top floor. Into the jaws of the same monster that had killed Jacaranda. No number of desperate rationalizations could change that, and no good would come of giving himself up no matter what Zella had done. Crowds and noise would hide him for a while, if his jaw did not flash like a neon on a bally.

If I'd been smart I'd have asked that Szüs where to find an outside line. Maybe I'd have been smarter to stay away from him altogether. He might have fingered me.

He went back down on the same escalator that had led him and Zella into the Labyrinths the night before. Halfway down he saw the two uniforms, Varvani this time, standing at the foot—watching riders boarding the up ramp. He turned his head away from them, looking at the streaming crowds until he hit bottom, then slipped around the pillar and lost himself among them. Those two might have been waiting for someone else.

He and the place had become different within fifteen Standard hours of this twenty-six-hour day. He felt so deeply the absence of Zella's touch at his side it was as if a part of himself had been torn away. The effort of keeping the turmoil of his mind below the boiling point flattened every-thing that reached his senses; the deep low roar of a thousand chattering good-natured human beings beat threateningly at his ears, he blinked in the flashing lights and the smokes of cooking caught his throat, the song of sweet rain turned bitter:

> *Savage rain, O savage rain,*

the lutolin player sang:

> *savage rain stains the city, and*
> *the country where it falls*
> *and the pain behind my eyes*
> *is the rain, the savage rain in*
> *the wilderness, the rain*
> *O the rain . . .*

He stopped in the doorway of a shop to catch his breath and pull himself together. Zella running toward the men and touching, Zella running—

He became aware of the darkness at his back without quite seeing it, and turned. The tiny shop, of less breadth than the span of his arms, was empty; the Lyhhrt, who had hammered thin gold bangles and woven filigrees that were beautiful no matter what the price, had gone, leaving no more than his shimmering gold-leaf world-symbol on the door.

This emptiness—beyond the glass was a blackness deep as space—struck Ned oddly, for no reason he could recall. He had never known this Lyhhrt, though he had bought plenty of Lyhhrt trinkets for women at other places. He had seen no Lyhhrt at all in Zamos's Palace, not even in the doctor's office where the mech had treated him.

It was the chilling emptiness of the place that touched him. He moved away along the walls and shopfronts where the noise ricocheted with multiple echoes above his head against the friezes of news reports and stock prices, looking across the moving thicknesses of bodies in all the colors and textures that thirty kinds of human flesh can show, handed, clawed, tailed and tentacled, some with eyestalks, some half metal or plastic, one or two double-headed.

He nearly tripped over the beggar.

She was crouched beside him. Not crouched, but sitting against the wall with her back straight, legs folded and head bent to look into the depths of her bowl, her hands were folded in it. One of his own species, dressed in neat blue denims, her hair braided and her mouth surprisingly rouged bright pink. She was thin, strung out probably on more than one drug, nowhere near smiling. Not Zella. The pale hair that shadowed into the braid was not blond but had whitened with age—she was half again as old as Zella. But he could see by the set of her body that she had been strong once, a fighter to begin with, God knew what else after. There was no way for anyone lost in the Labyrinth to find a passage home.

Ned could not keep himself from tearing a leaf from his book and giving it to her. She raised her head and looked at him with eyes like smashed glass, and whispered thanks. He hurried away feeling like the coward he had pretended to be when Jacaranda had let him beat her at the entrance to another labyrinth.

Before he had gone three steps there was a scuttling back of him, and a squeeze-box voice that he recognized said, "Ah-yee, here is that healthy boy again who needs nothing from me, not even work!"

Ned looked around to find the Sziis in the act of circling him like the stripe on a barber pole. "What do you want?" He could not be sure this was the one who had cashed his card for him; he had never seen another.

The Sziis's head was dancing at eye level now with his tongue frilling out through his tiny sharp fangs, four of his little feet jigging to keep balance, tapping their rattling claws.

"He seems me different in his new goodies, but my sharp tongue smells him the same!" The silver scales writhed in the flickering red, blue, and green lights.

"You got your cut, didn't you?" Ned said. "Let me go by!" He kept his arm up but was careful to make no offensive movements. He dared not get into a fight down here, and those little teeth had very sharp points.

He turned away from the dancing colors, half-hypnotized—more than half. He had not kept watch on the crowds, and if the two thugs working their way forward with their eyes fixed on him were not the ones who had punched him up on the gym floor, it made no difference. The Sziis had fingered him.

He grinned and snarled, "Smarted me up, percentnik? Sold me to the bull-chuckers for a grab of my cashbook?" In the instant that the Sziis blinked and listened, Ned thrust out his foot and swept it under the serpentine body. The Sziis flopped with his four hands thrashing and his six feet pumping wildly.

Ned grabbed a handful of tokens from his pocket and flung them over the heads of the crowd at his pursuers, a Varvani who was a half head taller than almost everyone else, and a Bimanda who was taller by a head. They were not uniformed but wearing the same kind of pugs' clothing he had discarded. Those around them, distracted by what seemed a shower of gold, set up a flurry of catching and scuffling, and Ned slipped away.

But the crowd blocked him as well, and the Bimanda, a pale shark-shaped woman with a lot of teeth, swam through the press of it and caught him by the ankle as he was ducking under a bally. There was a mixed troupe from five worlds dancing, and the music and spielers were so loud that no one noticed what was going on beneath.

Ned twisted on his back to face the Bimanda; a flicker of

light from between the bally's slats caught her staring gold eyes and the triple racks of her teeth. He saw in the shadows that she was armed with a knife and reaching for it, but she did not have quite enough space to move her massive arms between her body and the platform, and could not thrust. While dancers thumped and trombones blatted above him he kicked her in the throat with his other foot, and when she let go his ankle and pulled away gasping, he rolled out from under the other edge, then jumped up and dodged away without waiting to dust himself off. His breastbone was as cold as if the knife had lodged there: whoever wanted him now wanted him dead.

He paused in a doorway to take breath and was almost knocked down by a clump of burly customers coming out. He realized that he was in the entrance of the grim tavern he and Zella had come through on their way to the alley. The figures that yesterday had been hunched over mugs of beer and *yoptai*, smoking *jhat*, were the same, or same as no difference. He would not have minded sitting down among them. He had not eaten since the early morning, or paused for rest since he had lounged in the barber's chair for that comfortable few moments.

He did not dare stop for that, but he tossed a brass token and took a handful of dried *kep* seeds while he fought his way through the smoke and made a side trip to the urinal, pausing for a few handfuls of brackish water. Coming out he heard voices raised in the smokedrifts: "Nobody come in here that you want! Sit down and order or get out!"

No one would talk to Security that way. He ran, and hard. Security at least would not fling knives at him. Their justice was rough, but over half their salary was paid by Interpol, and they balked at murder. He pushed out into the alley and did not stop at the cupboard he and Zella had found refuge in the night before. He heard the pounding steps of his trackers too close behind him and the sound of shattering when the tall Bimanda ran into one of the hanging lamps and swung it against the wall.

The alley seemed to stretch endlessly without branching off, but as soon as he had the thought, he saw not twenty paces away a robot cleaner swinging around a corner to fill the breadth of the corridor and coming forward head-on fast with flashing lights and quivering antennas. He paused an instant to catch his breath, and a stunner bolt hissed over his shoulder and scored the wall. He took three springing leaps and vaulted over the big machine like a Cretan bull-dancer.

After that everything he had was used up and he had twisted his knee landing, but his pursuers were thick-bodied probable wrestlers, who had as much chance of flying as of leaping. The machine would not run them over, but would not let them pass either. They could do nothing but go back and duck into whatever door they found open.

Ned hobbled to the passageway the robot had come from and found a dead end leading to a closet like the one he had sheltered in. Panting he went on half-skipping down the alley, wound up with terror of another machine and afraid to try the latches on any of the doors he passed.

At the very end there was a door with an EXIT symbol straight ahead and to the left a narrow passageway leading to the open doorway of a restaurant kitchen. Clouds of steam were coming from it and he could see the shadowy outlines of bussers scraping food from plates and bowls. The smell was of garbage, too rancid to make him hungrier.

He lingered for a moment, not knowing where the exit led, not willing to cause a stir in the kitchen. A noise of crashing pots and clattering dishes broke out and two tall figures who did not care about making a stir burst through the clouds of steam yelling obvious obscenities in a language Ned did not know.

He pushed the heavy bar of the door. It opened with a hiss and let him into a small square space lit only by a dim red light, and leading only to a similar door. The first one shut behind him with a breath like a sigh. Only an electronic key would open it again. He heard faint laughter on the other side, and the words, "Got him now!" With dread, he began to realize where he was.

One of the thugs was pushing down the latch. Desperately he lunged at the bar of the outer one and fell, he thought, into space. The thin cold air dried his sweat in an instant, and as he rolled down three steps and landed flat on his back on concrete, the white sun Shen dropped beyond the world and the copper rim of the sky turned black and blazed with stars. It seemed to him that their lights were lancing themselves at him while he gasped for air beneath them.

Ned bit down on his panic and forced himself to take slow breaths that did not satisfy his need for air. He picked himself up achingly, and after a moment his oxygen capsule switched on. He dared not breathe too deeply or it would be used up before he could move far. He was shuddering in the freezing cold.

Shen IV had no moons, and the lights in its night sky were those of stars or other worlds, doubly bright because the air was so thin. Ned saw that the square of concrete was a buzzer landing pad, marked with tire tracks and fuel drippings. The area surrounding it was thick with ground trees furred with small grey leaves, twisted stems of wood swarming over the terrain ankle-thick as far as the eye could see. On the far side of the massive building was the long stretch of wharfs lining the seacoast.

His pursuers had not followed him out. He looked up at the huge arched windows on the upper floors; they were full of life and warmth. No one could see him out here, and not many were eager to save him. Tomorrow if he survived the night he would fry in the sun's furious heat when it reached the peak of noon. Trying to calm the fear clawing inside him like a cat in a sack, he climbed the steps again and looked around. He saw a narrow stone pavement along the wall, half overgrown by twisting branches. It led away from both sides of the door and neither direction looked better than the other. His capsule sounded a warning ping! that told him he had only half a Standard hour's worth of oxygen left. He went down the steps to his left calculating that it would bring him to one of the Labyrinths' entrances.

The wall was still faintly warm. He kept it at his back, sidling along the narrow passage to avoid stray branches; parts of the flagstones were cracked and forced up, and some of the blocks of the wall had cracks thrusting with grey lichenous growths.

When he passed several broad porthole windows set into the wall and found them completely dark he realized the direction he had chosen was wrong. He had reached an old section that did not seem to be inhabited at all. The capsule pinged again. He rested for a moment and heard the hiss of the airlock door, and a sound like oxygen tanks banging against it, then several voices. His trackers had not given up.

He kept going. Zella was far away somewhere on this world, so far away he could not find her, would not think of her. Ping! He stopped again but heard nothing of the searchers; perhaps they had gone in the other direction, or the sounds had come only from his imagination.

Suddenly the wall disappeared; he stumbled backward reeling to keep balance and found himself in a shadowy recess. There was a door here but the stems of the ground-trees had woven themselves across it. He crawled over and tried to wrench them away, but they would not move, felt at the door, but could not find a latch. Ping!

Three lights flashed on, in off tones of primary colors. They were set into the walls of the recess at points half a meter above his head.

"Traveler—"

He jumped. The voice came from speakers beneath the lights, but the image appeared just beside him. It was the old hologram of Zamos—Ned had not seen it on the floors above—shaking his beckoning hand free of his sleeve in a dramatic gesture, sapphires and rubies glittering on his wrist. He looked deeply faded and aged, like a weathered statue; the three transmitters were coated with dust and salt from the offshore winds, and the image was eroded. It spoke again.

"I am Zamos at your service, always ready to guide you. Do you need help, Traveler?"

Ned hesitated for only a second. He needed help. "Yes."

The figure said, "Guest of Zamos, this is an emergency exit. Have you become detached from your tour group?"

"Yes!" The word hissed through his chilled teeth. It was true enough.

There was a moment of silence while the computer controlling Zamos weighed the answer to his question. Ned listened for the sounds of the hunters, and thought he heard a faint cry.

"If you wish to return to your tour, please place your Zamos Tours Identicard against the sensitive plate in the left side of the doorway."

Ned swallowed and said, "I don't have it with me."

"You may also use any other I.D. bearing your retinal pattern. Always keep your Zamos Tours Identicard on your person at all times when you are with us."

Ned fumbled the I.D. disc from his belt with thick stiff fingers and pressed it against the faintly glowing square in the lintel. After a moment the door slid open, grinding fiercely on unused runners.

He heard the snort of a buzzer's engine starting up and the bright flash of its searchlight over the dark cold terrain. He had no idea where he was going but stepped quickly over the tangled branches into a dimly lit airlock with dust and dead leaves in its corners. The door closed behind him and another opened in front; he came through it into a broad corridor where the air was warm but musty.

The moment his foot touched the floor the colored lights quickened to life above him down the hall, startling him, and the image of Zamos beckoned once again. Ned glanced ahead and back; there was darkness in both directions. He followed.

Fans began to hum, and the lightstrips lit before and faded after Zamos as he floated down a hall floor gritty with dust and spattered with long-dried stains. Not far away thousands were eating, drinking, gambling, coupling, singing, dancing, fighting . . . Zella was very far away. Zamos's step was noiseless, and his own seemed too loud.

Zamos pointed to a dark open doorway. "There you see a demonstration of cattle cloning for species of twenty-three worlds. We have been engaged in such work for over two hundred years Standard." At his gesture a dim light illuminated an empty room littered with twisted shelf supports and warped glastex tank panels. Ned felt cold again. Here the silence behind Zamos's flat synthetic voice was palpable, unreality deeper with every step.

"And here you see scientists attending a course of lectures on the deadly virus-molds that pollute the jungles and tundras of Kemalan Five and Six." A door opened into a wilderness of toppled lecterns and scattered books and cassettes.

Ned listened for the clamor of his followers and said aloud, "This is crazy. What am I doing here?"

Zamos's image turned and looked him in the eye. "If you follow me, Ned Gattes, you will be safe."

"I am crazy," said Ned.

"Here is the highlight of this tour," Zamos said. He raised a finger and a door slid open. The hallway had ended.

Ned was hit by a hot burst of stinking air. In the ceiling yellow lightstrips brightened, and he saw the barred cages. A roomful of them.

"It is the very heart of Zamos," said the image. "Here we create life that—" Ned stopped paying attention to it. He was standing by the bars of a cage where two naked figures lay bedded on straw, snoring faintly. They were the pair of one-armed fighters who had attacked him, nested like spoons with their long single arms crossing over each other, their greyish bodies glistening with sweat. A clumsy apparatus wound with pipes and studded with dials and gauges hung overhead and dropped water and food pellets into pans.

"—have engineered many new species easily bred for cattle or hunting . . ."

In a clear-walled enclosure beside them a hairy male figure with its arms tightly wrapped around its head twisted in a dream and thrashed out with thick blunt feet like hooves; the walls had many kick marks. It flung out its arms and Ned saw the pale curved horns, the squared bull's snout of dark red hardened flesh that was not truly a bull's and not quite half-human, the heavy pelt spreading over the head and shoulders like a bull's hide. Ned wanted to wrench his eyes away and could not. He had seen a creature like this at a mall freak show, bellowing in terror, and thought it was a strange species, but this naked half-man had genitals like his own. It opened huge bovine eyes for a moment, saw nothing, and whipped at the straw with a sinewy tail; then raised the thick clubbed hands to wrench at its horns as if it would tear them from the skull, and burst out with a lowing cry of agony that was smothered by the thick plastic walls.

"—and so you see—"

"Shut up!" Ned yelled. Zamos's image stopped speaking. "You promised to lead me to safety, Zamos. Which way is it?"

"I will take you there this very moment," said Zamos. Ned followed him past the cage of some whimpering female creature all breasts and buttocks, with a minuscule head and limbs, and then something completely different with too many heads. After that he went down a narrow hallway lined with dials and control panels, and faced one more door.

"You may open that door for yourself," said the image of Zamos. "I am leaving you here, Ned Gattes. I am pleased to have met you. You need not reply. I don't exist here except as a hologram." Zamos bowed with a flourish and blinked out.

Ned pushed the door aside. Beyond it was a small round office lined with one huge cylindrical monitor screen in five panels. It was dead and cracked in places. The one light came from the ceiling and reflected off the lenses and antennas of a cleaning robot.

Ned stared. "What is this?"

"Did you enjoy the tour, Ned Gattes?" the robot asked in a crackling voice.

"Is this some kind of joke?" Ned saw his reflection on the slick surface around him, warped by the cylindrical shape. He was sweating from the heat in the room of cages. "What are you?"

"I am the last Lyhhrt on the world Shen Four. Perhaps the last on any alien world."

"I don't believe you."

"Do you not? I know that you are a Galactic Federation agent."

"Why do you think that? Who told you?"

"I sent for you, fellow! Or let us say that I/we did so. This entity received special permission to split, and my other half is on his way to the home I will never know again."

"I don't understand. Anything." The robot/Lyhhrt extended a folding limb and pushed forward a round stool for Ned to sit on. It was big and low to fit Varvani, but he sat down on it.

"Listen. Zamos made us sign an oath to serve them, and then made us their slaves. It is because we are so timid and fearful, and we would have been hideously destroyed."

"A lot of people think you're frightening!"

"We do our best. We served Zamos for a hundred and twenty-nine years. At the beginning they taught us everything, and we learned so fast they say now that we know too much."

"You made all those monsters—and the O'e."

"We helped develop the technology that made them. At first we were subtly tricked by Zamos, because the Research Foundation was set up for us, and Zamos wanted to sweeten its name. Those of us who worked here became separated from our fellows and lost touch with the Cosmic Spirit. We were so fearfully lonely. Our minds became as warped as those of Zamos's people. Zamos wanted to know how far they could go in making undifferentiated protoplasm become animals and persons, anything they could control. And we were so out of control that at one time we even thought that we might make independent organic bodies for ourselves instead of these metal ones. Disgusting thought!

"We told ourselves that we were serving humanity, and perhaps we did, a little, but we have committed terrible wrongs, and I know it is not enough that we tried to minimize the harm."

Ned said bitterly, "Nobody could minimize any harm to Jacaranda, and that swimming thing was—was more—"

"Yes, was more important. Jacaranda was aware of the risks, and we did our best to warn her."

"Did you," Ned said dully.

"The swimmer was the only definite evidence of a coerced being." The Lyhhrt said. "The O'e could be called indigenous, or a world of origin could be faked up for them. But the swimmer's species is known. It was created from your genotype of human stock on your own Old Earth, by the founders of Zamos, some hundreds of years back, not us, and bred for a few generations, then became sterile. The genetic data were saved, the type modified and cloned again and again because it had once been fertile. Slaves created on demand are immensely more valuable when they are self-breeding. This one is. She is pregnant.

"Once we realized her significance we had her put in the brothel window to attract Skerow. We were desperate to find ways of attracting attention to Zamos's crimes before they destroyed us in a manner just as terrible as the one we feared so much. We showed you on that machine, the 'pornograph,' what happened to Jacaranda in order to warn you that you were known and must take care. We were afraid to speak out against Zamos though they broke the oath they forced us to make. We hinted! Waiting and waiting for anyone to notice! Is no one outraged? Do all of you people of flesh want flesh in your power?"

The O'e woman's lip rouge burned on Ned's mouth. He had thought too often of Jacaranda and Poll Tenchard. But he did not think Zella would be flesh in anyone's power. He felt confused and gritty-eyed, not in shape to debate with Lyhhrt.

"But no—"

A hoarse voice outside the door yelled, "Gattes! Gattes, say something, Gattes! Tell us you aren't in there!" The door rang with kicks and another voice snarled, "Move away!"

"O God, they've found us!"

"I am unjust," the Lyhhrt went on, as if nothing had happened. "You are not all that bad—"

"Listen to that!" Ned said through his teeth. "You said I'd be safe here, and now we're both trapped!"

"No, no! You will escape quite easily! You must hear me out, it is my last chance to repent! We did not sink entirely into sin, because—"

There was a sound Ned could not quite identify. "They're going to come—"

"—because at the time we discovered the swimmer Kobai in Starry Nova we were able to find Skerow and Lebedev as well as you and your friend Jacaranda, who were not only willing but insisted on taking risks for us. Perhaps in places I do not know of there are others!"

The edge of the door began to spark, to shrink and soften, and in a moment the plastial was running in drops like rain down along the edge, and a voice cried, "Idiot! Don't touch it yet!"

"There must be others!" the Lyhhrt's voice went into a high whine, his limbs extended clattering and his antennas trembled. "Others!"

"You've gone crazy," Ned whispered.

"Keep in back of me," said the Lyhhrt. "I will save you." Ned maneuvered to get the bulky robot body between himself and the door.

An opening appeared and the snout of a Karnoshky flamer passed through. The Lyhhrt in a swift reach grabbed it and pulled, dragging a hand with it, and there was a scream.

The Lyhhrt howled in a huge earsplitting voice that woke chords of resonance in every surface around him, "One hundred and twenty-nine years of slavery! Imprisoned in impervious barriers! Going mad in loneliness! Endlessly falling in sin!"

He tossed the gun aside with one metal hand, hooked another in the soft edge of the door and folded it over like a sheet of paper. With the first he pulled in the Bimanda woman, knocked her down, then pulled her up by one arm and flung her against the screen; the impact widened its cracks, and she fell slumped. "A Cosmic Cycle of terror!" the Lyhhrt howled and reached out again.

"Watch it!" Ned yelled. There were two others with guns, the Varvani with a machine pistol that looked like a tiny thing in his massive hand. Ned reached for the Karnoshky, though he had no idea how to use one, had never before seen one up close.

"No, no!" The Lyhhrt pushed him roughly under the bank of controls that rimmed the screen, and Ned heard the whack-whack-whack of one gun and then another. Pieces of antennas and smashed sensor lenses flew against the walls but the Lyhhrt ran forward on his treads through the open doorway over these fragments, with his voice rising into a whine beyond hearing: "Say that you will testify, Ned Gattes! Say it!"

"I will!" Ned gasped. He heard a soft crunch and another scream, and more shots.

"Push that part of the console just behind you," said the Lyhhrt in quite a sane voice that quavered only a little from the blows it was absorbing. "You are not to be harmed."

"But you'll be—"

"Push it!"

Ned rose in a crouch and shoved at it; it swung back squealing from a hundred years of forgetfulness, and opened into a narrow dark passageway.

The Lyhhrt's limbs rattled once more and died. He had lost his voice control and bellowed: "NOW GET OUT! IT IS OVER!"

"But you—"

"GET OUT!"

The Lyhhrt was through the doorway, running toward the attackers with all the energy left to him. A stunner bolt hissed by Ned's ear and he waited no longer but backed out on all fours through the dark opening, then stood to push back the console where it formed part of a wall. He leaned on it in the darkness, catching his breath while his eyes accommodated to the light. He heard nothing from the other side.

After a few moments he saw that he was standing in another circular chamber at the top of a winding ramp. A light was slowly mounting from below, casting strange shadows as it came. He shrank against the wall.

A voice said, "It is I, Spartakos."

Ned swallowed on a dry mouth. "He—the Lyhhrt—"

Spartakos was standing half a head below him. The light was coming from his forehead. "Follow me," he said.

"But he—"

"He does not wish or intend to be saved. Did not. I have alerted Security and I doubt that you want to meet them. Come along." He put a hand on Ned's wrist. It felt like warm satin.

"Where are we going?" Ned pulled back.

"There is a local freighter here that has been delivering supplies and will be taking patients with serious ailments to Portside City Hospital. You will be among them: I have an understanding with the autopilot, and it is delaying its flight for you. Then you will be sent to the Galactic Federation representative."

"No, I can't go! I've got to find Zella!"

"You must finish your assignment! We have just barely enough time for you to reach the landing. After that I will find Zella and bring her to you even if I must steal a ship and pilot it. I promise. Come!"

Ned snarled, "Damn you, why didn't you do all this earlier?" Sweat was running off his scalp, and when he wiped it from his forehead he saw that his fingers were flecked with gold. He thought for a moment that it had come from Spartakos's touch, but the gold was only the dust in his hair. He followed Spartakos down the ramp, limping on his twisted ankle.

"It was difficult to place you where you would find evidence and swear to testify to it without giving everything away to Zamos. The Lyhhrt would not show himself in the open when he is the last one in the Zamos's power, and I am only a machine."

Ned looked into the lens eyes and said bitterly, "You have a terrible lot of arrogance for only a machine!"

"I did my best to be a friend to you, Ned Gattes, and I think of you as my friend. I was built by the Lyhhrt people to be a guardian and a lighthouse, and when the Lyhhrt are safe and the O'e are free then I will perhaps have been more than just a machine."

Zella's Walk

Zella woke up on a hard bunk with a bruised arm and a hand she thought at first was broken. But she had been lying on it, in sleep or unconsciousness. Her mind was blank, and slow to put the world together. The grey-walled room, cell, had few features: a dim lamp in a wall bracket, a camera high under the ceiling in one corner and a small round window in another, showing a thin line of deep blue eastern sky at the bottom and a star in the deep blackness above; a small sink, a w.c. without a lid, a wall hook for hanging clothes. A set of denims was hung on it. She was lying on the narrow bed in her underwear—a brassiere and briefs. The air was hot and poorly filtered. She sat up dizzily, not remembering much, knowing she would not want to remember when she did.

The room was a holding area for miscreants, usually drunks or swacked-out dopers, sometimes a too-violent fighter. She stared at the stark grey walls and they bounced back terror and dread. Stood up. More dizziness, a memory flash, she had been running, running . . . she ran some water over her face and hands, put on the blue pants and jacket, an old set of her own, and found her thick-soled shoes under the basin.

Yes. She had bought the clothes, foolish, whorish clothes. Coming to meet Ned had caught sight of him, then the Security men—"That face—" one of them had said, flipping open a wallet with Ned's hologram and pointing down, Ned standing looking up, catching sight of them with his face going white but for that odd dark part of his jaw, and she running with her arms open to embrace them, touching that one on the back of the neck with a red-gloved hand and laughing as if they were her dearest johns.

They'd humored her just for an instant, one of them had given her a feel before he blinked and said, "Hey, this is Sztoyko!" and the other snapped, "That was Gattes down there, you shithead, and he's gone!" Then they'd really grabbed her, and she had fought like a demon. Things after that were confused, she thought they'd used a stunner, and now there was a bit of a bruise on her arm where she'd been given a dermcap or a needle.

She drank some water to work the fog out of her head and sat on the bunk with her hands on her lap working to push the fear away . . . away from Ned. She could not think what more there was to do for him.

Time passed and when she opened her eyes again someone was saying, "Here's your breakfast, Sztoyko," and a tray was being pushed in through a flap at the bottom of the door. She picked it up and lifted the cover; breakfast was the same sausages, eggs, and grilled tomatoes as usual from Zamos's hydroponic farms. Not prisoners' fare, but she had not expected rusks and water. She sat down again and ate, beginning slowly, and then with a sharpened appetite. When she had finished she replaced the tray near the flap and waited.

Someone came and pulled it away eventually, and after that the lock whirred in the door. It slid back, and an ordinary-looking hefty fellow came in. His hair was red and his mouth a deeper color from chewing something, betel, perhaps, and one wrist was tattooed with some emblem of the Brotherhood of Goons. He had a small low-grade stunner tucked in a sling and hardly seemed to need it. "Come on," he said.

"Am I a prisoner?"

"Your sheet says violence"—he spat red juice into the sink—"but I know you aren't gonna be violent with me, sweetheart."

"No, I won't be violent."

"Somebody wants to talk to you," he said, and raised his arm toward the open door. He came out after her and walked beside her, his hand not quite at his side, ready to grab if she strayed.

The corridor was a place she had not even seen before; there were only two other cells she did not have time to look into. Her mind was running like a—not a computer but the adding machines they used on New Southsea World in her home colony, Eden II, with their glimmering brass-toothed wheels and steel-rimmed keys. She had a deep stab of longing for all the old hicks and yokels there.

When she came out of this section with her warder behind her the more familiar halls were quiet, in a depth-of-dawn near stillness where few were moving about, and the sky through the huge arch of window the color of a peacock's neck. *Maybe my last morning.*

Only the Khagodi were up early doing exercises, or pretending to, in slow and sluggish movements, stopping every once in a while to scratch their unhelmeted heads. They were a surly lot, and the dim thoughts they emitted were cloudy with resentments and old grudges. No help for her there, not anywhere, she thought. Most of the hardiest revelers had staggered away, and the only one she saw was a very old man being supported by a woman bodyguard; his ancient face had been recreated so many times that it seemed to have been seared by hot irons, and its touches of makeup might have been done by an embalmer. The flat-eyed woman with him was from the same stable as her own escort.

Sweet was doing pushups on one of the workout floors; he had not shaved yet, and there was a sleepy grin on his face; probably he had spent the night with a woman from one of the lower floors and stopped on the way home; he looked happy with himself, still enough of a pretty-boy to give some woman a thrill. She wondered that no one had stolen his diamond tooth. It flashed when he turned his head as she went by. "How you doing, Zella? Hey, where you been?"

The muscle said, "Don't. Say. Anything."

"Wherever I've been, I'm back now, all right."

Red Teeth grasped her arm, she tensed and twisted. They stared at each other for a moment. "He's my friend," she said. He let go, and they went on as before. A grey matte-finished cleaning robot that was coming toward them wheeled as they passed and followed them with a crackle of static.

He looked around. "What the hell's that thing doing?"

"Are you addressing me?" The machine asked. "I have been assigned a task in this direction."

Everything at once became surreal to Zella. The world Shen, the Palace of Knossos, the fighting, gambling, and whoring, Ned far and gone, her life. Her whole life. She went along as if she were something flat on a screen, seeing tableau on tableau, Sweet with his diamond tooth, one old whore or another, one muscle-bound bully or the next. Her mind seemed separated from her eyes, running on a flat screen behind them with flickering gears and spindles. In a moment the corridor would turn and broaden past the coaches' offices into the concourse that led to the escalators down the hall on the way to the Front Offices . . . *She was walking along, Jacaranda, just like this, first with him, and then that woman, letting that woman touch her with those claws, letting her . . .*

"That way," Muscles said, pointing to the last office in the corridor, where Kati'ik was standing in the open doorway, with Gobo just behind her.

"So, dems'l, you are back," Kati'ik said.

Zella stared. Expecting this encounter farther along on a different level, she was disoriented once again. All of the sores flamed on her face and jaws. *Letting her at my face with those filthy ripping claws.*

She climbed over the fear in an intense effort, and said in a low voice, "What do you want from me?"

"I thought once that I wanted you to fight in the arena, what you were hired to do." Tiny white lights shone off Kati'ik's eyes. "I had even planned to invite you into the Lottery we are pulling today, the fight in blood. Believe me, you would have preferred that to what you will do now: answer my very pressing questions."

"I didn't apply for the Lottery, and—"

Gobo broke in. "Kati'ik, I don't think this—"

"Shut up, Gobo! Sztoyko, you were brought here at great expense in one of the largest ships in the Galaxy to work under our terms as a respected fighter. What's left of you after debriefing will be grateful to find yourself a beggar in the Labyrinths or a filthy bawbee in one of the mud-duggets there!"

"You've done your best to make me a whore already! Making me screw that filthy Ned Gattes with his wormy face," *Forgive me, Ned!* "telling me he was a spy when he wouldn't lay out a lead *pista* to buy me a cup of clean water!" She fought to keep her voice down before she descended into hopeless shrieking and used up all her strength.

"Trax! Get her in here and shut her up."

Trax grabbed her arm again and the robot cleaner, which had paused behind him, began to hum and rock back and forth on its treads.

Kati'ik said, "What is that damned thing doing here?" and Trax twisted to aim a heel at one of its lenses. "No, no! I never told you to ruin it!"

The machine backed away. Kati'ik cried in a high odd voice, "GET INTO THAT OFFICE, SZTOYKO!"

At the same time Zella yelled, "No! You're not going to drag me in there and rip up my face like you did yesterday!" She rubbed her sleeves harshly across her face on both sides so that the four raw sores flashed out seeping blood and serum. After that wrapped her arms around herself tightly and lowered her voice. She felt dizzy again. *It was never any use, you fool!*

Her hope had been to attract attention and help, and if that did not work to kill Kati'ik with one hard blow. Disturbances meant nothing here and Trax would not let her near Kati'ik.

Gobo, who was staring at her, said, "Kati'ik, stop—" but Kati'ik had grasped Zella's arm, while another set of muscles came from the workout areas with an O'e foreman.

This is it, Zella. The long walk with the depthless onyx

eyes reflecting her. She snarled, could feel her mouth muscles working like a trapped animal's, "Let go of me!"

The robot began rocking again and another one drew up beside it. Trax grabbed a baton from the O'e foreman's hand and advanced on one of the robots. Three or four O'e had gathered, and there was a moment of stillness as if everyone was in check.

It was broken by a spy hawk that flew with a pneumatic pop out of its nest beside an airshaft, fluttering and squawking, "*Awk-ik!* Front Office asap!" There was a startling sense of the ordinary in the cry of this messenger, and every one twitched as if coming out of a spell.

"Kati'ik! Front Office asap! *Awk!*" The spy hawk flew home.

Kati'ik stood in a stillness of her own. "Me?"

"Hello, Kati'ik! You're wanted at Front Office." Spartakos's warm cheerful voice came down the hall before him.

Kati'ik whirled. "Don't give me orders, you machine!" She spun her head on her twisty neck and scoured all those around her with her black onyx eyes. "Get back to work, you! And take Sztoyko into that office and keep her there!"

Gobo pulled himself together and yelled, "I'm damned if I will! You can go fuck yourself! No fighter of mine is going to be abused!"

"We'll see about that!"

"Sztoyko is to be reassigned," Spartakos said. She gave him one fierce look and scuttled down the hall with her clogs clacking.

Zella stood still. Just stood, with her arms wrapped around her and the sores burning on her face.

Gobo came up, staring at her. "You sure you're all right, Zel?"

"I don't know," Zella said, "I guess I'll find out soon," and bit her lip to keep from giggling.

Gobo scratched his head and went back into his office. Trax and his companion were still confronting the two robots. The O'e moved off without fuss or hurry, but the robots remained crouched where they were. There was an odd staredown for another moment of silence. Perhaps the two bullies with stunners had heard of the rebellion of a thousand powerful robots in the Biological Station on Barrazan V, but the machines made no move in their direction. They shrugged and went off to other tasks, and almost immediately after the robots went off as well.

"Come along, Zella Sztoyko," Spartakos said. He urged her toward the escalators.

"Is that all there was?" Zella asked. "It's all over?"

"For you it is."

"Nothing happened."

"What did you want?"

"She wanted to kill me. I'd thought it all out. We were going to walk down that hall, and I was going to fight. I was going to smash her face till it split and watch that damned slimy orange blood-stuff run out."

"It would not have happened that way. Of course, you knew that. Come quickly now, before Kati'ik discovers that I am the only one who wanted her in Front Office."

"I'm really reassigned?"

"I am sending you to Portside City. You will find work there if you want it. You will have to go by way of the underground rail to Athenae Mills because there is nothing flying from here, and the Freightmaster will give you a lift. It is not first class travel, but I promised Ned Gattes that I would send you to him if I had to pilot a ship myself, and this is the nearest I can manage."

Zella murmured, "Ned . . ." But relief did not quite lift her heart yet, and she was left to dispose of her fury and hatred however she could. *It's like having sex and calling it off just when you've started to come.* An unpleasant thought that described the feeling too well.

Fthel V: *Manador and Maggie*

YOUR HEART'S DESIRE. SATISFACTION GUARANTEED.

When the message turned up on Manador's terminal it did not excite her much. It was a damned boring rainy day in Starry Nova and nothing new had come along for a tenday. A lot of spongers and PAYMENT DUE notices, solicitation from the Friends of Shanghaied and Marooned Workers, the business as usual.

HOW MUCH DOES MY HEART'S DESIRE COST? she asked.

YOU MUST SAVE AN IMPORTANT PERSON AT SMALL RISK TO YOURSELF.

She sat back and looked at the symbols saying these words, and remembered the deadly little streamer showing Jacaranda . . .

HOW?

GO INTO ZAMOS'S GAMBLAR AND BRING OUT ONE OF THE O'E.

THAT'S NOT EXACTLY SMALL RISK. O'E ARE BONDSERVANTS. I'D NEVER BE ABLE TO BRING ONE OF THEM OUT.

THEY ARE NOT BONDSERVANTS. YOU KNOW HOW TO TAKE CARE OF IT. YOU HAVE DONE THAT SORT OF THING BEFORE.

AND WHEN DO I RECEIVE THE HEART'S DESIRE I DON'T EVEN KNOW ABOUT?

THIS MOMENT IF YOU WILL PROMISE. WE MUST HAVE THE O'E WOMAN VERY SOON.

WHO ARE YOU, COMMUNICATOR?

THE LESS YOU KNOW THE HAPPIER YOU WILL BE.

YOU MAY BE AN ENEMY.

NO EVIL ONE TRIES TO SAVE THE LIFE OF AN INNOCENT PERSON.

Manador did not push further.

I'M NOT SURE I LIKE THE LOOK OF IT.

YOU ARE AN EXTREMELY CAPABLE WOMAN WHO HAS ARRANGED HER LIFE VERY WELL EXCEPT FOR ONE THING AND YOU WANT THAT MORE THAN ANYTHING. YOU SHALL HAVE IT. ONLY GIVE US ONE WORD.

WHAT DO YOU THINK I WANT SO MUCH?

A RECORD OF EVENTS.

She considered for a moment. The day was very dull.

YES.

WATCH CAREFULLY.

Without pause she was looking at the body of Jacaranda lying in the Florence-flask tank, and the dark red woman with the tail, dead or alive she could not tell, being lifted out. Apparently alive, for she was dropped like an exotic fish into a transparent bag full of water and carried away quickly by two Varvani.

They went away and came back, or two others came—Manador could not tell them apart through a camera usually angled in the corner of a ceiling—and the thinner one climbed down by a knotted rope, tied it around Jacaranda's ankles, and the other Varvani hauled her up. Then the rope was let down again, and the first one climbed up. There was sound with this sequence, as rough and unedited as the camera work, and the Varvani were muttering in a language of their own.

The camera drew back and showed a group of Miry, or some other Solthrees coming up to the platform. They were wealthy and ravaged by the depths of their pleasures. In spite of the poor sound it was clear that they were complaining about the performance and—Manador was not quite sure which—wanted their money back or another ticket.

Cutaway, a new scene. She recognized the bouncer who usually lurked by the gateway, along with another bruiser with the same kind of build and tattoos; his mouth was red from what he was chewing. This was the one who had come to meet and accompany Jacaranda on one relay toward her death.

They went down ever-narrower halls lined with doors, finally paused at one and Red-Mouth pounded on it. It was deeply solid, but did not seem to hurt his knuckles. There was no answer. He thumped it again. After a moment he twisted about, bent one leg for purchase, put both sets of fingers in the hand-well and wrenched. Manador watched the muscles swarming under his skin like animals. The door hissed open, rammed back into its socket with a *thunk!* rebounding to slide closed and back open, and he reached in and hoicked out two shivering, squeaking Kylkladi into the arms of the bouncer.

Manador recognized them by their green and purple dyed feathers. The green one was the brothel's Keymaster with the sore eyes and dark glasses, and the other the madam who had escorted Jacaranda, with those little claw-flicks, into the amphitheater. These wretches were dragged along corridor after corridor while the curious watched, a Bimanda woman dressed in iridescent *uki* scales, two Kylkladi with feathers dyed pink and vermilion, a seven-world score of others. Some were hugging themselves with sudden cold.

Finally the procession reached a door opening into a more spacious office where the two Kylkladi were shoved in to face a triumvirate of two Solthrees and a Khagodi, a big Southern woman and the tallest person in the room.

The Solthree woman launched herself at the Keymaster, screaming, Put her in the window? Who did you think would buy her? And you other one, brainless turd? tried to use her for a snuff act? what did you think you were?

But the Solthree male snarled and pulled her aside, punched the beaked face till it split and bled orange. All the while yelling while the Keymaster squawked and feathers flew, then wrenched off the dark glasses to bare the sore blinking eyes. While the two thugs held the Kyklad's shuddering wing-arms this Solthree plucked the eyes from the shrieking Keymaster's head with thumbs and fingers. Piri'irik, secured in the thick hands of the bouncers, had been screaming long before the first blow fell.

Manador watched steadily until the two bundles of ragged feathers and broken limbs were tossed in the trash heap. The screen abruptly went blank until the symbols appeared:

ARE YOU SATISFIED?

YES.

WOULD YOU LIKE A REPLAY?

NO.

ARE YOU STILL WILLING TO BRING OUT THE O'E?

DO I HAVE A CHOICE?

OF COURSE YOU DO IF YOU CAN SHOW CAUSE. BUT YOU ARE AN HONORABLE WOMAN AND ONE WHO IS WILLING TO TAKE A DARE.

YOU FLATTER ME. BUT ENLIGHTEN ME ANYWAY.

HERE IS A PICTURE OF THE O'E. HER NAME IS AI'IA.

Manador looked at the still of Ai'ia for a moment.

WILL YOU ALLOW ME TO TAKE HARD COPY?

YES BUT DESTROY IT AFTER YOU USE IT.

CAN YOU GET PICTURES OF ZAMOS WOMEN RIGHT AWAY?

YES.

Inside worker.

SHOW ME EVERY WOMAN THERE OF AI'IA'S FACE AND BODY TYPE.

They turned up on the screen, blue, bluish, greenish, pink, creamy, brown, and tan, with red, blue, green, orange, yellow, white, pink, gold, brown, black, and purple hair.

Going through them a second time she pushed STOP and wrote:

THAT ONE. MAGGIE MELADY. SEND HER TO ME TONIGHT. CAN YOU GET SOME MONEY IN A HURRY?

I CAN ARRANGE CREDIT BUT IT IS VERY RISKY JUST NOW.

REAL MONEY I MEANT.

NO. YOU MUST FIND THAT FOR YOURSELF. YOU WILL BE REIMBURSED.

WHERE DO YOU WANT THE O'E DELIVERED?

KEEP HER WHERE YOU PLEASE UNTIL SHE IS CALLED FOR. IT WILL BE LESS THAN ONE DAY. PREFERABLY NOT IN YOUR HOME.

YOU CAN BET ON IT.

YOU WILL NOT HEAR FROM THIS SOURCE AGAIN. I WILL MAKE ARRANGEMENTS TO REIMBURSE YOU.

HOW?

SOMEONE VERY FAMILIAR WILL BRING IT TO YOU.

THERE'S STILL NO LEGAL DOCUMENT.

YOU HAVE MY OATH AS THE DESCENDANT OF AN ANCIENT RACE. IF THE MONEY IS NOT PAID WITH INTEREST WITHIN ONE YEAR I WILL ANNIHILATE MYSELF.

THAT'S A VERY WEIGHTY OATH. GOOD ENOUGH. I GUESS.

ONE MORE THING. DO NOT BE INSULTED MANADOR BUT WHATEVER PLEASURE YOU TAKE IT IS NOT TO BE WITH THIS ONE.

NO FEAR. SHE'S NOWHERE NEAR MY TYPE. AND I'M SAVING HER FOR JACARADA'S SAKE.

THANK YOU FOR YOUR COOPERATION. FAREWELL.

GOOD-BYE.

Manador did not thank the communicator for the fulfill-ment of her heart's desire. She shut down her terminal, lit a dopestick, and spent the rest of the afternoon thinking long thoughts.

Maggie Melady was a cheerful young woman with a coarse

face framed by brown curly hair. "Who wants me, you? I don't do much fancy stuff." She grinned. "I'm the basic training course for young muggsters from the Urgha Mines that wants to brag they had a whore at a Zamos house."

"I want something fancy from you, dear, but it isn't sex. How would you like twenty-five big yellow ones?"

"Russki rooblies, real toothbiters? I'd take lessons in fancy dancing for them! Shit, I could even open up my own house!"

"Better not let Zamos find out."

"Nyet, back in the mines I meant, when I'd earned passage. No fucking at all?"

"Not with me. I want to play a trick, not be one. Here's the game: look at this picture."

"That's Ai'ia, she's one of the O'e. The house put her on the job bussing the Joint, but she gave somebody a kind hello and offered a drink, and they kicked the shit out of her, thought she was," Maggie sniggered, "trying to rise above her station."

"I want to bring her out of there."

"You do? That's theft! I'd never be able to do that!"

"Theft? You mean the O'e are property?" Manador put out a bottle of Kemalan brandy and offered a glass and a dopestick to Maggie.

"Well, like . . ."

"Slaves, you mean? I just want to understand, Maggie."

"There was," Maggie shivered, "that one called Yoya, they made her do some kind of . . . anyway, she tried to run away, I heard them beating her, Piri'irik yelling, 'You belong to US! you dirty piece of cattle!' and in the next day or so she sort of disappeared . . . but then so did Piri'irik, the old screwdaw! Can I have another glass of this? It's good stuff."

"Take all you like. Slaves, then . . . some kind of law is bound to be biting at Zamos soon. It might be safer to be running a whorehouse in a mining colony—but I never said you had to bring her out. I'll do that.

"What I want you to do is this: tomorrow night after your dinner I am coming into Zamos's with a mixed group of people. First we'll arrange to hire some take-outs, including yourself. Then we'll go into the main gaming room at the Gamblar, where the tables are. We'll mix around for a few moments and then split into two groups. When the first group is passing the checkout you will go out with them and suddenly remember that you've forgotten something. Got that? You will check out with the first group."

Maggie fingered the gold heart at her neck and nodded doubtfully. "Go out with the first group and turn back. Then what?"

"You will have found Ai'ia and dressed her to look as much like you as possible. Don't flinch! If you feel she doesn't look enough like you, find someone she does look like and get her to do it, you'll still have the money. Of course you'll have to pay whoever does it. I want her out of there, and I don't care who she looks like.

"If you are doing it you will have her ready and send her out in your place. She'll slip out with the first group around her, there will be a lot of people milling about; it's tendaynight tomorrow, and I'll be with you the whole time, taking the same risks. When they've checked out you'll dash over to the second group that's been hanging around with me and call, Yoo hoo, here I am!—but not too loud. Got that?"

"First group, dash back, send out Ai'ia, fidget around till I see the first group going, run out and give you the high sign. Right?"

"Good!"

"Gonna be fucking tight setting up her and the others in the right places for all that."

"If you think you're capable of running a whorehouse in

the Urgha Mines you'll be able to arrange a few whores in a pretty pattern. Now go take a look at my wig collection and see if you can find anything useful while I run through my pri-V codes and collect the money."

"What? You been arranging all this without no money?"

"No fear, Maggie. You have a saying about skeletons—I may not know where the skeletons are buried, but I do know all the dirty closets. When I call in my markers I'll have twice and a half twenty-five Russky rooblies."

Kobai, Lyhhrt

Here's Kobai to say good-bye, going, gone again . . . little fish is swimming, flicking his tail at me all night and day, round that fishbowl in my belly. 'Little Fish,' some dumb thing to call my son that will be every bit as big as that Crazylegs Om that threw the lump of gold, only not stupid.

:What have you got there, Iron Man?:

:It is a bottle of coldsleep.:

:Looks very blue and cold. Must I drink that?:

:No, Kobai. I will drain most of your water and mix it in. There will be nutrients and other drugs and chemicals to keep you alive and safe on your long journey. I will be doing that tonight.:

:I'm afraid.:

:I know you are—but believe me, you have much less to fear on this dangerous voyage than you would if you re- mained here.: He left the flask of coldsleep on the work- table and went into his office to call the Front Desk.

"Please remove the guardians you have placed with the delphine. I am going to decant her for transport and they are in my way."

"Why hurry? She won't be leaving for three days."

"I must monitor her sleeping heartbeat and the fetus's until they have reached the proper depth. I have not enough room for my equipment in this cramped place. Perhaps you would prefer to take the responsibility yourself."

"Never mind, I'll call them off."

Within a standard hour the watchman folded and pocketed his mini-skambi and the Varvani woman rolled up her ball of purple silk and speared it with her crochet hook.

:I am glad those are gone,: Kobai said. *:They would never even look at me.:*

"Now you may have a rest and a few dreams to yourself."

:No, Iron Man, I want to look and feel and think as my true self until I sleep. I think I will have too long a while in darkness.:

The Lyhhrt left Kobai to her daydreams and went along the hall and down a ramp to the office of the Recordmaster. She was a hearty Miry woman with straight hair in a bun. She looked up from an endlessly scrolling display of vital statistics.

"Hullo, Doctor! Haven't seen you for a while. Been wondering what you mean to do about the deadhead we've been supporting the last four tendays. A sister has turned up to claim her."

"I had been saving her for autopsy but have had no opportunity. That is the reason I came. I will have her finished and packed for shipment by tomorrow."

"Good! Those Pinxin never seem to last. Clients are always asking for them because they're exotic and they'll do anything that's kinky, but they just seem to have no stamina. Get on drugs and OD before they've earned their money's worth. Too bad we can't get decent clones off them." She looked glum for a moment but cheered up. "Got a new batch of Varvani coming. Less than zero on looks, but real hard workers—and tough! You won't find any of them among the deadheads."

"Quite," said the Lyhhrt. Solthrees sometimes called this woman the Dead Reckoner. He went past her and down through long ranks of steel boxes, most of which contained the dead, until he reached one rack of narrow tanks that looked little different from the coffin cases. There were no more than four or five in suspension, waiting on the disposition of relatives. The Lyhhrt paused before the Pinxid woman's body and extruding a sensor from the end of one fingertip plugged it into a socket and listened: Lubb-a-*dubb*-flick-*dubb*-flick-flick-lubb-a-*dubb*, said the two hearts.

Pinxin were the only two-hearted people beside Khahgodi that the Lyhhrt knew of on this world. He did not look at the woman's flat-line brain signal, but summoned the gurney and had it load her, then called up a robot wagon carrying a life-bearing capsule. He directed these two containers past the Reckoner and her automatic checkout. "This lifecase is being loaded and shipped to Shen Four," he told her. "I have a requisition for it."

"Yes, I see that. Go ahead."

The two robot bearers carrying the steel case and the capsule followed him along the corridor and up the ramp; the three of them made a small cortege. In the upper passageway he passed the room where the Ix was staying, and before he noticed that the door was ajar his sensors perceived the sharp electric smell by which he knew that people.

:Lyhhrt!: the terrible mindvoice called.

"Yes?" The Lyhhrt stopped the gurneys and waited while the door opened. In the dim light even he saw little more of the Ix than the glittering of the jeweled harness; its surface negated light.

:There is a new agreement for your next term of service, Lyhhrt, waiting for you to seal it.:

"I know nothing whatever of that," the Lyhhrt said steadily.

:Now you know it. It has been arranged with your superiors.:

"Is that so?"

The Lyhhrt went on and delivered the body and the life-capsule to the room where Kobai was waiting for coldsleep, then went upstairs to his laboratory office. He prepared a nutrient bath with a special mixture of neurotransmitters, and from the safe took a triply sealed vial of the hormone that would allow him to fission. He considered this for a long moment and returned it to the safe.

After he had fed and refreshed himself in the calming bath and placed himself in the plainest of his workshells, a dark matte grey with a few gold scrawls, he picked up his calls and found two impatient ones from Administration. "At your earliest convenience!" they cried, a degree of haste much faster than "asap."

He presented himself there, to the tall Khagodi woman and the two Solthrees who formed the present triumvirate. "With all celerity," he said, "I present myself."

"Ah, Doctor," said the Solthree woman, "you are the Doctor, are you not? You look somewhat less exquisite than usual."

"I have been speaking to the Ix," said the Lyhhrt. If the Ix had had a name and he had troubled to learn it, the Lyhhrt would not have addressed or referred to him by it. He considered names dangerously individualistic; Kobai and Lebedev were the only people he used them with. "I had not been told about a new contract."

"An unfortunate oversight," said the Khagodi woman. "The Ix are very eager to have you keep serving us."

The Lyhhrt did not ask what new trade Zamos and the Ix were engaging in that needed his talents so badly. "I and my progenitors have served you for a long time. Are there no others you would find useful?"

The stocky slab-faced man said, "We need Lyhhrt and there are no others. It will not go well with you if you refuse."

"And for how long?"

"As before, one of your cycles. We have the contract and we want it sealed now."

The Lyhhrt's workshell rattled and he said in a shaking voice, "I will agree if I must, but I have so seals with me, and there is still one day and ten Standard hours before my present contract ends. I beg you for one half-stad of freedom, so that I may say prayers and make my peace with the Cosmos and its Spirit." Before anyone could answer he said, "Please. Allow me this much. Please."

He could perceive that the triumvirate were amused to see the magnificently arrogant Lyhhrt begging so humbly. After a moment of collective thought the Miry woman said, "I think we just might allow that much."

"Thank you," he said quaveringly, and backed out of their presence, leaving them smirking with thoughts of further torment and plans for sliding out of this agreement.

"How disgusting it was, Lebedev!" the Lyhhrt said. His movements were jerky and his voice genuinely trembling. "I begged them! I said *please,* and again, *please,* as if I had learned to love slavery."

Lebedev said, "If the oath binds you so strictly as you believe, it is destructive."

"Yes, I know it, but I cannot help that."

It was nine days since Lebedev had met with the Lyhhrt. Not a pleasant nine days, spent looking forward to being inhabited by the Lyhhrt. For some reason the thought had made his ear hurt.

"Nothing is wrong with your ear," said the Lyhhrt. "Your

pain is caused by fear. Do you think I have no fear of—" He stopped. Both he and Lebedev had been seized by mutual revulsion and would spend their whole lives in this bond. "We need not discuss it. Do not eat any more food today, Lebedev." He took a flask from the desk. "Here is a potion I have prepared. There are nutrients and tranquilizers for both of us, and you must drink it tonight before you retire. When you wake it will have been done."

Lebedev accepted the flask. It was a flat silver one with classical engraving, and looked as if it contained whiskey. *How I wish it did! Ai Lebedev, what are you letting yourself in for now? and however did you get into this fix?*

"In my room? You will look strange coming into that area."

"I will take care not to look strange."

They parted for the second last time without another word.

When he went to his room to change for his afternoon session at the *skambi* table, Lebedev found a little card shoved beneath his door: it told him his services were no longer required as of tomorrow. He did not know whether his discharge had been arranged by the Lyhhrt; it was his pass out of Zamos's Gamblar. He stared sadly at his soup crock. He had eaten the last of its contents for lunch and it stood empty. It was too heavy to carry under his arm out the front door when he meant to leave quickly, and he had nowhere to deliver it, though he supposed for the sake of appearances he ought to make some kind of gesture. It was not expensive or valuable like a silver samovar passed down through the family for hundreds of years, but . . .

Dressed in fresh linens and closing the door behind him, he found Tally coming down the corridor toward his room. He had spent the night with her again half a tenday ago, and their coupling was one of comfort and warmth rather than passion, somewhat like eating a good soup. The thought of sleeping with Manador came into his head suddenly and made him grin; Tally took the grin for her own and her face brightened.

"Hallo, Lev!" She turned to match his walk and tucked her arm in his. "I heard some talk."

"What kind?"

"Not very good." She was smiling and nodding, leading him toward a sofa in Employees Common Area. "They like to have me serving them at private parties . . ." He saw that she was wearing an impervious net of very fine wire with, he thought, real diamonds in it; it fitted close to her scalp and her hair had been combed through it so all that could be seen was the occasional glitter. The gift, perhaps, of some old friend. "They get me to dress up like a whoremaster's idea of Marie Antoinette, only at my age I don't have to take the clothes off like the others do. And they like it if I have something to tell them, whatever I pick up at the stables. They don't much like me screwing you—"

Lebedev, who had been sitting knee to knee with her, pulled away sharply. "Why then, Tally—"

"You think I give a shit? I'm just telling you what they're muttering about. I don't know why they're worried about you talking with Ai'ia and the Doctor . . ." She did not look at him while she said this, and it seemed to him that she was warning him against telling her why. "Sometimes I've wondered if they didn't give you this job just to keep track of what you're doing? You know? Just because you were a rozzer?"

"You have a very good ear. Have you yourself ever thought of looking for another job?" She did not answer and he added, "At any rate, I have just received my notice."

She murmured, "They'd never kill you inside here after

the flap about that whore." She turned to take his face in her hands and kiss his mouth with a dart of her tongue. "Goodbye, Lev. Watch your backside." And she was out of his life in a flurry of lace and lilac talcum.

Kobai had been dozing, and when she woke she found the Lyhhrt standing by the coffin case, unsealing its hasps. *:Iron man, what is that?:*

"It is a dead Pinxid woman whose body has been kept working."

:Her skin is very blue, blue as cold sleep. I think she is far from home.: She did not ask any more questions.

From his cupboard of marvels the Lyhhrt called out an insectile robot that lifted the Pinxid's body out of the coffin case and placed it in the life-capsule. He covered it carefully with a blue gel of nutrients, reattached all the indicators, and sealed it with a metal plate engraved with instructions for handling the Enclosed Delphine en route to Shen IV.

He sterilized the coffin case with a blast of hot air, checked the spy monitors, which had been set to broadcast clips of him going about various tasks for his masters, and when he was satisfied that he was safe turned to the tank with the genuine delphine in it and placed his hands flat against the glassy surface, as Kobai had done so often.

:Now, Kobai, you are going to sleep, and when you wake up you will be free.:

:Yes!: She was deeply weary of all the long days in this prison, but her eyes were alight *:I am thirsty for water that is more wild and cold than this . . . I am sorry I said all those mean things to you before I knew what a good friend you are.:*

:You are not the first. But I have forgotten them.:

:You are the only true friend I have ever had and I will remember you forever, Iron Man.:

:And I—Kobai, dear friend . . . I will remember you as long as I/we can.:

He drained half of the water and added the sedative; she was only too willing to sink into a dream of home, where she saw herself in the tasks that had been a labor and now were a longed-for pleasure, carrying the sea-bladder lantern to light up the vein of gold, with the child against her belly and clasping her breast to suck . . .

With the water barely covering her he pressed a switch that lowered the tank wall into the floor, and his insect robot reached in over the free edge to pluck her out and put her into the coffin case. Before she could gasp, the Lyhhrt had the water-respirator tube in her throat to top up her lungs, and was listening with his sensor:

Lubb-a-*dubb*-flick-a-*dubb*-flick-a-lubb-a-*dubb*, said the two hearts of mother and fetus. He covered her body quickly with the blue gel and sealed the case with the metal plate informing shippers that the body of Io Adilon of Pinaxer would be outbound on the Miry ship *Aleksandr Nevskii.*

He followed the coffin on its trestle down the dim hallways of midnight to the kiosk of the Dead Reckoner. Her night replacement was a cheerful Varvani named Groad, who was free of morbid interests; the Lyhhrt almost liked him.

"Is that a gift for me?" Groad asked.

The Lyhhrt had learned that this kind of remark was humorously meant. "Only if you want a dead body."

The Varvani peered at the record number on the plate and keyed it into his registry. "That's Adilon, the one you were flatlining for autopsy. I guess she's dead now." He checked for heartbeat and did not hear any, the Lyhhrt made sure he would not. "Poor woman. She was alone and far from home. Was she ever a friend of yours?"

"Yes." The Lyhhrt let the coffin run along the tracks into

its niche with almost reluctant fingertips. He did not know that Kobai would not be discovered and reimprisoned, or that, if properly loaded and maintained, she would connect with the *Blessed Themesta* bound for Khagodis, or that once she was successfully in flight she and the fetus would survive these journeys. He was launching her as any alien child might send out a boat of leaves or bark down a stream that led to a great river.

Lebedev, Gold Copper and Silver

Moist from the bath-house, Lebedev found that his hammock had been replaced by a bed, too late for comfort. He sat on it and regarded the silver flask. He was trying to find a point at which he could have turned away from this course of action. It was not the particular moment when he had agreed to harbor the Lyhhrt for a day, he thought, but that instant when he had conceived the plan of risking everything and installing himself in this place. Half his motive was to expiate guilt for sending Jacaranda in here with insufficient defenses. *As if you had more, Lebedev, you schmuck.* And here he was.

He opened the flask and smelt the liquid. It had a mild "chemical" smell, like a doctor's office. He poured it into a tumbler; it was brilliantly clear and very slightly viscous, like glycerine. Not to make a drama of it he drank it, rinsed the cup and flask, and lay flat on the bed. He did not think it deserved a *na zdrovya*.

The cleaning robot, embarked on midnight rounds, paused in the dim grey corridor outside Lebedev's door, and several latecomers who could not see straight banged into it and cursed. "Executing self-repairs, self-repairs," the robot muttered apologetically. When the curses had been replaced by snores and no one was stirring about, it extended a limb to push open Lebedev's door and opened a hatch to let out what looked like a giant tarantula. The tarantula scuttled into the room and shut the door behind it, and the robot rumbled off.

This spider shape scrambled up on the bed and switched on an imager and a small intense lamp, then whisked the covers off to regard Lebedev's huge repulsive body with its lens eyes, minutely examining the vast expanse of hair and skin.

It palpated and listened for resonance, found the area chosen for entry in Lebedev's abdomen above the groin crease, extruded a nozzle to spray the skin and its own limbs with sterilizing liquid. Now the abdomen of the spider-machine split and the Lyhhrt reached out holding a tiny case of minute medical instruments in one pseudopod; he opened this, selected an almost invisible scalpel, and made his cut. This was merely familiar landscape: the flashing blood, the slithery layers of tissue, the webby membranes suffused with capillaries that flowed red at every touch, but beyond that—

The Lyhhrt tightened his resolve and quickly—

—quickly insinuated his body into the cavity, into the new universe between the external and internal oblique layers of the superficial muscles, steeling himself to control his hideous terror of the burning heat, the acid bite of the tissues, the drumming heart, the blood singing in its vessels as its thickly streaming cells swarmed through them, their bitter taste of iron, the bubblings, rumblings, pulsings, spasms—but his tormented nerve endings were already stimulating the secretions that would thicken his integument to insulate him from the horrors of this alien hell.

Clutching his remote-control system and his instrument case while he cut through tissues, snipped and tied off thready blood vessels, and fought through the fat cells in waves of nauseating tastes and smells, he forced pseudopod after pseudopod into tiny spaces until he was almost as attenuated as a membrane himself. Finally he was able to pull in his last tendril and use his controls to let the spider seal the wounds with collagen adhesives.

Then the spider's lens eyes cast about the room. There was no disposal chute here, and the Lyhhrt, with a flinch of regret, sent his beautiful machine scurrying up the side of the waste bucket and dropping in, where it expired with a magnesium-flare of light into white ash.

Lebedev snorted gently, dreaming of his year in prison, a happy time in retrospect.

He woke with a sore belly that was swollen by the damage inflicted on it rather than the Lyhhrt's mass. All of the mass was tucked to one side to minimize damage between the muscle layers, but did not make Lebedev look or feel grotesque. He had lost a couple of kilos in the last tenday out of anxiety, the way he had gained the earache. Except for the soreness and the tiny scar he could almost believe he had imagined everything.

:*Not quite,*: said the Lyhhrt from his torment.

"If I go around muttering to you like this everybody will think I'm as crazy as I think I am."

:*I do not expect you to mutter at me except to inquire about my condition in this terrible place.*:

"It wasn't my idea," Lebedev said. :*And you seem to be your usual self.*:

:*Your conversation with the woman Tally Hawes indicates that you are to expect an attack. You must avoid violence.*:

:*I intend to.*: Lebedev set about cleaning his teeth.

:Please eat bland foods. Your digestive system disturbs me.:
:You're lucky, I'm not very hungry. All that consoles me is, today, whatever else happens, is the last day of dealing skambi.:*

Down in the vaults where the Dead Reckoner worked, the stevedores had come to collect coffins and flat-line cases for loading. "Ahoy, Recordmaster!" one of them called.

"What now?"

"This cadaver you're shipping to Pinaxer, the *Nevskii* doesn't run the shuttle out there this route."

"Well I have it down, Doctor got it ready and it says right here, Pinaxer, bound on *Nevskii.*"

"That's wrong, and you better check."

"I'll call."

When the copper figure with the sunset face appeared, the Reckoner cried, "These fellows say you've made a mistake with that Pinxid woman, Doctor, no stops at Pinaxer by the *Nevskii!* If that's the case, we'll have to burn her here."

"Impossible. She has a reserved space on tier eighty-six, slot five hundred and twenty-two. She is to be delivered with supplies to the Sector seven-eight-seven Spacelight on the Outer Instar Route, and a shuttle will collect her from there.'

"Yeh, that's the place she's to be stowed in, the numbers check. We do connect with that Light, so I suppose we'd better take her along," said the stevedore.

While the Lyhhrt's copper shell was walking back toward his office the Ix's door opened and blackness stood within its darkness. *:Lyhhrt, have you signed the contract?:*

"Not yet."

:You will sign it before midnight.:

"We shall see about that," said the Lyhhrt, speaking through his shell.

:You will sign or I will crack that shell of yours, Lyhhrt:

The Lyhhrt picked up his calls from the office and once
again there was a summons from Administration. "NOW!"
it screamed, in the person of the Khagodi woman, whose
eyes were inflamed. There had been arguments among the
Triumvirate, he thought. He checked his attachments to the
cardiographs, encephalographs, and sphygmomanometers,
and switched his logic into the humble matte-grey shell.

"You are going to sign that contract before midnight,"
the Solthree woman said. "It has occurred to us that you
were trying to play a trick with your hour of freedom, your
prayer-time when you were free of your oath, not of your
service. We see through you. You will sign or we will hand
you to the Ix for a gift."

"The Ix has already told me all about your plans. Has he
become your new Keymaster? Or is your Triumvirate now
a Quadrumvirate?"

"Watch your arrogance, Doctor, or your people will
suffer!"

"A thousand pardons!" the Lyhhrt said cringingly. "I will
come to you in all humility on the point of the twenty-fifth
hour." His shell backed away from them as if it had been in
the presence of majesty.

During the afternoon Lebedev had no communication from
the Lyhhrt and only the merest flutter of movement. *:Sleep,
Lyhhrt, sleep.:* There was no answer. He was mildly surprised
that he felt so much at ease about providing the Lyhhrt with
a home away from home, and it struck him briefly that the
Lyhhrt had willed this, but he found his mind unable to
dwell on it. After a mild supper of scrambled eggs on toast
and even a glass of soy milk to placate the Lyhhrt, he dressed
himself in the same suit he had worn on the day he had applied for work at the Gamblar and went out to deal the last
round.

"Dear friends and gentle hearts," said Lebedev, "the number today is twenty-nine."

During the shuffling for the third game he saw a familiar face—unpleasantly familiar. The brute he had fought with on the first night sat down in South's position, still wearing his business uniform with its little company crest. Lebedev had not seen him since that night, and began to feel real urgency. *:The violence we need to avoid is running at us,:* he told the Lyhhrt.

:Hold him off as long as possible. I have work to do.:

It was while they were playing the second spindle that South pulled down the smoke-cone, pulled a case of *ge'iin* sticks out of his pocket and lit one. Lebedev's heart sank. Whether this was a deliberate provocation or not, he was forced to act. Smoking *ge'iin* was unlawful in Starry Nova's public rooms not only because it was a powerful narcotic; its allergens were also powerful, and mixed with the air pollutants of a port city, often fatal. West was already coughing and covering her mouth and nostrils.

"Stop play," Lebedev said. "Sir, the substance you are smoking is illegal. You must stop or leave." His toe was resting on the alarm switch.

South's face was flushed, but he grinned and shrugged. "I'll stay in, Dealerman." He extinguished the black stick carefully and put it back into its amber case. When he lifted the cone and the biting white smoke drifted away Lebedev saw looming in back of him three or four hulking figures, one of whom was a Security guard he had noticed earlier in the brothel.

Lebedev thought he understood what had happened with South. He was a sanctioned bully who had provoked and then attacked him the first night to ruffle him, then been told to lay off while Lebedev gradually revealed himself. Whether or not he had really given himself away, Zamos thought he was dangerous and ought to be shrugged off for good. He dreaded the intermission after this game. :*It's coming too fast, Lyhhrt.*:

:*It is the point of the twenty-fifth hour. I need a quarter hour more.*:

West fainted at that moment, and North cried out in Russian, "Oh my God!" He reached for her, and began to gather her up.

Lebedev had jumped up, shocked. His first thought was that the Lyhhrt had struck down a harmless woman, but North, obviously her husband or lover, said, "She's pregnant! I've got to get her out of here!"

He struggled to lift her and at the same time twisted his head toward South, snarling, "You bastard, with your goddam filthy smoke!" South gave him the finger, but by that time Lebedev had toed the alarm and was between them, shouldering back South with his body half-turned to protect his belly. South had had it in mind to give him a knee.

Help came quickly for West and North, and at the instant in which Lebedev realized that he had been enabled to read South's mind, the attention of the Lyhhrt was sharply withdrawn from this tableau. Two eager players filled the empty seats, and Lebedev decided to ride out the intermission, in defiance of the Entertainment and Recreation Workers' Union, and shuffled the disks.

"Citizens of the Galaxy, your number for today is twenty-three. Your wild numbers are forty-six, fifty-one, and twenty-eight." Lebedev shot his cuffs and dealt his last game.

On the point of the twenty-fifth hour, the Lyhhrt's golden shell presented itself to the Triumvirate.

"You are here to sign this contract," said the Khagodi.

"No."

"What do you mean, no!"

"The Doctor has always done everything that Zamos has asked, but in his contract there was no option to renew it, and he does not feel any such obligation."

"He? What do you mean by 'he'?"

"The Doctor no longer inhabits this shell. I am a robot. Of course the Doctor is serving according to his oath: other robots are monitoring patients at risk, but after the fourth Standard hour of this coming morning that will stop, and you must find a new Doctor." While it was saying this the shell reached a hand in back of itself to lock the door and seal it with a laser bolt.

The two Solthrees jumped up and reached out, the woman with a stunner in her hand, the man raising a machine pistol. The robot extended its free hand to flick it away, but did not bother with the stunner; its neutral poison was harmless to metal. The gold shell wrenched away the table where the triumvirate was sitting, and lasered the alarm switch in the floor, then went about the room gutting the communications devices. The Solthree man was yelling and red-faced, threatening with his fists, and the woman shrinking back in her chair, while the Khagodi was thrashing her tail and cursing, but afraid to attack.

"There is no need to be so alarmed. I do not mean to touch you. I have left the lights on and you will be found in the morning. You have cots to rest on and running water as well as the use of a lavatory." The robot folded its hands for a moment; the three quieted down and watched it sullenly.

It said almost shyly, "Now you must excuse me while I deconstruct myself. I am a marvelous and beautiful artifact created by the Doctor for his uses, but now my work is complete and I am not needed anymore, nor will my master's skills keep serving you through me." And with this last word the robot grasped its sunburst head in its two hands and wrenched it from its shoulders.

At the moment that the gold shell began to take itself apart the copper sunset shell presented itself at the Ix's door. The door slid open and the shell stepped into the darkness.

:You bring me good news, Lyhhrt,: said the Ix.

"I am not the Lyhhrt," said the shell, and closed the door behind it.

Between one moment and the next Lebedev felt an almost paralyzing jolt of euphoria. For a second he thought that either the Lyhhrt or some other source had given him a drug, but after a few gasping breaths, which he masked by coughing, realized that the Lyhhrt had suddenly and for the first time turned his attention to Lebedev's surroundings. "West plays three, but South puts down twenty-eight wild," he said breathlessly, while the crystal clarity of all the minds around him increased and intensified with explosive force. Oh the power! as if he were a Creator standing on a mountain looking down on all the beasts below.

South, waiting to smash Lebedev as the prelude to a violent encounter with a woman; West, a Bengtvad woman with two new children, a bureaucrat husband, and a mountain of debt; North and East, locked in a hate that was as valuable to them as love; over there a male Dabiri couple spending at Zamos's what they had stolen from the Kylkladi GamePlex, being watched by a croupier-detective and unaware how near their capture was; in back of Lebedev a bartender skimming the till; and, eyeing the barman while she spent the evening on a drink and a token, a richly dressed woman too old to be a whore who had once been one and needed somebody. Anybody.

After this first great rush Lebedev understood that he was feeling all this from a Lyhhrt's point of view strained through his own understanding. Seeing it through a rozzer's eyes, Tally would say. The glow passed as if a bubble had burst. He did not want this kind of power and he had learned nothing that he did not know already.

No. He had learned one or two things: one, a woman named Maggie Melady had come over from Zamos's House and was dabbing rouge on Ai'ia's trembling mouth to prepare her for Manador; and two, Tally had been mistaken when she reckoned that he would not be attacked inside the building. South had complete permission to choose his arena. Lebedev's own lips were trembling as he called, "And South's number five takes the game, good players! That concludes play for tonight!"

South grinned and punched buttons for his cred and I.D. cards; he lit up a dopestick and sat watching, with his friends lurking behind him, while Lebedev racked the disks, sent out the night's take through the pneumatic tube, and slowly removed the dirtied white gloves and the mauve armbands with pink *yeye* flowers. *:Do something about him, for God's sake. What's keeping Manador? Do something!:*

:Would you like me to punch his face for him with your fist, Lebedev? I am exhausted from what I have already done. Get away as fast as you can!:

Lebedev twirled his chair about and stood up. So did South. The Security man and the sleepy bouncer from the poor man's gate came around the table alongside him. There was nothing to be gained here by sounding the alarm; Lebedev was in deeply hostile country.

"Good night, gentlemen," he said firmly, and stepped away from the table.

A thick hand grabbed his arm. "What's your hurry, Dealer?" Almost before he knew it South was pulling at him, and Sleepy butting him in the back of the shoulder with one hand while the other pulled a steel spiked knuckle-duster out of a pocket, the three surrounding him, hustling him away from the tables and lights toward the shadows behind the gaming machines. Buffeted about, Lebedev could feel the Lyhhrt's fear as well as his own, and tried to dig in his heels and at the same time twist his body away to protect his belly, with the result that he had no leverage to move freely in whatever reckless way he might have found for himself alone.

Desperate to stay out of the shadows at all costs, he wrenched to pull his arm out of South's grip and launched the straight edge of his other hand in a chop against the bridge of Sleepy's nose, but both these moves were muffled by his caution, and did not have enough energy behind them to make the least difference. One heavy hand pushed down on the back of his neck, another clapped his mouth shut so that he could neither struggle nor call out, and the knuckle-duster grazed the side of his head. All of this taking place between one breath and the next, and hidden under the lights by the three bodies.

In the instant in which Lebedev went from desperation to despair the room began to boil with the influx of a new crowd. Again he had one of those flashes of revelation that whitened the world like lightning. But before he had time to tell himself what it was, a boozy lazy voice was calling, "Yoo hoo!" and being answered by Manador's whip-cracking accents:

"Hello! *Skambi* table closed already? Is this the way to run a casino?" A new tenday-night flurry of players flowed around the tables; a wreath of young women from the House in brightly colored silk gowns mixed in with a half score of Manador's gladiator clients of all sexes, came swarming through past the poker tables, the latter group separating themselves long enough to surround Lebedev's escorts and in a few moments—Lebedev could *feel* South being punched in the kidneys by one of the pugs—he was free, pulling himself together enough to be able to bow and kiss Manador's hand.

As he did so he realized what his flash of perception had told him: that the Lyhhrt had been saving his energy for the last-ditch effort of giving illumination—or at least information—to his rescuers.

"How gracious of you, Lebedev!" Manador said. She had gotten herself up in black leather and a flat brimmed hat; with her pale-blue powdered face and dark red mouth, she looked like a vampire who had tasted some good times.

"For you, any time," said Lebedev, and they both snickered.

The Lyhhrt became urgent. *:Now hurry and get us both out of here!:*

Lebedev did not have time to enjoy the scuffle in which Manador's guard was attending to South & Co., but he paused to whisper, "Ai'ia? You have her?"

"Any time, for you, Lebedev," Manador said coolly.

Lebedev nodded and turned; then he found himself surrounded by a crowd of revelers who were laughing and giddy and for one moment, it seemed to him, innocent. Next moment he was inside a freight elevator rising to the rooftop. As its door opened he smelt marginally fresher air and on the roof saw the Lyhhrt's plainest workshell with its metal hand holding the bottom rung of a ladder that hung from a hovercraft puffing warm jets of air around itself.

The skin of his stomach began to itch. The Lyhhrt said, *:Yes, Lebedev. In a short while both of us will be free.:*

It was not long afterward that Lebedev woke up to find himself in the clean sparely furnished room of a hostel run by the AlphOmegan Ecumen, a grab-bag religious organization that provided priests, shamans, rabbis, mullahs, *tin-katui*, Blessed Sisters, and many others to give service and counseling. Lebedev picked himself up and got dressed; he did not miss the presence of the Lyhhrt, but thought that for a while the world would seem opaque rather than transparent as it had been with that mind alongside his own. He recalled the last words the Lyhhrt had spoken when he said good-bye: *:The "I" that you know will no longer exist, Lebedev, but I/we will not miss it. Farewell.:*

His head ached where the knuckles had grazed it, and his mind felt battered and dull from contending with so much fear.

It was not until he was out in the street that it struck him: the Lyhhrt had put the inhibition on him to keep him from revealing information and now he could not quite think, let alone tell anyone, about it.

He had a moment of fresh panic. Unaccountably he felt an urge to reach into his pocket and pull out the little card that gave him notice. The We-regret-that-we-no-longer wording had not changed, but when he turned it over he saw that something had been written on the back. He brought it close to his eyes and squinted under a street-lamp whose light had become watery as the dawn rose in the stark grey sky. The tiny exquisite letters engraved on the square of parchment said:

Barley Soup

At once a long stream of numbers tumbled into his mouth: the Lyhhrt's security account code through which he was to repay money advanced by Manador. He stood staring at the card and after a moment said to the empty air: "Zamos is creating slaves in the vaults of its brothel."

A few days later when he was reading the local news in

the *Intergalactic Herald Tribune* Lebedev found the item about the strange doings in Zamos's Gamblar. Not the dust-up, which was not strange at all, but the discovery that three high administration officers had been found sealed in their office and in a hysterical state, along with a mysterious heap of machine parts. In another room, sealed from within in the same way and believed to be the quarters of a mysterious alien from another galaxy, there was nothing at all but a ceiling, a floor, and four walls dusted with a white powder presently being analyzed. Business had dropped off for a day or two but then increased due to a surge of curiosity-seekers. Lebedev by then was safely on the other side of the world and had no curiosity about that place whatever. He never went near another game of *skambi.*

Shen IV: *Portside City*

In Portside City Ned was debriefed by his GalFed contact, a shrill-voiced Kylklad woman named Tui'ireet.

"I am most satisfied with your work in Zamos's establishment," she was saying.

"Thank you," Ned said. He would have liked to add that he hardly knew what he was doing the whole damned time, but did not think that would improve his record.

Tui'ireet went on, "So clever of you to realize what was going on alongside you while drawing fire from the Interworld Police agent!"

"Hm?"

She tittered. "You may feel quite free to discuss that here! This room is completely sealed and has its own power sources."

"Ah . . ."

"Realizing that you had been mistaken for that Police Agency fellow—what's his name? Yes, Smugger is it? a chap who had something wrong with his face?—and all because, this I think you did not know in every detail, Zamos's people misread the warning they had been given by one of their spies to *look out for that man with the poor facial reconstruction!* But you caught on and completed your mission without giving him away! First class work, Gattes! That fellow what's-his-name's superior has asked me to put you in line for a Special Commendation, and I'm very pleased to do it! What do you think of that?"

"Very grateful," Ned muttered, rubbing his jaw and hoping he did not sound as stunned as he felt, or as pissed off at Smugger.

"Tell me, Gattes, what do you have in mind for the long term?"

"More of the same, I suppose." He had never more than glancingly thought of running a string of whores, or of coaching a stable of pugs who would learn everything from experience anyway. If he married Zella, perhaps . . . something more settled. "I'll fight for a while and then I'll find something steadier."

"If you want to go further I can tell you that Galactic Federation has a fine career ahead for you in the future if you want it." She offered a handclasp.

"Thank you, Madame," he said, and took it. He felt breathless, and relieved that the interview was over.

While he waited until his transport landed he had rented quarters at a cheap Travelers Rest (7—Complete Pollution-free Environments—7) in the Shen IV spaceport; some day he would be called on to testify, someday he might find Zella, maybe. She seemed transparent now, an ache beneath his breastbone. Right now he wanted only to fly off the world, and until then lose himself somewhere, perhaps in the city, anywhere not to be jumped by a Zamos thug. But he had not had enough sleep and his mind was lumbering along heavy and sparkless.

Down the corridor near the Travelers Rest was a boozer called the Humanoid Bar. Anyone who breathed oxygen and could stand nine Newtons of gravity went there. It was run by a Praximfi shapeshifter called Loui, who today had put on the shape of a velvety blond chanteuse, and was singing, with a display of finger-snapping:

> *I never loved you*
> *baby**
> *just said I did ***
> *you never knew the many*
> *many masks that hid*
> *me, baby**
> *you never did . . .*

It was a song that made Ned melancholy and wrapped him in a shroud of doubt; the way she had run toward those men . . . the bright future in the Service offered by that fatuous Tui'ireet looked only grey and empty.

The bar was sleazy, its tropical air was hot, the drinkers looked—like himself—as if they had been collected from *Wanted* trivvy clips. He looked out the big port windows at the rain and thought of another song.

He was sitting with the songs winding themselves about in his mind and nesting his chin in sweaty hands when they were clasped in turn by two cool ones. Cool firm hands that had touched him where he lived.

A voice said in his ear, "I never just said I loved you, never."

"Zella!"

Her face seemed thinner, and, scarred as it was, dimly

shadowed. Like his own. "Ned! I've been waiting and looking for you everywhere, everywhere. We're both free!"

He clasped her, she was herself, no shadow but whole and
fleshly, and he grew a hope like a green plant. "I love you,
Zella."

She rained kisses on him, and he was happy to be rained
on in this way.

You be sure Iron Man is having hot chills and rust attacks on
the way to sending me down into that long cold sleep that
give me those winding around and sickmaking dreams of
the Monster and the Demon and every other one that want
to slice me and my Baby up down and sideways to find out
what make us the Live Ones. But they don't.

I wake up with the kind ones who want to drop me into
my Bay where I pick the gold, where they have taken away
the net to let us be free, and I learn I am not just some stupid
nothing, that drop down like a lump of shit from some big
Lord Upthere, but a person, a kin that has been made long
ago of those that come here from that world called Earth,
Terra, Mir, a place that have a lot of names instead of just
one like what was given to us Folk. It's not bad to pick the
gold when you are paid with good food and medicine and
have somebody to love. It is not so good to learn that you are
not a fish that has the whole freedom of the deep sea, and that
most of the world you really belong with is Upthere where
you cannot live, but no one of us is free in every way . . .

As years ago in Mean Galactic Standard Time, several of
them had passed before Skerow again found herself in the
Interworld Court on Khagodis—not as judge, but as a witness, watching the center of the huge bowl-shaped courtroom where Kobai was giving testimony. Skerow was a
World Supreme Court judge by then, still in exile from her

own desert land where scientists and technicians had not yet finished digging the immense deep-space ship out of the rocky bed where it had slept for an eon. Fearfully they listened for sounds from within, wondering whether it was that longed-for beacon, The Great Egg, or only some nest of demons.

But beyond this world there had been other developments: Skerow had during this trial watched Zamos's empire splitting to show its spilling corruption. She had looked at the faces of evil, who had been brought to plead here not as snarling pirates like the Boudreau she had condemned so long ago in Starry Nova for smuggling, but as mild corrupt men and women disguised in business suits who dealt not in drugs and flesh but in transmuting them to gold; who, through the Goldyne Corporation, only one of its monstrous arms, had in the end infected the heart of the Interworld Trade Consortium with gangrene that could now never be cleanly cut away.

The brothel in Starry Nova had vanished as though it had never existed, racks of embryos seized in evidence, the shadowy unlit one in Burning Mountain Station seemed to have folded itself away and disappeared. She had regarded all this with a certain irony. Of course Zamos would always exist under one name or other.

Skerow still occupied the wife-house given her by Evarny, whose wife had died and whose son lived far away; she shared his dinners and part of her life with him, not quite in the old way, but still. She could see him down along the line of lecterns, several tiers below, in the section reserved for Galactic Federation officials. She wondered if this vast complicated case, this nested box of cases, would ever be completed. For her the prize was simply to watch the swimming woman in her cylindrical tank, speaking in her own way, sometimes by signing, sometimes raising her head above the surface of the water to gulp air and speak, stretching her limbs, making ripples with her shimmering tail, telling the last chapter of her own epic.

This baby that come out of me, he was one just like me but very small, not like those ones the Lords used to drop down from Upthere. Then he got bigger and bigger and everyone says, He will be a man one time and must have a name, a new Name, not just Baby. I got to think of all the names I could call him, everything new, but you know, maybe you will laugh at me but I call him Om. Yes, after that stupid one! I want to call him ten and ten and ten again other names but it has got to be Om.

Because when I come back I find that everybody got older than me in some way that I don't know why about, but two other women have these babies that are already a boy and a girl, not just little ones. So I think: that Om that was so handy with his this-here and going after all the woman all the time, maybe he is their father!

He is the one that want the knife, the one that picks up the gold and throws it, the one that want something so much even if it leave him dead! Because the whole world is changed forever when Om throws that one piece of gold.